FIREBALL

OTHER BOOKS BY PAUL DAVIES

FIREBALL

Paul Davies

HEINEMANN:LONDON

William Heinemann Ltd
10 Upper Grosvenor Street, London W1X 9PA

LONDON   MELBOURNE
JOHANNESBURG   AUCKLAND

First published in Great Britain in 1987
© Paul Davies 1987

ISBN 0 434 17701 6

Photoset by Deltatype Ltd, Ellesmere Port
Printed in Great Britain
by Redwood Burn Ltd, Trowbridge
and bound by WBC Ltd, Maesteg.

PROLOGUE

THE MEDICINE MAN crouched low in the centre of the long-house, his face dimly visible in the gloom. Slowly he swayed back and forth, chanting the litany of his tribe. Against the walls sat the assembled group of elders, restive and apprehensive.

Had it not been handed down from time immemorial that their people would succumb to the wickedness of the intruders? Was it not so that even now the devil-men from the place they called the city were corrupting the young ones, casting spells upon them?

Not one man among the elders doubted that the day of judgment would come, when all would pay for their evil ways. And no one feared that judgment more than the one they called Biame, for he had committed the worst treachery. Driven by a mixture of doubt and curiosity, Biame had gone to the place they called the Mission, where there lived the white man who wore the cross and spoke of marvellous happenings in a far-away country. Biame had turned away from the ancient spirits of the tribe, and even now he secretly wore the cross symbol, hidden beneath the snakeskin pouch that hung around his neck.

The medicine man wailed and clawed at the air as though in a paroxysm of agony. The old men in the long-house shrank back in fear and expectation, watching the lone figure wrestle with the evil forces that assailed them all. Each knew that the medicine man had the power to strike any one of them

1

down by the mere expedient of marking his sign at the entrance to their hut, or by pointing the bone strapped to his belt. But none of them expected the terrible punishment that even then came forth.

The soft glow in the long-house began to redden and grow brighter. Shafts of pink light pierced the gloom. The medicine man chanted louder, his eyes screwed tightly shut, his face contorted in concentration.

The old men turned their heads towards the source of the light, their eyes widening in terror and astonishment. They gazed upon a devil.

The red globe hissed menacingly as it bobbed along the floor of the long-house. Its intense light seared the eyes, but every eye remained riveted, save that of the medicine man whose frenetic chanting now reached fever pitch.

The devil globe hovered motionless for a moment, then began to swing slowly from side to side, like a pendulum. Suddenly it rose upwards, lurched to one side, then sank purposively towards one of the trembling old men. Biame.

A single shriek of unspeakable horror rang through the village. In the long-house the old men cringed like children, quivering with shock and fear. Amid them lay the body of Biame, his bare chest terribly burned by the now vanished fiery sphere. And at the centre of the burn a metal cross glinted in the half-light, proclaiming the treachery that had invited this dreadful visitation.

The medicine man sat silent and immobile, fixing the elders of the tribe with his gaze. Never had he witnessed such a portent. Never had the terrible fate foretold by his ancestors been confirmed by such a clear and visible sign.

Now he knew for sure. The end was at hand.

The roar of the rocket motors rumbled across the frozen Russian steppes. Nobody cheered as the colossal craft lifted slowly from the ground in fiery splendour. The titan powered its way skywards, over the snow-covered wastes that ringed the cosmodrome, gathering speed all the time, until it shrank into a tiny glowing speck in the bright blue canopy overhead.

In the control room stood only two men, hand-picked and trusted. Both craned their necks upwards until the rocket was lost to sight. The older man, squat and greying with wide Russian cheekbones, turned to his companion.

'It is done, Alexei Petrovitch.'

The younger man, tall and dark, kept his eyes on the sky. Presently he said, 'Is it right, Viktor, what we do?'

'It is not for us to judge such matters, my friend. We are scientists, not politicians.'

'But the waste . . . '

'It is dangerous to question the decisions of the leadership.'

'Indeed.' Alexei lowered his gaze, almost reluctantly, and smiled at his companion. 'Are we really the only ones who know?'

'Outside of Rogachev's group, yes. The only ones.'

'The technicians, the rocket engineers?'

The older man shook his head.

'Then we carry a momentous secret to our graves, comrade.'

Just then the door opened, and in stepped a soldier of the General Secretary's personal guard. He was dressed in full military uniform, and in his hand he held a standard issue officer's pistol. The soldier closed the door gently behind him. The two scientists stared at him in incomprehension.

'I have come to convey my congratulations from the General Secretary personally, comrades.'

Two shots rang out in the still air. Both scientists arched backwards, a neat round bullet hole in each forehead.

Science Report – London *Times*, February 17 1990

Astronomers from several countries, including a number of amateurs, reported the appearance, on 14 February, of a plume of material emanating from the bright eastern limb of the moon. Unfortunately the source of the outburst seems to lie just beyond the limb and therefore out of sight of direct observation from Earth. Speculation that the outburst was a volcanic eruption will no doubt renew the controversy about the moon's internal structure.

The possibility of lunar volcanism was supposedly laid to rest many years ago when it was established that the moon's craters were caused by meteoritic impact. It is widely believed by scientists that there is no significant tectonic activity on the moon, a conclusion supported by the general absence of substantial seismic events (moonquakes).

Planetologists will want to study the data of the 14 February eruption very carefully before revising their long-standing assumption that the interior of the moon is cold. The quantity and distribution of ejected material were reportedly quite unlike that of terrestrial volcanic eruptions, and scientists are not ruling out the possibility that a novel process was involved. The event recalls the fortuitous observation in 1979 of a peculiar eruption from the surface of Io, one of Jupiter's many moons, during the fly-by of an American Voyager spacecraft. On that occasion unusual electromagnetic effects were thought by some to be responsible.

In the absence of direct observation of the moon's surface, the cause of the eruption seems likely to remain a mystery.

1

ANDREW BENSON WATCHED his luggage disappear on the conveyor with a deep sense of depression. There was no going back now. He turned away from the airline check-in desk and ambled aimlessly around the terminal. He checked his watch. A whole hour to kill.

Benson hated Kennedy airport. In fact he hated all airports. But travel was a necessary evil that every active scientist had to put up with. It was part of the job, flying out and back to this or that conference. Except this time he wasn't coming back. Ever.

Something made Benson recall his father's words, solemnly delivered many more years ago than he cared to remember while on a fishing trip in Maine. 'Andy,' his father had said, 'life is what you make it, only making it is a hellavu lot easier in the US of A than in some places I know. This is the land of opportunity, they say. Don't let those opportunities pass you by.' Well he'd made it all right. Then blown it.

Benson headed for the Flight Deck bar and ordered a bourbon on the rocks. He slumped disconsolately into a wicker chair and stared into space. A voice startled him.

'You're a hard man to get hold of, Dr Benson.' He looked round at a large man in an expensive suit.

'Good.' Benson replied.

'May I?' The man indicated the stool beside him, offering a business card: 'Henry B. Foster, associate editor (features), *Time* magazine.' Benson nodded, refused the offer of a drink and waited while Foster ordered himself one.

'Transworld Booster, huh?' Foster said to the menu. 'Wonder why they bother? I'll settle for a beer.'

Benson said nothing, waiting for him to come to the point. 'I hope you don't mind this intrusion but, as you didn't return my calls, I thought I'd catch you here before you left.' He handed over a plastic folder. 'You knew we were preparing a profile on you, I suppose?'

'I'd heard.'

'This is the page proof. It's planned for our next issue.'

Benson drew it out and glanced at a photograph of himself. It was three years old, taken on the occasion he received the Einstein Medal. He looked ten years older now.

'We make it a matter of policy,' Foster said, 'to show the profiles to our subjects before publication.'

'In case the subject decides to sue?'

'Forewarned is forearmed. We did mail you a copy, but since you didn't reply . . . ' He let the words hang in the air as Benson concentrated on reading.

There was a moment of silence. Then Foster said, 'Well? What do you think?'

'"A contender for the Nobel Prize",' Benson replied. 'Are you sure?'

'We've got contacts in Stockholm.'

'Well, well,' Benson said softly.

Foster leant closer. 'I trust everything is accurate. We pride ourselves on our accuracy.'

Benson shrugged and read aloud. ' "Andrew Benson's character does not permit him to suffer fools gladly. He has not a trace of the politician in him, which is both a strength and a weakness. Colleagues say that he sees life from a pinnacle of excellence and consequently does not inhabit the real world." ' He looked up at the journalist.

'Sounds like Hendricks speaking.'

'We did interview him.'

'But you're not quoting him.'

'Most of our interviewees insist on anonymity.'

'Yes,' Benson said. 'Of course.'

'So?' Foster continued. 'You don't object?'

'I don't like the title, "Genius in Exile".'

'You don't like being called a genius?'

'I don't like the word "exile". Exile means I've been forced out.'

'Well, that's the way we . . . '

5

'No.' Benson leant forward, suddenly menacing. 'Nobody has ever forced me to do anything. I'm leaving because I won't work in a system which places people like Hendricks in positions of power.'

Foster drew back involuntarily.

'Self-imposed exile, then?' he offered.

'If you like. But it sounds clumsy to me from someone who's supposed to be an expert on semantics. I'm merely emigrating.'

'Okay, Dr Benson,' Foster conceded, and there was an edge to his voice now.

Foster looked at him for a moment in silence. 'I suppose it's not for me to say, but I think you're not emigrating. You're running away.'

'Perhaps.'

'So what are your future plans? Surely this British – what do they call it? – "redbrick" university isn't your scene, Benson?'

'I've got books to write.'

'Well. That's something.' He looked around the bar. 'And there's no one to see you off?'

'Like you said. I don't inhabit the real world.'

Foster smiled and tapped Benson's shoulder. 'They're calling your flight,' he said.

Benson looked up at the TV monitor. It was time to go.

Benson knew instinctively that something was wrong. The ululating whine of the aero-engines had changed subtly and he glanced in a panic out of the window. The stars were in confusion. He searched in vain for the familiar constellations but the cosmos was in anarchy and from the depths of the universe Hendricks's bloated face stared accusingly at him accompanied by a chorus of laughter . . .

He awoke with a start. The plane was going through some turbulence. A metallic voice announced that it was only temporary.

Benson yawned and rubbed his eyes. How he loathed flying. Checking his watch he calculated that there were still three hours to go before he reached Heathrow. He glanced around the cabin at a scene of familiar tedium: passengers slumped across each other trying to sleep, or staring morosely at the movie, anonymous-looking stewardesses gliding around with drinks in plastic cups, harassed mothers attending to infants.

A woman mouthed noiselessly from the movie screen; Benson's headphones had fallen off. He retrieved them, clipped them back on, and fumbled with the control. After several channel switches producing nothing but static he flung down the headset in disgust, rose and stumbled into the aisle.

6

A pretty stewardess was busy dispensing cokes. A few years back Benson would have fancied his chances there. Tall and slim, with a mass of blond hair and piercing blue eyes, he had once been described by a girl friend as good-looking in a craggy sort of way. Since then he'd degenerated; his eyes were glazed by too much drinking and a cynical disillusionment with life. His general appearance, once endearingly dishevelled, was now positively unkempt. A broken nose did nothing to enhance his attractiveness. The stewardess handed him a coke without so much as a second glance.

Benson flopped back into his seat with a sigh. He stared at the woman next to him. She was chuckling distractedly at the screen, absorbed in some news report tagged on to the end of the movie. Benson gazed absently at the screen, without the benefit of the earphones, watching a man standing in the smouldering ruins of a house pointing agitatedly at the sky. The CBS interviewer was familiar. The sign on a passing truck suggested it was somewhere in Kansas.

'Fireballs, my ass,' said the woman next to Benson.

'What?'

'Fireballs,' she repeated, leaning towards him, removing her headset. 'On the news.' She nodded at the silent screen. Benson didn't understand and wasn't interested. He never followed the news anyway.

'Did you hear the story of the woman from Oklahoma?' she continued. 'Figured she'd seen a flying saucer land in her backyard. Local sheriff asks how she knows it's a flying saucer and she says, "Cos it had UFO painted on the side, dummy." '

She grinned at him and he smiled back at her. 'Very good,' he said.

The woman stared at him for a moment, silently chewing gum. 'You going on vacation?'

'I'm emigrating,' replied Benson.

'No kidding? Why's that? Dontcha like living in the States?'

'My job.'

'Oh,' she said, and thought about that for a moment.

'Whatcha do then?'

'I'm a scientist.'

'Really? That's nice.'

Benson reached for his headphones but she said, 'There's some real neat places in England. I took a tour last year. I'm from Boston by the way. I . . . '

'Excuse me,' said Benson, cutting her off. He fixed his headset on firmly and studied the screen intently. The woman shrugged, turned away and opened a lurid-covered paperback. After a few moments Benson sneaked a glance at the opening line: 'The astronomer was not a religious man. When he

7

gazed through his telescope, he saw the sky and not the heavens.'

He settled back into his seat. '. . . the sky and not the heavens.' From now on his exploration of the sky or the heavens was over, his career in ruins. All that was left was teaching in a backwater university and the occasional obscure conference to learn about other people's discoveries. He closed his eyes and drifted into a fitful sleep, full of threatening images and desolate landscapes.

When he awoke again, a stewardess was handing out landing-cards.

Benson took out his passport; he saw Stratton's letter folded inside. The man had insisted on writing it, in order, he said, to assist him through Immigration.

It was a single sentence, typed, by the look of it, on an old machine on the university's headed notepaper, addressed to the Chief Immigration Officer, Heathrow Airport and informing him that Dr Andrew Benson would be arriving on 15 May to take up a position as Professor of Physics at Milchester University, and requesting that he be given every assistance.

The captain came on again, announcing that shortly they would be starting their descent towards Heathrow where it was 15 degrees and raining hard. A group of Englishmen cheered.

'Set your watch back a hundred years,' whispered his neighbour.

It was an old joke and Benson didn't laugh.

Thirty thousand feet below, Charlie Pike cursed savagely. Few jobs are better paid but worse loved than a pipe welder for an oil company. For such worthies, the worst task of all is known as 'the grovel'. Pipelines are welded in precast sections, mainly from the exterior, and inspected systematically as the pipe grows in length. From time to time, however, a section of the tube well back from the open end suffers accidental stress, and some unfortunate individual has to grovel along the inside of the pipe back as far as the suspect section to check it out.

It was purely by misfortune that Charlie Pike was grovelling that day, for it was not his turn. His mate who should have been up the pipe was down with the flu instead. So it was that, amid much foul language and resentment, Pike lay on his back in a three-foot-diameter steel tube, fifty yards from the open end, inspecting a lousy welding job with the aid of an electric torch. Big pipes have little trolley devices to facilitate passage along them, but, in such a restricted space as the one where Pike worked, the only recourse was to a hands and knees affair, ameliorated somewhat by the help of large sponge pads.

After a certain amount of random tapping, probing and cursing, Pike arrived at his prognosis and began the arduous and time-consuming task of crawling backwards down the tube to the open end. It was the shouting and bellowing echoing down the metal casing of the pipe that caused him to glance beneath his shoulder. Pike's heart missed a beat. It seemed as though the entrance to the pipe was on fire. The bright white aperture of daylight had turned an ominous orange-yellow.

Gradually the glow seemed to advance, until Pike could see clearly that the fire had entered the pipe itself. Nervously he began to crawl forward again. The glow came on. Pike crawled faster, but the mysterious ball of fire seemed to be gaining on him, almost as though it were hunting him. He cried out in alarm, but no one could hear – there could be no help.

Faster and faster he scrambled, until his hands bled, their flesh torn savagely into strips by the jagged metal edges around the pipe joints. Still the ball of fire bore down on him. Pike was screaming uncontrollably now; he could see clearly the dull orange glow illuminating the black depths before him. He knew there was no escape that way – the far exit of the pipeline was two miles distant.

Suddenly he felt a searing, roasting pain enveloping his trailing legs, and he turned in helplessness to face the full horror of the fiery thing. A huge glowing ball filled the interior of the pipe. The sharp, sweet smell of ozone pervaded the air. The screams seized in his throat, and he could only watch in paralysed terror as the ball slowly engulfed him in a nightmare of boiling agony.

2

'IT's 8.12, TUESDAY, 27 May, and the Embankment is a mess,' said a cheerful voice on the radio.

'Absolutely,' agreed John Maltby.

'The Kings Road and the Fulham Road are both at a standstill too. So if you're in it, grin and bear it.'

'Thanks,' replied Maltby.

'So bye-bye from the Flying Eye.'

Music now blasted out of the twin speakers of the little Porsche convertible and Maltby hummed along with it. It was a warm morning, a gentle breeze coming off the river, thinning out the car fumes. There were worse places to be stuck than the Embankment on a summer morning. As he waited for the lights to change at Chelsea Bridge, Maltby stretched. Parts of him still ached from the exertions of the past week on leave, spent hiking in the Lake District.

The lights changed and the traffic moved slowly eastwards. It took almost ten minutes to reach the next set of lights, at Vauxhall Bridge.

A red jeep squealed to a halt beside him and made him look up. He saw a dainty foot on the jeep's brake. The girl was 18 maybe, flaxen-haired, her lipstick the same shade as the jeep. She flicked a wisp of hair from her face and turned to see him gazing at her; she granted him a quick up-and-down stare and then turned and pouted at the lights. As they changed she accelerated hard and swung the jeep left into Vauxhall Bridge Road with a wave of her hand over her shoulder. He smiled and watched the jeep pick up speed, then let out the clutch and sat back. Ten years ago, when he was still in his 20s and chasing girls like that, she would have been an Amanda or a Claire or a Lucinda. The names had changed now, but the new generation would be the same: arrogant, noisy and delightfully promiscuous.

To his right, above the river, a police helicopter clattered, banking north, sending a cough of static through his radio. He eased the Porsche through a gap and began singing, convinced that morning, as his father and grandfather and great-grandfather had been, that being born English was the first prize in the lottery of life.

Fifteen minutes later he turned into the Ministry of Defence car park and waited at the barrier for the security guard. Maltby produced a computer card with a coded magnetic strip. Although Maltby was well known to the guard, the man insisted on going through a daily ritual of feeding the card to the computer for clearance. It took only a few seconds for the computer to identify him, then the barrier was raised and he drove deep into the basement. The old timers occasionally told nostalgic tales in the local pub of the pre-computer days when there were doormen at the Ministry of Defence with names like Bert and Bob, when the IRA was still a joke and you had to check a map to find Libya. The old good days maybe, but Maltby preferred to work in the age of high technology; more complicated but more professional.

Maltby pushed open the door of his office and crossed the room to his desk. It was a cubby-hole of a place, just the desk, some shelves and a couple of chairs, with one window overlooking the well of a courtyard. The bookshelves were crammed with White Papers and files of memoranda. There was a sheaf of telexes and memos in his in-tray. He briefly went through them. There was nothing that gave any clue as to why he'd been recalled from leave, nothing that smelled of urgency.

The intercom buzzed. Sir William was in and would see him now. Maltby got to his feet and straightened his tie in the mirror.

Sir William Peebles was the most senior civil servant at the Ministry, had seen Ministers come and go and had treated them all with patrician disdain. He was not liked, but popularity did not concern him. The only thing that bothered Sir William was the good name of the Ministry and the reputations of successive Ministers. He had served eight and, rumour had it, all eight had been terrified of him.

Sir William's door had neither name nor number on the panelled mahogany, just a small, red light sunk into the top left-hand corner. Maltby knocked and waited until the red light changed to green, then went in. His superior was standing by the window, 6 feet 3 inches of him, the gaunt figure shredded by sunlight slicing through the venetian blinds. Maltby muttered, 'sir,' and waited. The old man was in his uniform pin-stripes, chalk on grey, with white shirt, starched collar and Eton tie; almost a caricature in this day and age, although those who thought so would never dare suggest such a thing openly.

'Sorry to drag you back, Maltby,' he said, nodding at his desk. 'The buff file tells it all.'

Maltby crossed the room and picked up the file. Sir William sat down in his swivel chair behind his huge desk and reached into an unseen drawer. Maltby wondered what the old man was about to produce, but it was only his pipe plus assorted apparatus. Sir William peered sceptically into the bowl of the pipe, then raked around with a dilapidated penknife. Eventually he crammed in some evil-looking weed, patted it carefully and struck a match. After a seemingly interminable series of puffs and coughs Sir William finally achieved ignition. Maltby stared in silence.

'Well don't stand around, Maltby. Sit down, for God's sake.'

'Thank you, sir.' Maltby cleared his throat. 'What's all this about then, sir?'

Sir William leaned back in his chair, and puffed his pipe for a while. Then he said, 'Something odd has been happening at a number of our installations.'

'Odd?'

'Very odd.' Sir William fixed the younger man with a stare. 'Maltby, you're a Classics man aren't you?'

Maltby nodded. 'Balliol, sir.'

'Quite. What does the world "plasma" mean to you?'

'Something in the blood . . . ?'

'Ionized plasma.'

Maltby grimaced. 'Physics . . . electricity.'

'Hmmm. Open the file to page four.'

Maltby laid the file out on the desk and scrutinized a set of photographs. The equipment was familiar: a submarine communications array in Cumbria. A ring of antennae like some monstrous latter-day Stonehenge. One of the pylons was in close up. A hollow vertical tube. Something had punched a hole about two inches across in the steel.

'According to witnesses, that hole was made by a fireball of some sort,' Sir William elaborated.

'A malfunction? Accidental discharge? They use some pretty high voltages.'

'The fireball came from the sky.'

Maltby looked up and stared at his boss.

'Now turn to page five.'

Maltby did so, and found photographs of a control room of some sort with an equipment console wrecked.

12

'Fylingdales early-warning station. The security staff described a glowing ball which floated across the control room and exploded when it touched the panel. One of them swore he saw the ball descend from the clouds.'

Maltby studied the pictures for a few moments. Then he said: 'Has anybody else reported these things? Is it just M.o.D. stations?'

Sir William shook his head. 'There have been quite a number of cases reported by the public. The newspapers have been carrying stories for a few weeks.'

'I remember, now you mention it. I thought it was just the usual silly season crap.'

'I don't think so. Anyway, it'll be your job to find out. I want you to follow this up as a matter of the highest priority. When you've read the file, contact Malone in Washington.'

'You mean the Americans have got fireballs too?'

'Oh yes. And they're taking the threat seriously.'

'Threat?'

Sir William's pipe had gone out, and he set about the whole rigmarole of relighting it from scratch. When he had finally finished he addressed Maltby's unanswered question. 'There is a belief in some quarters . . . ' Sir William didn't say precisely to which quarters he was referring, ' . . . that these fireballs are not acts of God.'

'You mean somebody's controlling them? But surely . . . '

'Control? I don't know. Causing them, maybe.'

'The Russians?'

'It's not us.'

'Is there any evidence of Russian involvement?'

'Circumstantial only. They have a big plasma weapons research project at Novosibirsk. Plus a few coincidences regarding personnel. It's all in the file.'

There was a moment of silence. The younger man got up to go.

'Oh, Maltby. Pay attention to the security aspect. We don't want the press to twig on that the military are rattled by these fireball reports, do we?'

'Indeed not, sir.'

Sir William stood up and resumed his survey of Whitehall from the window. He was no longer shredded by sunlight. Storm clouds had moved in from the west and, as Maltby went out, the lamp on the old man's desk automatically switched on.

Maltby sat back in his chair and tried to let it all sink in. His mood kept oscillating between scepticism and alarm. In a world grown used to Star Wars the idea of directed energy weapons no longer appeared fantastic. Yet it was scarcely credible that the Russians would actually deploy such weapons in peacetime. Who knows what it might lead to?

Perhaps they'd released these fireballs and then lost control of them? Certainly the Russians had been unusually tight-lipped lately. Or maybe they were gambling on the fact that, with civilian reports coming in too, the fireballs would be dismissed as some freak atmospheric phenomenon.

Speculation.

The file offered no physical explanation for the fireballs, only that they varied in size from a centimetre to a metre, made little or no noise, and were generally yellow or orange in colour. Their lifetime could be a few seconds or as long as two minutes. They either faded harmlessly away, or exploded violently on contact with metallic objects. Fireballs had been seen both inside buildings and outdoors, where they were occasionally witnessed falling from the sky. They seemed to move of their own accord, often at low speed with a curious bobbing motion. Five people had died and seventeen had been injured after coming into direct contact with fireballs during the preceding month.

The file contained a summary of the American research project, cryptically named C7, that had been established to investigate the spate of fireball reports and evaluate the security implications. Most of the personnel were civilian scientists, university professors and the like, mainly physicists and chemists. Maltby didn't recognize any of the names.

He checked his watch. Too early to phone Washington. He'd leave it till after lunch. Meanwhile he'd run the list of C7 personnel through the M.o.D. computer to get some more background.

Going up in the lift, he met a young man named Brook, from the press office.

'Back early from leave, aren't you?'

'Yep.'

'Nothing to bother me with, I hope.'

'Don't worry,' said Maltby as the doors opened. 'You'll be the last to know.'

The data room was almost empty, just a couple of white-coated technicians at their monitors. Maltby nodded at them, sat at a console, tapped in a security number and entered the first name : Stanley Hendricks.

The data came up, words chasing themselves from left to right, line after line, papers published, committees chaired, honours awarded.

'Busy boy,' Maltby whispered. Hendricks' file finally came to an end and Maltby tapped in the second name on the list, then a third until he had reached the last. He sat back, something niggling at the back of his brain, a name that was missing, someone who should have been there, but it wouldn't

14

come to mind. It was like the games he played as a young man with his friends in a bar, trying to remember who played for what soccer team in what year, trying to go through the players of famous teams. It always seemed to be the number six that was the problem. Who was the number six missing from this team of scientific all-stars? This was getting him nowhere. It was lunchtime. A visit to the pub was in order.

The day had turned sour. The sun had gone and drizzle seeped into him as he crossed Whitehall and sheltered, at the corner of King Charles Street, in the entrance to the Home Office. Pedestrians scuttled past, each one carrying an umbrella, their heads and shoulders encased in a semi-circle of material, like walking mushrooms.

He looked through the glass in the main door at the uniformed security men. He knew none of them. The guardians of the Home Office, the Ministry of Defence and along the road, the Foreign Office kept themselves to themselves, drank in different pubs, maintaining a sense of rivalry, in much the same way that a paratrooper wouldn't drink with a marine or one regiment of guards with another. Only a common enemy would unite them.

Maltby shivered in the damp air and suddenly felt hungry. A pie and a pint, then it would be time to wake up Washington.

An hour later he was back at his desk. The pie seemed to have re-formed his stomach and he felt the first spasms of heartburn. He checked his watch. Malone started early. He would surely be at his desk by now.

A machine answered and he gave his name. A moment later Malone came on the line, growling, 'Hello,' at him in a voice like Louis Armstrong.

'Fireballs,' said Maltby.

'I might have guessed.'

'Sir William's put me on to them.'

'Then the best of luck, John; you'll need it.'

'There's a touch of anxiety about it all over here.'

Malone laughed. 'Good old British understatement, I'll bet.'

'Yes, well, it seems we've started to take some rather strategic hits.'

'So I heard. So you've come to Uncle Sam for help?'

'That's right. I've read the file. It's long on descriptions, short on explanation. What's going on, Sam?'

'Damned if I know.'

'Is there anything new I should know about, anything not on the file?'

'Another miss. An oil tanker in the Indian Ocean just blew up. You'll hear about it on the news. What you won't hear is that a fireball got inside one of the containment tanks by squeezing through a duct and ignited the accumulated gas.'

15

'Blimey. Why do you call it a miss?'

'We list all civilian cases as misses. Only military reports make it to the hit column.'

'What about this C7 outfit – your top scientists? Haven't they come up with anything?'

'Nope, but they're going hard on the Commie ticket. It's got the President running scared. He thinks the Reds may have outclassed him in the SDI stakes. I suppose you've seen the stuff from security.'

'Got it here.'

'Right. Well, the smart money's on either mini-nukes or controlled plasmas. You know what I'm talking about?'

'I know about mini-nukes.'

'Okay. Hendricks – he's the brains behind our little outfit – favours mini-nukes.'

'And the plasmas? What about them?'

'That's complicated. I'll fax over some background for you.'

'Thanks, Sam.'

'Anything else I can do for you Limeys?'

'I don't think so. Not yet. I'm just beginning. I've been told to set up a unit over here.'

'Forget it,' said Malone. 'You got nobody qualified enough. This is one of those dumb subjects where no one seems to know very much. It's what you might call a speculative area.'

'Sam, don't you think everybody's over-reacting a bit on this one? I mean, so there's a few weird explosions . . .'

'Don't you believe it, John.' The flip tone disappeared as Malone replied. 'I think this could be more serious than any of us yet comprehend. The effect of one of the larger fireballs hitting a chemical plant or a nuclear installation doesn't bear thinking about. And between you and me, no one here has the least idea what these things are, let alone how to stop them. So far, we're getting nowhere.'

'I gleaned that by reading between the lines of the report. Any joy with the Russians?'

'Zilch, buddy. Can't even raise the bastards. The hot line's gone ice-cold all of a sudden.'

Just then a light flashed in Maltby's mind. He did not know any physics, let alone any physicists, but once, long ago as a student in Oxford, he'd attended a lecture by a young whiz-kid physicist from California. Maltby had been there as a member of the committee that had voted the lecturer some sort of prize. Though he hadn't understood a word of it, he remembered the lecture well because the man's name was the same as Maltby's cousin. And the topic of the lecture was . . . plasmas.

'Sam. Why haven't you got Andrew Benson working on this?'

'That crazy bastard?'

'Isn't he supposed to be good?'

'Maybe he's a genius. But he won't have anything to do with us, or with anybody for that matter. He hates the military. Anyway, he dropped out in a fit of pique and is sulking in his tent.'

'Mind if I talk to him?'

'Go right ahead; can't stop you. He's in your jurisdiction, buddy boy.'

'Eh?'

'Yeah. He just emigrated to Britain. He's on his way to work at some university in the north of England.'

'Really?' said Maltby in surprise. 'Can you remember which?'

'Er, Milchester, I believe.'

'Well, I'll be damned.'

Milchester University Physics building was situated on the outskirts of town, quite close to the centre of the campus. It was a drab rectangle of concrete and glass set back twenty yards from the car park, with a small service road at the rear. Rumour had it that the building won an architectural award when it was opened in the sixties, which said a lot about British architects.

Benson climbed out of the cab and stepped straight into a puddle. For a moment he stood in the gutter, looking at his sodden shoes, then at the rain-soaked gravel path that bisected a weed-ridden lawn in front of the building. He trudged along it, scowling. Ever since he was a boy and his family had moved to southern California he'd taken good weather for granted. Now, within hours of his arrival in Milchester, his shoes were wet.

He pushed open the glass door and stepped inside. The reception area was painted a dull green which gave the porter a faintly nauseous appearance. He was a big truculent-looking man and he eyed Benson with disdain.

'Sir?'

'My name's Benson.'

'Indeed.'

'I was expecting someone to meet me.'

The porter put on a pair of half-moon spectacles and peered at a large note-book.

'Professor Benson?'

'That's right.'

The big man picked up a phone and spoke briefly.

17

'Just take a seat, Professor. Someone will be here shortly.'

Benson declined the offer and ambled around the reception area, idly reading the poster display proclaiming the latest discoveries made by the Department's research staff.

Presently a tall, balding figure in a green sports jacket appeared, beaming genially.

'My dear chap, so sorry to keep you.'

The man wrung Benson's hand as though he were a long-lost brother.

'I'm Ken Stratton, Head of Department. I've really been looking forward to your joining us.'

Benson muttered something polite and trailed along behind an effusively gesticulating Stratton, who waxed lyrical on the virtues of life in the north of England in general, and his Department in particular.

Soon they came to a busy corridor of staff offices, the familiar clatter of academic life enveloping them.

'You've picked the wrong day to arrive, old chap', said Stratton. 'I've got a Faculty meeting at ten and then I'm off to a Research Council committee in London after lunch, so I'm afraid I'll miss your reception this evening. I thought I'd get young Quenby to settle you in. He was one of poor old Ramshaw's graduate students.'

Poor old Ramshaw was Benson's predecessor, who'd vacated the Chair of Physics somewhat prematurely when he'd had a heart attack while in bed with a neighbour's wife. Or at least that was the story Benson had heard. No doubt Benson would inherit the poor sod's students if, alas, not his mistress.

Quenby appeared from a side office, bearded, bespectacled and blustering. He seemed intent on giving Benson a complete guided tour of the entire Department.

'Just my office for now, if you don't mind.'

Quenby led him up a flight of stairs, leaving Stratton muttering apologies. On the stairs they ran into a freckled girl of about twenty-five, clutching a sheaf of papers. She shook hands limply with Benson and flushed.

'This is Sally,' explained Quenby with a grin. 'She's your secretary. She'll do *anything* for you, won't you Sally?'

Sally looked flustered and hurried on.

Benson's room was at the rear of the building, facing north over a derelict factory. By standing on the desk it was possible to see the rusting cranes near the old dockyard.

'I know it's not like Caltech,' said Quenby, apologetically, 'but the countryside's beautiful.'

'So I've been told.'

The room seemed cramped and bleak. Empty filing cabinets lined one wall; another was devoted entirely to bookshelves. A new blackboard had been installed in Benson's honour. On a table next to the desk stood a computer terminal, which Quenby assured him was connected to the main frame. Benson's packing-crates sat in the middle of the room, slightly battered from their long voyage and looking strangely forlorn.

'You were lucky,' Quenby said. 'They arrived last week. You hear a lot of stories about pilfering.'

Benson scoffed. 'Anyone interested enough to steal that lot is welcome to them.'

Quenby smiled tentatively as Benson wandered around the room, looking up at the television video in the far corner. Quenby followed his gaze.

'We got it specially,' he said. 'We'd heard about your, ah . . .'

'Eccentricity?' Benson offered. It was his one peculiarity. He always worked with the TV on, a habit he'd picked up as a student and never thrown. He paid scant attention to it, but, if it was not on, he would notice and become uncomfortable.

'Audio-visual wallpaper,' Quenby said. 'That's what they wrote in *Time* magazine.'

Benson snorted, went to the window and looked out at a desert of one-storey buildings in decay, some with windows boarded up. There was no sign of life.

'The new industrial estate,' said Quenby. 'Only the new industry never came.'

Benson felt a sudden overwhelming desire to be alone, away from this bumbling acolyte. He shook his head, then shook the student's hand again and said he hoped they'd meet again later that evening at the reception. Quenby left, walking backwards, stumbling against the desk, the classic combination of a clever mind and an uncoordinated body.

The swivel chair behind the desk was old, and it squeaked annoyingly when Benson either tilted or swivelled in it. He sat there motionless, staring miserably at the atrocious view. The rain ran in rivulets down the plate-glass window.

So this was it. His new career had started. *Jesus.*

He thought of the palm-lined avenue outside his old office at Caltech, of the vast airy laboratory he'd had at his disposal, of the easy drive down to the beach at Santa Monica or Malibu . . .

Leaping up, he flicked the venetian blinds shut and switched on the light. Then he went over to the television and switched that on too, without sound. From now on, he vowed, he would never look out at that terrible view again.

Picking up a piece of chalk, he crossed to the blackboard. On impulse he scrawled up an obscenity in large block capitals. The chalk screeched in protest.

Then he sat down in his squeaky chair, put his feet up on his desk and waited, feeling like some small animal at the beginning of a long winter of hibernation.

Samantha soaped her slender legs. Not bad, she thought. Her legs and breasts were her best assets; as far as men were concerned, the rest seemed of less importance. She sank back beneath the warm bath-water contentedly.

Last night had been better than her wildest dreams. She'd guessed from his smooth telephone voice that her blind date was . . . how to say it? . . . up-market. When she saw the flashy car, the flowers and the expensively cut suit she could barely contain her excitement. This time there would be no cheap evening for two at the run-down local cinema and a trip to the chip shop on the way home.

They'd dined extravagantly at Esters in Mayfair, then gone on to 'a little place' he knew, which turned out to be a discreet nightclub for the 'in' people of London's wealthy West End set. They danced and drank and drank and danced till at least three, he patiently expounding on the intricacies of the stock-market, she burbling on about life in the travel agency where she worked for a pittance. When they finally got back to her flat she played along with the quick-coffee-settee-bed routine with scarcely a second thought. This one was a real catch.

Samantha smiled to herself and wiggled her toes. The radio next to the bath blared a song called 'Gotcha', and she thought it most fitting. Deep in her reverie she failed to notice the soft orange glow that suffused the tiny bathroom. It was the annoying crackle of static on the radio that first gained her attention. Cursing, she reached a dripping arm over the side of the bath and froze.

No more than six inches from her hand there hovered a weird radiating orange ball. Samantha had never seen anything like it. It resembled some fiendish object from the depths of her unconscious. Its surface was diffuse and pulsating, and the interior a turmoil of motion. She could feel the heat of it scorching her bare arm. The radio squawked and hissed.

Instinctively Samantha withdrew her arm. The fireball followed, as though deliberately targeting her. She screamed in alarm and scrambled to get up, then slipped and crashed back into the water, sending splashes over the side of the bath. She wallowed helplessly for a moment as the glowing ball remained motionless above her, and then watched aghast as it slowly descended.

When the fireball touched the water there was a furious hissing sound, and

20

a plume of steam rose in front of her face. She felt the scalding water against her legs, her beautiful legs. Oh God! She was going to be boiled alive.

Her next scream was heard in the street. A passing window-cleaner hammered ineffectually on the front door of Samantha's flat for a minute, then noticed the open window. Hefting his ladder from the van he deftly climbed into the young woman's bedroom. Ten seconds later he found Samantha slumped naked in the bath. Ugly red burns disfigured her legs, stomach and chest, as though someone had poured scalding hot water in a trail up the length of her body. Her face was contorted in terror. She was dead.

3

THE RECEPTION WAS dreadful, everything Benson loathed. Never at ease socially, he particularly disliked formal occasions, especially those given in his honour. He couldn't bring himself to be polite, so he just stood around grunting and grinning stupidly as a seemingly endless succession of people introduced themselves.

Benson armed himself with a drink and a sausage to avoid shaking hands, and countered every leading question with a reference to the weather, in good English tradition. It seemed to work.

The key figure, who, for reasons ill understood by Benson, was known as the Vice-Chancellor rather than the Chancellor, turned out to be an avuncular, retired army general with a thin moustache and a wife to match. Benson instinctively disliked him, but forced himself to be civil. At least the guy had given him a job, he thought.

The Vice-Chancellor made a short speech of welcome, during which time Benson stood stiffly, feeling silly. Then the hubbub resumed as people's glasses were refilled. Benson drank too much as usual, and began upsetting people with indelicate remarks. He didn't much care. After all, he was washed up anyway.

A woman approached him. She was short and dark, with penetrating brown eyes, long but neat hair and delicate features that rewarded closer scrutiny. There was also a subtle but unmistakable sensuous quality about her. He wondered why he hadn't noticed her before.

She pressed another drink into his hand.

'It's a bourbon on the rocks,' she said in a smooth, confident voice.

'How did you know?' asked Benson.

'I read *Time* magazine. It said that bourbon and physics are your only passions.'

'Not quite.' He fixed her gaze.

The girl glanced down momentarily. Then she said: 'You don't look like the guest of honour. I mean you don't look too happy to be here.'

'It's the rain,' he said. 'Once I hopped in a little plane around the Windward Islands, everyone singing and dancing and drinking rum. Except in Dominica. Seems there was some kind of freak weather. The place was always under cloud. In Dominica everyone was punching each other.'

'Melatonin,' she said.

'Huh?'

'It's prescribed to combat jet-lag. It's a hormone produced by the pineal gland. When the weather's bad, and the days are short, the pineal produces less of the stuff – makes you depressed. Then, in the spring, you get more of it. The sap rises, so to speak.'

'Is that so?'

'I know these things. I'm a biochemist. The name's Tamsin Bright.'

They shook hands.

'Biochemistry, eh? Another one from the Faculty of Stamp Collecting?'

Her lips tightened. 'At least I'm not running away from my subject,' she replied acidly.

'*Touché.*' Benson grinned disarmingly and raised his glass. He liked women who could hold their own.

'What made you become a biochemist, Dr Bright? A yearning for the white coat and the test tube?'

'It's the subject of the future, Professor. Didn't you know?' She smiled sweetly, revealing a dazzling set of white teeth.

'What made you become a physicist?'

'I'll tell you over dinner.'

'In the refectory?'

Benson shook his head. 'At your place.'

'You've got a bloody nerve.'

'Yes, Dr Bright. So they tell me.'

They drove to her place in a little red Fiat. She had the top floor of an old Victorian house of red brick with huge chimney-stacks. The décor was tasteful, feminine and low-key. In the corner of the living-room, a glass tank incarcerated two terrapins, whose only purpose in life seemed to be a futile struggle to scale the sides of their enclosure. Benson empathized with them.

Over the meal she told him that she had graduated from Oxford, got her doctorate at 24, spent two years in America, another four back in London and she had had her present position as a lecturer in biochemistry for five years.

'Very good,' said Benson. 'And now the sexist question . . .'

'Divorced,' she said, interrupting with a smile. 'The classic dilemma. He's a computer engineer, very bright, very ambitious. Upwardly mobile, I believe the term is. Three years ago he was offered a job in Germany. I couldn't work over there, and I had no intention of becoming a *hausfrau*, so . . . ' She smiled wistfully. 'Now it's your turn, and I'm curious as to why a man of your reputation ends up in the sticks.'

'I screwed up.'

'How?'

'Let's say I precipitated a sort of crisis.'

'Personal or professional?'

'Both.'

'Do you want to talk about it?'

Benson shrugged. 'Hell, why not. You see, I had this nice little set-up in Caltech, couple of postdocs, three technicians on call, NSF grant for five hundred thousand a year. More to the point, we were going places. I'd already gotten a really neat result about magnetic storms. Then I made a big discovery about plasma confinement that breathed new life into the controlled fusion programme. We were all psyched up over it. You know, like we were headed for a Nobel prize or something. Then I went and blew it.'

Tamsin eyed him silently.

'There's this guy Hendricks, Stanley Hendricks, top-notch physicist at Fermilab. You must know of him.'

'I do – Adviser to the President on Defence, or something.'

'Yeah,' said Benson grimly. 'That's the guy. Particle physicist really, but he's into astrophysics, plasmas and Christ knows what else. Big brain, big shot in the US of A establishment. Pulls a lot of strings does our Stanley.'

'Including budgetary ones?' ventured Tamsin.

'Correct. Anyway, couple of years ago Hendricks came up with this theory about cosmic rays and geomagnetic reversals.'

'I remember now,' she said. 'There was a lot of media publicity about it. Something to do with the death of the dinosaurs.'

'Well – that was just some crappy spin-off by a few hangers-on. The thing is, Hendricks' essential idea was a bit of a bombshell. He was obviously pretty pleased with himself; nobody else had spotted the mechanism he'd discovered.

24

'The first I knew about it was at a conference in Baltimore. APS thing. Hendricks had given this jazzy title for his lecture, so we all knew he had something important to say. The place was packed out. When he wrote down his main result I thought to myself, "Christ, Hendricks screwed this one up." '

'You mean you didn't believe it?'

'I don't know what I believed. The trouble was that Hendricks is a lousy lecturer and he'd put over a really half-arsed argument so you couldn't tell what he was actually driving at. He just sort of dropped this bombshell into a mish-mash of dubious-sounding gobbledegook.

'Well, at the end of the lecture everybody clapped enthusiastically for the great man. The chairman drivelled on with some ingratiating remarks about the revolutionary new discovery, and most of the audience were left completely baffled.

'I figured Hendricks had gotten a bit into my territory and that there were some pretty basic questions about his result left unanswered. Like, about stability, and the boundary conditions and all that. So I got up during question time and said I thought it was kind of odd that his result seemed to conflict with the laws of thermodynamics and that there seemed to be something a bit mysterious about his boundary conditions.

'Well, I guess I never did get on with that Chicago crowd. They're so bloody arrogant. Anyway, Hendricks obviously felt insulted that his great result was being challenged in public. He brushed off the questions in that big-shot way of his, and a few people gave me steely looks.'

'And that got you fired? Surely not.'

'No. There's more. That evening I went for a walk along the harbour, found a little fish restaurant. There were a few faces I recognized from the conference and a woman on her own. Smooth brunette. We got talking. Eventually we got dancing. She danced close. I'd had a lot of wine so I kissed her and she didn't object.'

'I can imagine,' Tamsin said.

'I discovered something at that moment. When a man is kissing a woman, he's pretty vulnerable to a left hook. I didn't see it. I'm kissing a pretty woman, then I'm on the floor looking up at a very angry guy.'

'Not Hendricks?'

'Hendricks.'

'She was Hendricks' girl?'

'Hendricks' wife.'

For a few seconds she gazed seriously at him, fighting for an expression of sympathy but she couldn't do it. She laughed, at first just a giggle then a squeal of laughter, then an apology.

25

'Don't be sorry,' Benson said. 'One of those things. You can guess the rest. Four papers rejected in a row. No more invitations to the big conferences. To cap it all, Hendricks' theory turned out okay after all. The whole bloody physics community's gone overboard about it. Every university seems to have somebody working on it.'

'And a certain Andrew Benson's been left out in the cold?'

'Yeah. After a year or so it became clear that my research group was falling apart. We couldn't get any postdocs, most of the good graduate students in our subject were going to Chicago. Then my director began hinting that, unless I got my act together soon, my tenure would be in jeopardy. I figured I was just about washed up. My work went downhill fast. I suppose I lost interest really. It's not easy to cope with a disintegrating reputation.'

'What made you choose Milchester?'

Benson shrugged. 'Oh, I knew they had a good ionospheric physics group here. Done some interesting stuff on plasmas. When the Chair became vacant I figured I'd be in with a chance. So here I am.'

'Do you regret it?'

Benson shrugged. 'Too early to tell.'

'Maybe your attack on Hendricks was self-preservation.'

He frowned. 'Huh?'

'They say that the brain can only take so many years at full throttle. Perhaps subconsciously you were protecting yourself. You rebelled yourself into temporary retirement if you know what I mean.'

Benson squinted at her. He'd never thought of it that way. Maybe she was right. It deserved thinking about over a bourbon some day.

He got up to go. 'Thanks for the meal.'

'My pleasure,' she smiled winningly. 'Can I give you a lift somewhere?'

'Oh no, thanks. I'll get a cab.'

'Where are you staying?'

'A hotel out near the airport.'

'When you've had a chance to settle in, I'll help you find somewhere more permanent, if you like. I know the area quite well.'

'Sure. Well, thanks again.'

She held out a hand and he shook it awkwardly, and left

It was raining again.

On a clear day the view from the top of the Eiffel tower is breathtaking. In the stormy weather that day, however, Marcel Dubois could only see as far as the suburbs of the great city – a chequerwork of starkly illuminated patches where the sunlight broke through the heavy cumulus, interspersed with sombre grey.

26

Not that his attention was directed to the view. Dubois was far too preoccupied with the demands of the task in hand. To the visitors at the top of the tower he must have appeared to possess nerves as strong as the framework to which he was strapped. But working at great heights presented no problems of anxiety to Dubois. For twenty years he had clambered over, scaled and hung from all manner of skyscrapers, towers and bridges with scarcely a second thought. The reinforced nylon straps that secured his harness were completely reliable, so that Dubois worked complacently, concentrating only on his work.

There is a folk story in France that the Eiffel tower is always being painted, for the job takes so long that no sooner has one complete coat of paint been supplied than another is needed. In fact, Dubois' company was contracted only once a decade for the job, and with modern high velocity jet sprays it took only about two months. They started at the top, which was where Dubois was working, like a spider on a wall. He was dressed in heavy-duty overalls, and his head was encased in a PVC hood welded to a perspex face-mask. On his back were slung two heavy steel cylinders of pressurized paint.

The force from the spray gun was vicious, and it was necessary to take long rests between successive applications of the gun. It was during one such obligatory interregnum that Dubois noticed the unusual stillness in the air – an oppressive, foreboding atmosphere. In the distance he could hear the rumbling complaint of a brewing storm. Knowing that heavy rain forced a complete abandonment of the work, Dubois returned to the spraying with renewed dedication.

Dubois enjoyed painting the Eiffel tower; it was a great national symbol. With a sense of pride, he would boast to his friends at the Café Rouens of an evening that he was helping preserve France's most renowned monument.

When the strange orange glow reflected from the wet paint on the steel girder in front of him, Dubois' first thought was that the sun had broken through the towering black clouds. It was only when he felt the searing pain at his elbow that he realized something was wrong. Terribly wrong.

With a cry of alarm he dropped the spray gun, which cavorted angrily in its liberation. Jerking around, Dubois was confronted by a luminous red sizzling ball of fire, about one metre across, rolling slowly along the horizontal strut towards the clasp where his harness was fastened. No sooner had his startled mind registered the presence of this terrifying object than the right strap of his harness melted and he collapsed backwards to dangle precariously from the single remaining line. Panic-stricken, Dubois grasped frantically for a hand-hold, just as the fireball melted the other strap. With a high, thin scream of pain and fear, he watched helplessly as the fiery shape glided on to his bare

27

hands and his flesh began to incinerate. The next thunderclap drowned his shriek of despair as Dubois dropped from the girder out into the chasms of nothingness high over the city.

Tamsin stared from her office window into the university quadrangle. It was a beautiful early summer day. The rain of the previous week had given way to clear bright sunshine, and students lay sprawled across the grass, resting between examinations. It was one law that all students knew: the weather is always hot and sunny during examinations.

One of the students waved up at her; a Turkish lad called Kemal. She half-smiled and withdrew to her desk. Kemal had once made a pass at her. Fortunately she'd managed to fend him off without damaging his ego.

A pile of exam scripts lay on her desk, ready for marking. Tamsin sighed heavily and sat down to begin the chore. She soon found herself humming light-heartedly in spite of the tedium. Was it just the sunshine? No. It was Andrew Benson. He'd affected her in the most peculiar way. It was clear to everybody that Benson was rude, arrogant and bigoted, with an almighty chip on his shoulder. He was openly contemptuous of the country, the University and its staff. He was also the archetypal male chauvinist pig. And yet . . .

The previous evening had been quite unlike any that she'd ever spent with a man. There was an electric energy about Benson that ennervated her. It was not sexual; definitely not. Intellectual. He set her head spinning; a delicious sort of intellectual drunkenness. And all of it overlaid with that terrible boorish exterior. Fascinating.

Tamsin couldn't get Benson out of her mind. She knew they would become lovers. Though she'd only known him a few hours there was a compelling inevitability about it. She was drawn to him like a magnet, but for mental rather than physical gratification. It would be an interesting experience.

After an hour or so, hunger invaded these musings. Tamsin normally ate sandwiches in her room at lunch-time, but today her routine was screwed up. It'd have to be the university refectory. She found an empty table near the window and ate mechanically, her mind on other things.

'Mind if I join you?'

It was one of the physics graduate students – the one who'd been hanging around Benson at the reception. Quenby she thought his name was. He grinned at her from behind a bushy beard. 'I've been meaning to tick you off for abducting our new Prof., Dr Bright.'

'Oh, well, he abducted me actually,' she replied. Quenby's eyes twinkled at her. 'What do you make of him so far?' she asked. 'He's pretty rude, isn't he?'

'We were prepared. I've known him for a couple of years. In a scientist of that calibre one can excuse some rudeness. We're jolly lucky to get him.'

'What do you know of him? That restless energy . . . '

'That's the key to his performance, I think,' ventured Quenby. 'You see, most people get into research because they're intrigued by the subject-matter. They like to solve riddles and make new discoveries. It's like a game, a treasure hunt, looking for clues, piecing information together, anticipating the thrill of discovery. With Andrew Benson it's different. He attacks a research project with ruthless efficiency. For him, an unsolved problem is like a toothache: he can't rest till it's been overcome. When other scientists complete a piece of work they go out on the town and relax. Benson just goes on to the next problem.'

Quenby stabbed at a potato with his fork and munched it reflectively.

'Sure he's rude and moody. That's part of it. Something drives him. He doesn't enjoy research, he's addicted to it, as though the mysteries of the universe are a personal challenge. He sees himself as one man pitted against the secrets of Mother Nature and he doesn't try to seduce them from her. With Benson, it's rape!'

Tamsin looked up sharply, and Quenby flushed. 'You seem to know him very well.'

'Actually, most of it's verbatim from *Time* magazine. They did a profile on him this week.'

'I know. I read it too.'

Tamsin excused herself and went back to her office. Raping Mother Nature. She'd forgotten that bit.

She heard the telephone ringing as she came along the corridor, and she fumbled clumsily for her door-key, eventually gaining access. The phone stopped. She sat down. The phone rang again and she answered it. A familiar voice said: 'Tamsin, it's John. John Maltby. Do you remember me?'

'Of course. How could I forget?' She'd met Maltby when they were both students in Oxford and they dated each other for a while. Then one day he took her punting and an excess of zeal had resulted in the punt capsizing, pitching them both into the river. After that she dated a chess enthusiast instead.

'I heard you went into the Ministry of something.'

'M.o.D. actually.'

'Is this a social call?'

'Strictly business, I'm afraid. I want to get in touch with a man called Andrew Benson . . . '

4

THE SOULLESS ROOM had driven Benson to the brink of despair. God, he thought, I'll never settle here. He stared morosely at the blank blackboard. Then in a fit of frustration he scrawled another obscenity on it and flung down the chalk. 'Three days,' he muttered to himself, 'and already I'm pissed off.'

After the rapturous welcome Benson had been left largely to his own devices. Which suited him. But any hope that the radical change of environment would somehow rekindle his desire for work was rapidly fading. Milchester University was going to be stultifying; he might as well face up to it. The only good thing about the place was the woman he'd met that first evening. She wasn't all that pretty, and was rather too old for his tastes, but there was something about her, something just beneath the surface. She'd had a most peculiar effect on him. That evening had been quite unlike any he'd ever spent with a woman.

A sharp rap interrupted his thoughts. A bearded head peered uncertainly round the door. Quenby. Benson grimaced.

'I've got a copy of my Phys. Rev. paper I mentioned. Would you like to go through it? I thought . . . '

'I'm busy,' snapped Benson.

Quenby looked at the board and saw the obscenities in large block capitals. 'So I see.' The bearded visage withdrew.

Benson groaned. 'Enough!' he said to himself, and he left the building, utterly dejected. After forty minutes waiting in the inevitable rain for an

30

apparently nonexistent bus he hailed a cab and went back to his hotel. He switched on the television and stretched out on the bed. He really ought to find himself somewhere permanent to live. A stone cottage up on the fells perhaps? Nice and isolated. Sod it. He'd start tomorrow. Really.

He closed his eyes. The voice on the TV droned on. A news reporter was interviewing a Frenchman at the base of the Eiffel tower. Some sort of accident.

Benson fell asleep.

He came awake slowly two hours later and glanced at his watch. He snapped off the television, washed and changed and thought about Joe. Joe would be polishing glasses downstairs by now. In less than a week, Joe had become a close friend, so close that Benson was already bored by him, but he was a good barman, didn't worry too much about those crazy bits of tin on the upside-down bottles. Benson still hadn't got accustomed to the things Joe called optics; didn't make sense to him, but not a lot of England made sense to him; it would take time to know a country that turned its booze upside down.

Joe smiled at him, as he came in, and said, 'Pleasant weather for ducks.' Benson grunted at him and looked around the bar. There was only one other customer, a youngish man sitting in the far corner, curly-haired with a pleasant smile and the build of a middleweight boxer. He was wearing a tennis shirt and baseball boots and reading the evening paper.

Later, thinking back, Benson could not remember who spoke first. It was something innocuous, one asking the other if he was staying at the hotel, a few moments of small talk before the young man introduced himself; an exchange of names: Andrew Benson, John Maltby. He had a firm, dry handshake and spoke with the distinctive well-modulated tones of the English public school. His first words, after the introduction, surprised Benson.

'I heard you lecture once. When I was a student. Ten or eleven years ago. In Oxford.'

'Is that so?' Benson accepted a cigarette and squinted at him. 'And what did you think?'

'I was rather baffled.'

'By me or the subject?'

'Both.'

Benson grinned. 'I'm not much of a lecturer.'

'Maybe not your strong point,' Maltby said.

'No damn maybes about it.'

There was a pause, Benson waiting for Maltby to continue. He wasn't from the University, too much self-assurance. Benson sensed the man wanted something from him. His guard went up.

31

'Journalist are you?'

'No.' Maltby replied, smiling. The man was quick, he thought, hoping he'd be able to keep his cover intact. Maltby had had a lengthy debate with himself on how to play it with Benson, whether to work on the 'humanity' angle or to play on Benson's weakness, present it as a chance for Benson to out-trump Hendricks. Finally he'd decided to present it as a straight intellectual puzzle. He had restructured the data to downplay the military aspects, highlighting the civilian incidents. Now he would see if his guess had been right.

'I'm a civil servant in the Home Office, Department of Justice to you.'

'Congratulations. I assume you want to see me about something. Why didn't you make an appointment? Pick up a telephone?'

Maltby leant across and tapped Benson's glass.

'Bourbon on the rocks,' Benson said.

A pause while Joe brought the drinks.

'Cheers,' said Maltby.

Benson nodded but said nothing.

'The thing is,' Maltby said, 'I know a few reporters. Occasionally bump into them. One thing I learnt from them is never to make appointments by phone if you think the other person may be, shall we say, unenthusiastic.' He smiled. 'Phones are dreadfully easy to hang up.'

'And I would have hung up?'

Maltby nodded. 'Your reputation, as they say, travels before you.'

Benson matched his smile. 'Who are they? And who exactly are you?' he asked quietly.

Maltby's smile widened. '*They* are just contacts. *Me*, they call a senior liaison officer, brackets science unbrackets.'

'Good for you.'

'It beats working.'

'And you decide who gets what?'

Maltby shook his head. 'Oh no. I just make recommendations.' He paused. 'I hope maybe I could interest you . . . '

'I can't imagine how.'

Maltby opened a black attaché case and extracted a file. He paused until the barman had moved away out of earshot.

'Let's get one thing clear at the outset,' Benson stated. 'I'm not getting involved in any sort of military science. As far as I'm concerned weapons research is a perversion of science.'

Maltby smiled deprecatingly and said, 'No, no, nothing like that.' He gave a little cough by way of introduction, then explained.

'About five weeks ago a radio communications facility in Cumbria suffered a sudden, though minor, malfunction. The damage itself wasn't serious, but the circumstances were, to say the least, peculiar. A metal pylon supporting a high-tension cable was melted through, leaving a ragged hole about two inches across.'

He leaned down, opened his bag, and withdrew a set of black-and-white photographs of the damage, taken at various magnifications. Benson studied them with evident scepticism.

'Probably lightning,' he muttered, scratching his nose.

'Possibly. Except that three weeks later exactly the same thing happened only the damage was more extensive.' He handed Benson another set of photographs, this time of a metal cowling encasing some switchgear. The pressed steel sheeting had been severely distorted and ripped apart in the centre.

'Lightning can strike twice, you know.'

'But this time there was a witness. An electronics engineer. He reported seeing a luminous orange ball, about the size of a grapefruit, sink slowly from the cloud base, zigzag a few times over the antenna array, and then dive suddenly towards the switchgear where it exploded with a loud report.'

Benson chewed his lip for a moment or two, vaguely recalling the fireball reports on the news, re-examined the photos and frowned. 'Ball lightning?'

'Maybe. The description is reminiscent of ball lightning – a glowing sphere exploding on contact with a solid object, erratic motion and so on. Yet twice in the same place seems odd.'

'Ball lightning is not as rare as many people suppose,' countered Benson. 'What were the weather conditions like?'

'Stormy on the first occasion, but only a low overcast the second time.'

'Well what do your lot think it is?' he asked.

'Frankly, Professor Benson, we don't know,' he said. 'If these two incidents were the only ones, we should probably write them off as freak atmospheric phenomena. But other strange events have been reported in the last month or two that have given us something of a jolt. For example, on the 18th of April a satellite-tracking station in New Zealand was disabled for twenty-four hours by an explosion in the antenna head itself. Then five days ago two ICBM early-warning radar stations reported exploding luminous balls near their main control cables.' He paused. 'That's serious.'

Benson looked unconvinced.

'You don't know that all these events are related. God knows, the military maniacs have scattered enough garbage around the world that something's bound to go wrong somewhere every week.'

Maltby ignored the slur and said: 'Any possibility of a threat to the West's communications system, however remote, must be taken seriously, Professor Benson.'

'What do you want of me? I really don't see how . . . '

'According to my sources you're the expert. If you'd agree to examine the evidence you might be able to advise us whether to take the fireball threat seriously.'

Benson's eyes widened a fraction. 'The fireball threat is it? What do you have in mind?'

'Some of our people see the Russians behind this.'

Benson was consternated. 'Oh, come on, Maltby. You people are paranoiac.'

'The idea of controlled plasma weapons is by no means fanciful, Professor, I assure you. Our intelligence has confirmed that experiments with plasma balls are taking place in at least three Russian secret laboratories, and we've had a number of reports of trials aboard military aircraft. Believe me, if they have found a way to produce artificial ball lightning to stabilize and direct controlled plasma at a distance, it could drastically tip the balance of power in the Russians' favour.'

Benson's eyes narrowed. 'You're not from the Home Office. You're State Department, aren't you,' he said accusingly.

'Ministry of Defence we call it here.'

'You devious little bastard.'

'Yes, well, I had hoped to leave the military aspects of this out until I had gained your attention.'

Benson got up to leave.

Maltby got to his feet too, unflustered. 'We think you are the man for the job, Professor. Ideally suited in fact.' He began ticking off points on the fingers of his left hand. 'By your mid-20s you had acquired an international reputation in the field of ionospheric thermodynamics. You had solved as part of your doctoral thesis one of the major outstanding problems concerning the transmission of energy through the upper atmosphere during magnetic storms. You then switched to low frequency radio wave propagation during thunderstorms, discovering a brand new technique for studying the atmosphere of Jupiter . . . '

'Believe it or not, I'm aware of all this.' Benson turned to go.

Maltby continued unabashed. 'You spent two years working on atmospheric and astrophysical plasmas. Then you built up a research group of ten people at the California Institute of Technology to study the effect of solar wind interaction with the atmosphere. You were on the threshold of major new progress concerning plasma confinement for controlled fusion

34

when . . . ' Maltby paused and smiled, ' . . . you rather made a mess of things with a senior colleague. Didn't you?'

Benson glowered at Maltby. He'd touched a raw nerve and Maltby intended to exploit it.

'Professor Benson. You know more about plasmas and atmospheric physics than anyone. For weeks our people, here and in the States, have been investigating all the available evidence of the fireball mystery. Eyewitness reports, on-site measurements and data analysis. Some progress has been made.'

Maltby looked into Benson's eyes earnestly.

'The problem is that several of the fireball phenomena remain puzzling. Indeed, I would go so far as to say that they are alarming. I am most anxious to obtain your specialist advice.'

Maltby smiled again. 'Believe me, Professor, I fully understand your feelings about military science. To be honest, I share your repugnance of the lunatic arms race. However, I must emphasize that the fireball mystery is not part of the West's armaments programme. What concerns us is a possible outside threat to our communications system.' He lowered his voice and made his appeal. 'Surely it's not unreasonable to expect a man to contribute to national security?'

Benson glared back at him, exasperated. 'Don't give me that patriotic bullshit,' he snapped. 'You spend enough public money on your infernal killing-machines. Now you come to me, expecting free advice, because you believe that the other side are one up on you. Well forget it.' He strode to the door. 'Leave me alone will you. I have some real science to be getting on with.'

The story had got out by chance. If the young man named Gregor from Ohio had been more accustomed to drink and could have held his liquor better the previous evening, he wouldn't have spoken out of turn. If he hadn't split up from his girl in Washington and come to visit friends in New York, he wouldn't have been in the same restaurant, at the next table to Peter Chalmers.

Gregor had been introduced to a young woman who had agreed to come out with him for dinner. By the third martini, she had regretted the decision. He had even come up with the canard about martinis and women's breasts: one's not enough and three's too many, and had laughed as if he'd just made it up.

At that point she had thought about leaving, then decided, what the hell, she'd stay. She might as well get a good three courses into her and then drop him. They'd ordered. But by the main course and second bottle of wine, he'd begun to confide in her. She didn't give a damn about balls of fire. She wasn't listening.

Nor, at first, was Peter Chalmers. If he had been more interested in the woman opposite him and what she was saying, he would not have paid any attention to Gregor; but the woman opposite was his wife. They had been married for eight years and they loved one another, but that evening she wasn't saying anything he hadn't heard ten times before.

'See, what it is,' Gregor was whispering, 'is nothing more than a massive cover-up.'

'Yeah?' said his date, eyes wandering.

'Yeah. Shouldn't be telling you of course. Like, I've taken the oath and all that.'

'Really?'

'Yeah.' He fumbled in his jacket and pulled out a badge. Candle-light flickered on silver lettering and caught Chalmers' eye. He glanced to his left, recognized the security pass and got interested.

'Makes that old Watergate stuff seem small beer,' Gregor was saying.

'Sure.'

'Anyway. These fireballs. They don't want people to know. They don't want it out that there's been over three hundred hits reported since April.'

'Is that so?'

Chalmers murmured to his wife that he was going to the men's room, got to his feet, stumbled, knocked over a glass on the next table, apologized profusely, apologies coming out of him rat-a-tat while he mopped the table and read the name on the pass and memorized the number. For the rest of the evening, he took a careful note of everything the young man was saying.

The following morning Chalmers had a problem. He had been a freelance journalist for ten years; some good years, but some not so good. This was one of the-not-so-good years. He could do with making some money from this tip and at first he thought of the supermarket rags, the ones in Florida that dealt in UFO stories and cancer cures; but this was too good for them. This was *Washington Post* material, but he'd lost his only contact there. And, besides, once he'd given it to them, they would do it themselves and drop him only a few bucks. So he decided on Larry who worked for the *New York Times*.

At ten that morning he was sitting in an O'Lunneys Bar and Grill with Larry trying to work out a deal.

'I'll give you what I got,' he was saying, 'so long as you bring me in on the story. Let me work it through with you.'

Larry shook his head. Trust us, or go to the guys in Florida.

Chalmers took a long pull of his beer, made his decision and started talking. Ten minutes later Larry was passing on the story to his features editor. The man took a lot of convincing but Larry had a name and a number in the State

Department. If they checked out, they had a story.

They checked out.

The editor held a morning conference at noon and listened to Larry's boss. He listened hard, then sat forward and arched his fingers. It was a good sign: meant he was interested.

'Okay, get every fireball story there's been,' he said at last.

'Even the crazies?' Larry's boss asked.

'Everything.'

Someone mentioned a story from Paris, France, about a guy killed on the Eiffel Tower. Someone else brought up the riddle of the exploding oil tanker. Maybe two and two could make eight after all. Then the oldest man in the room, a veteran from the days of hot lead and professional ethics, a man who kept refusing offers of early retirement, spoke:

'This could create a panic.'

He was laughed at and he shrugged. He should have known. Panic sells newspapers; a good bout of hysteria and maybe they could sell more copies than the *Daily News*.

Then Larry knocked, poked his head round the door and came up with the clincher. The State Department would neither confirm nor deny Chalmers' figures. Couldn't confirm or deny meant couldn't deny, which, as they all knew, meant the story was copper-bottom true.

Within four hours the streets of New York were filled with stories of fireballs; front page and centre spread, even encroaching on to the sacred space of the sports pages with an item on fireballs on golf courses. The hoardings screamed at the passers-by: 'Fireball Cover-Up'.

The story had finally broken.

5

BENSON WOKE THE next morning in a foul mood. He punched the TV buttons by his bed and stared absently at the flickering screen. At first he thought that he was watching a recording of a rock concert. Thousands of rapt faces were staring at someone on a platform, the camera flitting amongst them. But this could be no rock concert. There were too many children and old people. He listened as the commentator told him that an estimated fifty thousand people had converged on Central Park last night after stories of unexplained fireball activity had appeared in the *New York Times*. The man who had brought them together was the preacher named Harry K. Leveridge.

The camera closed in on him, a wild-eyed man, his chin speckled with white stubble, arms outstretched as he roared: 'Fire and brimstone!' the last syllable echoing in a whine of amplified feedback. Benson reached for the remote control and turned up the sound.

'These balls of fire are a warning from God,' Leveridge roared. 'The plague known as AIDS has destroyed the sodomites. Now comes the wrath of God in its most virulent . . .'

Benson groaned and switched Leveridge off.

An hour later he turned into a street of Victorian three-storey terraced houses, and pulled up at the door of number 56. There were two bells. He pressed the top bell and waited a full minute, wondering if she had forgotten. Then the answerphone squawked and he heard her say, 'Come up.' She was sorry but she was in the shower. He couldn't help wondering, as he climbed the stairs, what she would look like in the shower.

The door was open. She yelled from the bathroom that she'd be with him in a minute. He went into the living-room and gazed around him. It was a big bright room, the walls painted pale grey. On the coffee-table, a bottle of wine sat amongst a clutter of magazines. On the mantelpiece, above an open fireplace with a log basket, a bottle of sherry stood next to a more familiar bottle – bourbon, the seal unbroken.

He ambled across to her work area; a wall of shelves and a desk with an expensive word-processor. On the shelves, text books were stacked at random between works of fiction. Graham Greene had half a shelf to himself. There was Mailer next to Gore Vidal; Thomas Pynchon, Kurt Vonnegut and some writers he did not know. He picked out a paperback: *Erotica* by Anais Nin. It opened to the touch, a bus ticket fell out. He stooped to retrieve it, stuck it back in and began to read.

'Interesting choice.'

He turned and saw her standing in the doorway. He long brown hair was wet. She was barefoot, wearing jeans and a floppy green-and-white football jersey with the number sixty-four on the chest.

'New York Jets,' she said. 'I thought I'd make you feel at home.'

He replaced the book. 'I go for the Giants,' he replied. 'But thanks for trying.'

'Right,' she said, taking up a sheaf of estate agents' hand-outs. 'Let's find you somewhere to hide.'

Tamsin drove them out of town in the red Fiat, seeking a quiet rural spot that suited Benson's antisocial frame of mind. The sun shone brightly and the hills were a vivid green. On the high ground sheep wandered about, contentedly grazing. The contrast to the drab city was striking.

'It's beautiful,' he said. 'I hadn't expected this.'

They drove along country lanes bordered by hedges and dry-stone walls. From time to time a pheasant or partridge would flee the oncoming vehicle. Eventually they pulled up in a tiny village, just a few houses clustered around a pub and a church. Tamsin consulted the hand-out given her by the estate agent.

'That's it, over there,' she said, pointing to a decrepit-looking cottage that looked a clear candidate for demolition.

They walked up the garden path for a closer look. The cottage was built of stone, with a slate roof and a wooden porch with honeysuckle growing uncontrollably over it. The place looked as though it had lain empty for months. Large damp areas were clearly visible on the north wall. The garden was a jungle of weeds.

'Let's give it a miss,' he said firmly, and they drove on to the next place. It was even worse. They grew steadily more depressed.

'We'll leave it for another day,' he concluded as they drove off.

'But you've got to get out of that hotel.'

'Why? I like it there.'

'You can't live in an hotel.'

'You meet some very interesting people in hotels. Take last night for instance . . . ' She looked at him sharply, but said nothing. 'Some government guy accosted me in the bar, would you believe.'

'Oh? What did he want?' she said evenly.

'He had some crazy notions about these fireball things that people are getting freaked out about. Seemed to think I could help. Wanted to enlist me into the British secret service or something. I tell you, it was really weird.'

'What did you say?'

'I told him to fuck off, more or less.'

She looked annoyed. 'Was that sensible?'

Benson shrugged. 'Sure. Why not? I don't want to get mixed up with the military. Those guys are paranoiac. Anything odd happens, they blame the Russians.'

She was quiet for a few moments, negotiating a winding road. Then she said: 'Would you be able to help, Andrew? I mean, these fireball reports . . . they seem pretty genuine to me. You can't just shrug them off. Isn't it your subject area?'

'It's just hysteria. People see fireballs all the time. There are books written about them. It's known as ball lightning, a perfectly natural phenomenon.'

'But people have been killed. There was a welder trapped in a pipe . . . '

'Look, Tamsin. People do occasionally get killed by ball lightning. It's a very nasty phenomenon. A ball of fire, floating along . . . it only has to set light to your clothing or explode in your face . . . '

'But why are there suddenly so many incidents?'

'It's just the newspapers building it up. You know, like UFO reports. Hey, did you ever hear the one about the woman in Louisiana, said she was taken up for a flip around the solar system in a flying saucer. The cop asked her how she knew it was a flying saucer and she said: "Cos it had UFO painted on the side, dummy." '

She didn't laugh.

'If these fireballs are only ordinary ball lightning, why are the Ministry of Defence so interested?'

'How did you know it was the Ministry of Defence?'

She blinked. 'Well, it would be, wouldn't it? They'd be the ones who would

40

have to check it out, make sure there's no risk. From what you said about this strange man at the hotel, it sounds as though they're very concerned.'

'Nah. They're just twitchy because one or two of their precious installations have been damaged.'

'Still,' she persisted, 'it's worrying, isn't it?'

'I'm not worried. Are you worried?'

'Yes, Andrew. I can't just dismiss it like you. I think you should contact that man and offer to help.'

'Well forget it, Tamsin. Nothing would induce me to team up with those military bastards.'

Her eyes flared slightly as she shot him a glance.

'What have you got against the military anyway? Why this holier-than-thou attitude? Somebody's got to defend the nation.'

He didn't answer for a long while, just sat staring out at the passing fields.

'I've seen too many nice guys perverted by military science, seduced by secure jobs and fat salaries. They get so absorbed in the technical details of the work they forget its purpose is for killing people.'

'Surely people only get killed if there's war?'

She waited, but he made no attempt to reply. Her words just hung in the angry silence until they reached the next cottage. Like the others, it was old and damp and in urgent need of renovation. For an instant the image flashed through her mind of Andrew dressed in overalls, mixing plaster and drilling walls. She dismissed it.

'I guess I'll have to settle for an apartment in town,' he said resignedly.

'A flat.'

'A what?'

'Flat. We call them flats here.'

'Oh. Have we exhausted the list of cottages?'

'No, there's one more. Sounds just the job for you. It says "the ideal retirement home".'

'Anything wrong with retirement?'

'No. It's just that I expected more from you.'

He glanced at her but she slammed the car in gear and lurched off up the road. 'I expected,' she continued, 'someone bursting with ideas and energy, someone who raped secrets from Mother Nature.'

Benson laughed wryly.

They drove on in silence for a while, then he said: 'Do you know a place called The White Hind?'

'Yep,' she turned and looked at him. 'It's expensive.'

'I'll buy you lunch.'

41

It was an old coaching house, the date 1633 chiselled into a beam above the door. Tamsin swung the car into the car park, and they got out. Benson smiled. This was more like it. This was the sort of place he was looking for – if his salary were twice what it was.

They walked inside to a smell of wax polish. There were old oak beams, low ceilings, leather armchairs in the reception room, and a well-stocked bar. The television set in the corner looked distinctly out of place. Benson glanced at it; he'd never thought of televisions as out of place before. There was always one around, wherever he went, all his life. But in The White Hind, it looked incongruous.

They sat at the bar with drinks and perused the menu. A large Alsatian dog came up to them and Benson dutifully patted it. He tried small talk with Tamsin, but her attention was on the television, her eyes narrowing.

'Isn't it obscene?' she declared in a tone of disgust.

He turned and saw scenes of a riot. It was dark, the night lit up by police spotlights.

'What is it?'

'Last night's CND rally in Hyde Park. Peaceful until they got attacked. Look, the police are doing nothing.'

She winced as the screen showed a young woman being punched and kicked by two men, then she glanced at Benson. His face was calm and detached.

'It doesn't affect you, does it?' she said.

'Too remote.'

'But that girl?'

'Very nasty,' he said dispassionately.

The scene switched to Geneva; shots of angry Russians pushing their way through reporters outside an hotel and getting into their cars, the voice of the commentator stating that the meeting had broken up amid violent scenes unprecedented in the history of arms reductions talks.

'I was in CND for a while,' Tamsin said. 'At Oxford. But I didn't stay long.'

'Why?'

'I agreed with the policies but I couldn't get on with the people. They were too earnest. Too much decaffeinated coffee, if you know what I mean.' She tapped his arm, brought him round away from the TV. 'There's a rally in Milchester on Monday evening. I'm going. Want to come?'

'Why?'

'You could be my minder.'

He frowned. The word was unfamiliar.

'My bodyguard.'

'Beats rape,' he quipped.

The InterCity 125 train pulled out of Peterborough station on the last leg from Edinburgh to King's Cross terminus in London. It was hot and stormy and the passengers embarking at Peterborough were grateful for the air-conditioning in the coaches.

The powerful twin diesel locomotives soon built up a speed in excess of 100 m.p.h., so that when the rain came it ran in horizontal streaks along the windows. In the driver's cab Percy Bilton munched a corned-beef sandwich and eased the speed up further. The train was designed to cruise at 125 m.p.h. but this could only be achieved on the relatively straight sections of track. They were eight minutes late and Percy was pleased to have the chance to recoup lost time. British Rail had become very fastidious about schedules since privatization.

He set the huge windscreen wipers on maximum speed, but even so they had a hard time coping with the deluge of rain that splattered forcefully against the onrushing glass surface. What with the heavy cloud and the screen awash, it was all Percy could do to make out the track ahead.

The train was entering a narrow defile. At the far end lay the bridge that took the B1091 main road over the track. A set of signals were situated about a mile beyond, and Percy automatically peered through the murk in anticipation: looking out for signals is a reflex action for train drivers.

Suddenly his eyes narrowed. That was odd, thought Percy. It seemed as though the sun were reflecting from something coming towards him. He could see the bright yellow glow framed by the dark brickwork of the upcoming bridge. His first thought was that this was a northbound train on the parallel track, reflecting the sun from the cab window – until he realized that the sun doesn't shine from the north even when the sky isn't black with thunder-clouds.

The train was closing fast. Percy looked more carefully, and with a shock he concluded that there was somehow a blaze *beneath* the bridge. A shimmering fiery globe about two feet across hung as if from the roof. This was a section of track that had been electrified for dual use. The electric trains operated by overhead pickup from high-tension cables strung above the track. As the gap closed, Percy could see the ball of fire clinging to the cable, and he realized that there must be an electrical fault, something discharging and causing a corona.

It was obligatory to report instantly all such incidents, and Percy reached for the radio mike. The train was now about fifty yards from the bridge. At that instant the fireball began to move, as if sensing the oncoming locomotive. Astounded, Percy watched as the pulsating yellow ball began to roll along the

43

cable in a southward direction. As the train plunged under the bridge, the fireball had already moved thirty yards downtrack.

As he studied the mysterious spectacle, Percy's bafflement changed to alarm. The fireball had detached itself from the overhead cable, and was floating gently downwards. His heart missed a beat as he watched the train rush towards the glowing sphere. He dropped the mike and flung his free arm instinctively across his face, expecting at any instant the windscreen to shatter as the fireball collided with it.

Nothing happened. He looked up, consternated, to see the fiery sphere hugging the front of the locomotive, racing along with it at 120 m.p.h. Percy stared at the shimmering object, spellbound. Slowly it rolled around the side of the cab and then, without warning, suddenly flew off to the side of the track. The noise of the train drowned out the sharp bang that the fireball made when it exploded against the low-tension wiring near ground level.

Unnerved by this weird experience, Percy leant down to retrieve the mike, still dangling on its flexible cord. With a trembling hand he flicked the switch to transmit, but couldn't raise the signalman. He tried again, but the transmitter was dead. In the excitement of the moment he completely failed to realize that he had passed the first set of signals south of the bridge, and that the signal had been red.

Fourteen miles to the south, in the large box at Huntingdon, Ted Armitage had pushed the button to halt the 1.28 York to London InterCity express at Holme. This train was running forty minutes late, and had missed its time slot to pass through a short section of track where engineering maintenance work was being carried out. The next train uptrack was the Edinburgh to London InterCity, which had to be halted at the signal lights just south of the B1091 bridge, to avoid it entering the same sector as the York train. When the warning light on the control panel flashed, Ted was taken completely by surprise. The Edinburgh train had evidently passed straight through the red signal.

Ted was puzzled but not thrown; this was precisely the sort of incident he'd been trained for. He knew there was a back-up set of signals four miles south of the B1091 bridge, and he rapidly checked their status. With a start, he saw the system registering a malfunction. In a split second he flicked the emergency circuit into operation. Nothing. Something had knocked out both circuits. The back-up set of signals was dead.

With rising panic, Ted reached for the radio microphone. At 125 m.p.h. the Edinburgh train had about a minute and a half before piling into the rear of the York express. He switched to transmit and barked a rapid warning into the mike, then repeated it more slowly, asking for acknowledgement. He flipped to receive. Only static came over the speaker. His voice now shrill with anxiety, Ted kept on repeating his warning, over and over.

In the cab of the Edinburgh train, Percy was recovering from the surprise of his experience with the fireball. He vaguely remembered reading about similar incidents in the newspapers. Perhaps he'd witnessed something important? He was very excited: this would make an interesting tale to regale his mates with in the pub that evening. Who knows, the local newspaper might even be interested. He could end up with his picture in the paper.

With a broad grin, he switched on the intercom connecting the forward locomotive cab with the guard, who rode in the rear locomotive. At least that circuit seemed to work alright.

'Yes Percy?' came the metallic voice of the guard over the intercom.

'Alf, I've just seen the strangest thing, mate.'

'What's that, Percy? A pair o' knickers on the line?' Alf referred to a now-famous story concerning an Eastern region driver dismissed for being intoxicated in charge of a train.

Percy began describing the fireball, keeping one eye on the track ahead. The overcast had worsened now, and the rainstorm was so fierce that visibility from the cab was down to fifty yards. The back-up signal light, had it been functioning, would still have alerted Percy in time to the blockage on the line, but given the gloomy conditions and Percy's preoccupation with relating the fireball incident to Alf, the train roared on through the blacked-out signals without so much as a second glance by either driver or guard.

At full speed an InterCity 125 takes nearly half a mile to stop, using maximum emergency braking power. When the rear of the stationary train emerged from the gloom some seventy yards ahead Percy knew he was a dead man. His reflexes took care of the brakes, but in spite of the instantaneous reaction, the train was still doing eighty when it ploughed into the York express.

6

THE CAB DRIVER taking Benson to work on the first morning of his second week was the talkative kind. Benson had had him before and automatically he closed his mind to him.

'Bloody liberty all this, isn't it?'

'Sure.'

'Diabolical I reckon. I mean, if only the government would tell us what's going on, but they don't. They just flannel. And your lot aren't any better, are they?'

'Worse,' said Benson.

'My missus reckons it's God.'

'Probably'.

'He's sick of the whole lot of us. That's what she says.'

Benson looked out. The streets seemed emptier this morning. House after house glowed a dim blue from living-room windows as though everyone was watching television.

'So what do you reckon then, Professor?'

'About what?'

'What I've been on about. Fireballs.'

'Jesus Christ,' Benson muttered. 'Not you too.'

'Yeh. Take that forest fire near Melbourne. Did you see it on the box?'

'No.'

'Terrible, it was. All them houses.'

'There have been forest fires in Australia before.'

'Yeh, perhaps. Maybe you got a point there.'

Benson was glad to get out. He worked all morning reading through a paper written by one of the graduate students.

At lunchtime, he wandered down to the refectory, ordered a sandwich and sat at a corner table, but there was no relief from the fireballs. Everyone was talking about them. The conversation gave him indigestion. He fled to his room, locked his door, took out a paperback and read throughout the afternoon. Around five the phone rang. It was Tamsin, sounding oddly cheerful, reminding him of their date. Six at the Rose and Crown, then on to the rally. He had forgotten all about it.

The pub had been designed to resemble a medieval castle: plastic swords, balls-and-chains, axes and crossbows decorated the walls. The bar counter was framed by cardboard turrets and battlements. Tamsin was sitting on a stool drinking red wine.

'Did you get across the moat all right?' she asked.

He nodded. 'Awful isn't it?'

'You should see the Jolly Brewers. It's done out like a Manhattan cocktail bar.'

Benson shook his head. 'Whatever happened to tankards of ale and guys wearing smocks?'

'They'll think of that soon enough,' she said. 'Beer?'

He nodded. The beer came up and Tamsin clinked glasses.

'Did you hear about the train crash?' she asked.

'No. What train crash?'

'Edinburgh to London InterCity 125 smashed into the back of a stationary train near Peterborough. It was on the news.'

'I never bother to watch. So what's new?'

'There are seventy-eight people dead, that's what's new,' she said tartly.

'Sorry. But there are crashes all the time you know.'

'Not caused by fireballs there aren't.'

'Oh Christ. You can't get away from them.'

'Andrew, it's getting worse.'

'Hysteria.'

'It's not! This man on the television, he was the guard on the train. He described what happened. You can't just brush all these incidents aside.'

There was an awkward silence while both of them peered into their drinks.

'Have you had any more contact with that man from the M.o.D . . . the Ministry of Defence?' she ventured, nervously.

47

'No. Why should I?' he snapped. 'I told him to get stuffed, remember. What's it to you anyway?'

'I thought you might have changed your mind, agreed to help.'

'No I bloody well haven't changed my mind!'

Benson's raised voice drew looks from the other customers, and Tamsin flushed brightly.

'Look, as far as I'm concerned,' he continued, 'these fireballs are nothing more than a few ball lightning incidents that the press has got a hold of and hyped up out of all proportion. It's just a freak phenomenon. You know, I wouldn't put it past those military guys to have set up the whole fireball story as a cover for their own weapons testing.'

'Alright, alright,' she said quickly. 'Let's change the subject.'

'Right. Tell me about this insane rally of yours.'

The platform had been set up on the wet grass in the local park. Two men and a woman sat perched on canvas chairs in front of the home-made CND banner, looking down on an assorted crowd of about two hundred. Most of the audience seemed to be either students or young mothers. Some of them had infants in push-chairs or suspended in slings from their shoulders. Tamsin chose a place near the back of the crowd.

It was dull and humid, with the threat of thunder in the air, and Benson regretted allowing himself to be dragged along. He found the speeches banal beyond belief, full of well-rehearsed clichés and familiar exhortations. It was the woman's turn now, the local branch secretary apparently. She stood up nervously, thin and grey-faced, like a caricature of a librarian spinster. Benson could see what Tamsin meant about decaffeinated coffee.

The woman's faltering tones competed with static over the loudspeakers. Her argument was sincere enough, but the delivery was dreadful. Benson recalled the messianic features of the Reverend Harry K. Leveridge and the sheep-like adoration of his audience. What a contrast. When it comes to public crusades, he decided, it was not enough to be right, you also had to be Right. What CND needed was a Leveridge.

Tamsin glanced at him and pulled a face.

'Had enough?' he asked.

She nodded and they turned to leave, just as the first sound of chanting began. An ugly, sneering chorus. Tamsin had heard the sounds before, on television – the soccer riots, the picket line, the National Front marches.

The obscene chanting was followed by a rhythmical clapping.

Then they saw them. Fifty youths, identical in bleached crew-cuts, denims and heavy boots, were swarming up the grass bank towards the gathering, some clapping, others with their hands ominously behind their backs. No police were in sight.

'Oh my God,' Tamsin whispered, grasping his arm.

The thin woman on the platform looked utterly bewildered. She broke off from the tedious monologue and began imploring everyone to remain calm, stand firm. This was a situation that tested the real strength of their resolve.

The result was a panic-stricken rout. The mob was only fifty yards away now, and closing fast. The yobs were swinging clubs and bicycle-chains menacingly, rushing at the crowd with piercing screeches, like a pack of crazed gorillas, light reflecting from their steel-capped boots. As they approached they split into groups and began the chase, lashing out at the defenceless supporters. Men, women and children scattered in all directions, desperate to find an escape route, women shouting, toddlers screaming in alarm. Benson watched, sickened, as a pram turned over, spilling the baby out on the grass.

Then there came a scream, thin and high, amplified over the loudspeakers. The woman on the platform was shrieking and pointing to the sky. Benson's eyes followed the woman's finger. There, about two hundred feet above them, was a glowing yellow ball, slowly descending from the thunderclouds. It hovered directly over the mayhem in the park, and for a moment the fighting calmed as the element of the unexpected was injected.

The fireball bobbed and swayed gently over their heads for a few seconds; then, as if obeying some unseen command, it veered off suddenly to the west, towards a line of trees, where it dropped out of sight behind the bank.

'Come on!' shouted Benson, tugging at Tamsin's arm, pulling her toward the trees. 'Let's take a look.'

'No!' she replied emphatically, shaking her head. He turned and saw that there was no colour left in her face. 'I must get out of this nightmare!'

Benson glanced back at the trees, and then around them at the strangely interrupted affray. At that moment there began a chorus of police sirens, and instantly the thugs began to scatter.

'Okay, let's quit,' he said.

It was just a short walk to Tamsin's flat, and she remained silent all the way. Once inside she sat stiffly on the sofa, ashen-faced. Benson could see she'd been badly shaken, and he scoured the living-room for some brandy. He half-filled a tumbler and she gulped at it.

He went to the window and peered out in the direction of the park. A thin column of smoke rose from behind the trees.

'I guess I'd better leave you to recover,' he said.

'No, Andrew. Don't do that. Please stay.'

49

He turned, walked back to the sofa and sat beside her, their thighs touching. 'Does the brandy help?'

She nodded, and smiled thinly. 'Sorry to be so pathetic.'

'Pathetic? Christ, I was scared out my wits out there. Mind if I have a brandy too?' She handed him the remains of hers. He downed it in one go. Then he looked directly into her eyes, and for the first time in years he felt a glimmer of real affection for another human being.

George Todd had boarded Alitalia flight 702 at Milan. He'd changed his itinerary at the last minute, having finished his business trip a day early. Anxious to return home to London, he'd taken a cab to the airport on the off-chance of getting a seat and he'd caught the plane with five minutes to spare. It was 9 p.m.

Always nervous of flying, his anxiety hadn't been helped when the passenger next to him, a diminutive Sicilian with a moustache, crossed himself vigorously on take-off. Todd ordered a double Scotch to calm his nerves and tried to relax. He distracted himself with fragmented fantasies about the girls on the beach at Alassio.

It was about half an hour out of Milan that Todd was abruptly shaken out of his reverie by a cry of alarm from the first-class compartment. He craned his neck to see. A weird orange glow emanated from the front cabin. 'A fire!' thought Todd, the adrenalin pumping instantly through his arteries. But he couldn't see because a stewardess was blocking the view. People were shouting, waving their arms.

The stewardess backed slowly down the aisle, her face fixed in a mask of terror. Todd could see now. The source of light was a swirling fiery ball, about a foot in diameter, drifting slowly and silently down the centre of the cabin two feet off the floor.

As the terrified stewardess drew level with his seat, Todd's mental inertia broke, and he grabbed the girl round the waist, dragging her unceremoniously on to his lap. The fireball slid by menacingly.

A second stewardess stood directly in the path of the ball. She tried to squeeze to one side but the glowing object brushed her skirt and instantly her clothing was ablaze. She screamed as the flames engulfed her, and fell writhing on the floor.

The horrified passengers were thrown into a frenzy of activity. Two Italians leapt up and desperately tried to smother the flames. A woman began to shriek and tear at her hair as though demented.

A middle-aged English businessman, smartly dressed ex-army type, rose from his seat, walked calmly to the galley area at the rear of the plane, and emerged with a large metal tray. He waited amid the hubbub until the fireball glided by and then swiped at it as though it were a football.

There was a deafening explosion and the lights went out. The man was flung on to his back and the plane began to lurch alarmingly. The stewardess on Todd's lap lost her balance and sprawled out across both seats, then slid helplessly into the narrow gap between his legs and the seat in front.

The plane twisted and turned, its engines roaring over the din of the hysterical passengers. They were losing height fast.

Todd was paralysed with fear. All his worst nightmares about flying were coming true. They were going to crash. They were over the Alps. All mountains, nowhere to put down. It would be the end. A horrible, painful death. Oh God!

A colossal impact sent a shock-wave down the fuselage, flinging passengers and baggage through the cabin. Todd was badly stunned and for a few seconds that seemed like hours his senses were a meaningless jumble. When he finally gathered his wits his first distorted thought was that he had fallen off his yacht which he kept moored at Devonport. His face was wet. Blood! No, water. Definitely water. The plane must have come down in a lake. He was still alive.

Suddenly his euphoria turned to renewed fear. The plane had broken in two on impact and flames were rapidly devouring the open end of the fuselage. There was no escape.

Then he noticed the water lapping around his feet, felt the fuselage tipping slowly backwards. They were sinking. He was trapped between fire and water!

Todd despaired, tried desperately to clear his befuddled brain. If the plane were sinking there must be a hole somewhere . . . near the rear.

He went to get up, but couldn't. Something was wedging him into his seat. The stewardess. He grabbed her clothing and even her hair and pulled frantically. She screamed in pain.

'Get up, for Christ's sake! Get up!' he bellowed at her, but to no avail. The Sicilian lay slumped in his seat, his face a mass of blood. No help there.

Todd peered through the flickering gloom at the prostrate girl. Her leg was wedged under the seat in front; probably broken. He had to get her off him.

The fuselage was tilted at about twenty degrees now and icy water was pouring all around them. Todd reached down and clasped the girl's leg, yanking viciously, oblivious to her screams, self-preservation uppermost in his mind. The flames were already scorching his face.

Her leg came free. He dragged her off him and stumbled out of his seat, the panic enveloping him. Todd saw one or two dazed passengers wallowing in the water, ducking under. He saw the jagged hole in the light of the flames, the inky black water swirling in.

51

Something clasped his ankle. He looked down. It was the stewardess. She was pleading with him in Italian. He tried to shake her off, but her grip was like a vice.

Cursing uncontrollably, he tugged the sprawling figure into the aisle. 'Get up!' he bawled at her. The girl struggled painfully upright, her injured leg dangling uselessly. Todd pushed her roughly towards the rapidly sinking rear of the plane. She stumbled and hobbled pathetically, clinging desperately to seat-tops and dead passengers.

They stood waist-deep in water. 'Go on! Go on!' shrieked Todd. The girl was blocking his path. The fuselage was sinking fast. In a few seconds the hole would be below water. He'd never find it. His only means of escape would be lost!

He shoved her violently in the back. The girl pitched forward into the water, gashed her stomach savagely on the jagged metal, and disappeared.

Todd wasted no more time. He floundered towards the dwindling aperture, took care to avoid the sharp edges himself and ducked below the surface. He caught his thigh painfully against something, but otherwise managed to pass through the opening effortlessly.

Several passengers were struggling in the water round the plane, coughing and spluttering. Todd could see the lights of a town at the edge of the lake. It wouldn't be long before help arrived, a boat to pick them up.

He swam gently away from the plane in the dark, his mind gradually clearing. He'd had a miraculous escape. No doubt about that. Probably the media would be on to him tomorrow. 'London man in plane crash drama.' He could see the headlines now. If he played his cards right he might even pick up a fat fee for his story. After all, he was a bit of a hero really, saving the stewardess and all that; always supposing the stupid girl didn't drown after his efforts . . .

'An amazing escape,' said the interviewer later.

'It was just a matter of remaining calm,' replied Todd, nonchalantly.

When he awoke it was dark, and for a moment Benson wondered where he was. Then he felt the warmth of her body beside him.

He lay there for a while, feeling strangely uneasy. It had happened so suddenly. Her love-making had been intense, frenetic, an explosive release of tension. He'd not really been in control and that disturbed him. Benson was unused to being manipulated, even in matters of sex. But that was less unnerving to him than the feelings that were surfacing in his mind. He actually cared about this woman, a woman who was still, in fact, nearly a stranger to him.

Once before, many years ago, he'd cared for a woman, cared more strongly than he ever believed possible. They had lived together for three years, and in that time he did his most important piece of research. Then she'd had the accident . . .

He slipped out of bed and began to dress quietly. He was not ready yet for small talk across the breakfast table. Tiptoeing into the living-room, he looked around for a notepad, finding one by the telephone. He picked up a pencil and was about to write something apologetic on the top sheet when he noticed in the half-light from the street lamps that something was already written there: a London telephone number with the word 'John' beneath. Something made him tense. On impulse he lifted the phone and tapped out the number. After a few seconds a voice said, 'Ministry of Defence'.

Benson put down the phone and swore savagely. He tossed the pencil on the desk and left.

7

TAMSIN KNOCKED ON Benson's office door and let herself in. The blinds were drawn tightly, shutting out the bright summer sunshine, and the television played soundlessly to itself. There were packing-crates everywhere. The blackboard was blank except for two large obscenities. Benson sat brooding behind a desk strewn with papers and discarded plastic coffee mugs. His eyes were hostile.

'Can't you see I'm working!' he snapped at her, ignoring the look of hurt and indignation on her face.

'I brought you some flowers', she said flatly, holding a small bunch of violets pathetically. 'To say thank you.'

'Save them for your boyfriend!'

'Who?'

'The one from the Ministry of Defence.'

Tamsin went pale.

'Did they actually pay you to get me into bed or did you do it for patriotic reasons?' he said sourly.

Tamsin struck him heavily across the face, scattering the flowers over the desk. Benson was so stunned he remained speechless. 'Jesus Christ, you're a disgusting bastard!' she shouted at him, her dark eyes flaring angrily. 'I don't pretend to know who or what has poisoned your mind, but if anyone can ever penetrate that self-righteous ivory tower of yours they ought to tell you that there are real people out here, people with feelings. You might be a smart-

54

arsed physicist, but that doesn't give you the right to play God!'

She tossed her long hair out of her face. 'So I happen to know John Maltby? And yes, I did put him on to you. That doesn't make me a whore!'

'You set me up, you bitch!' Benson was shaking with rage.

'As a matter of fact, Professor bloody know-all, I thought you might welcome a new project. You know, like making a fresh start in a new country and all that crap. I wish to God I'd never bothered. How was I to know you'd be so high-and-mighty about the military?'

'Stay out of my affairs, will you!'

'Oh, don't worry. I will.'

She slammed the door behind her and Benson sat in eerie silence, staring unseeing at the flickering television screen. Jumbled images chased each other through his mind: a crazy preacher, a panic-stricken crowd, a ball of fire descending from the clouds, Tamsin clinging to him, Tamsin crying out as they made love, Katy crying out as . . . No! He screwed his eyes shut and pounded his head.

He opened his eyes and recoiled with shock. A familiar face stared at him accusingly, mouthing abuse. Hendricks! Benson pulled himself together and hit the TV sound control.

' . . . wish to assure the public that the fireballs will abate as soon as this unusual period of sunspot activity is over.'

Benson gaped in consternation. Sunspot activity! What the hell was the stupid bastard on about?

The interviewer asked what could be done to protect the public meanwhile. 'We're investigating a number of counter-measures', intoned Hendricks. 'Experts from all across the United States have been cooperating in an attempt to understand the properties of the fireballs and devise adequate protection. There is no need for alarm.'

'It's a cover-up,' muttered Benson to himself.

The news clip ended and the programme returned to the London studio.

'And now for more details on last night's plane crash in Switzerland, over to Peter Crowe in Geneva.'

The reporter stood in front of the lake, interviewing a dishevelled man of about thirty who was evidently a survivor from the crash. 'At first I thought it was a fire, I could only see an orange glow. People started screaming and that. Then I saw this big kind of luminous ball, floating down the centre of the plane . . . '

Benson's brow furrowed, and he looked away from the screen as the man went on to describe his heroics. 'How the hell did it get inside the bloody plane?' said Benson to himself.

He sat there immobile for a further ten minutes, then he jumped up abruptly, locked the door and began rummaging through the half-opened packing-crates that littered the room. It took him an hour to find the folder with the yellowing hand-written notes he'd made all those years ago. He'd only dabbled in the subject then. Ball lightning was never quite respectable . . .

The pin-board behind his desk slowly filled as he pinned up papers, photographs and formulae. There was an engraving of the death of a certain Dr G.W. Richmann of St Petersburg in 1752, struck on the head by ball lightning as he was experimenting in his laboratory, then a diagram of a water barrel hit by a fireball: four gallons of water had boiled on impact, and the water was too hot to touch for twenty minutes; a woman burned in her home by a four-inch ball that melted her polyester skirt and caused her gold ring to heat up, burning her finger; a gruesome photograph of a woman burned so badly that only her lower torso and legs were recognizable, the death being put down to a bizarre phenomenon known as spontaneous combustion. Benson scrawled 'ball lightning' across it and a question mark. Then there was another series of photographs of a trail of burnt grass ten yards in length ending with a burnt, punctured light-bulb under the eaves of the house, the puncture hole a quarter inch in diameter.

He worked on, pinning up photo after photo until the board was covered, then he picked up a list of names of the phenomenon: *Kugelblitz, globes du feu, tonnerre en boule, coup de foudre en boule, sharovoyi molnii, globus igneous* . . .

There was a knock on the door. Benson shouted, 'Come in.' The knob rattled and Quenby mumbled: 'It's locked.'

Benson let him in and stood back as Quenby shambled into the room.

'Sorry to trouble you,' he said, looking curiously at the scattered flowers and at the papers pinned to the board.

'No problem,' Benson replied in clipped tones.

'It's just that the computer's down again, so I though I'd have a crack at that research problem we talked about the other day, you know, the solar wind thing.'

'Fine.'

'I took a look at that suspect coefficient, but I'm stuck on an integral. I can't find it anywhere in Gradshteyn and Ryzhik.'

'Have you tried the Russian book?'

'Yes, that too. Let me just show . . . '

'Forget the integral, Nigel,' cut in Benson. 'I'm working on something new now, and I may need your help, okay?'

'Sure.'

Quenby straightened, his face lighting up. It seemed to Benson as if the man was actually standing to attention.

'It might mean long hours.'

'That's alright. What do you want me to do?'

'For the moment, nothing.' Quenby's face dropped. 'I'll call you, right.'

'Right.'

When Quenby had gone, Benson picked up the phone and dialled the Biochemistry Department. A voice said: 'Bright.'

'It's me.'

The phone went dead. He dialled again.

'Look I'm sorry, right?'

'An apology from Andrew Benson! I should have taped it,' she replied acidly.

'I want you to contact Maltby. I need some data.'

There was a long silence. 'Don't tell me you've changed your mind?'

'I won't work for those military bastards, but I need the data. Are you going to help or not?'

'I don't see why I should.'

She hung up.

Five minutes later the phone rang. A smooth female voice informed him that Mr Maltby would be on the two o'clock plane and would be at Benson's office before four.

Maltby eyed him warily. 'Do I take it that you are prepared to cooperate after all?'

'No,' replied Benson. 'I'm not going to work for you. You are going to work for me. I need all the data you have so I can figure out how the hell a fireball can get inside an aircraft.'

'Then you accept there is something odd about the fireballs?'

'I accept nothing.'

'Do you at least concede it's possible that these objects don't have a natural origin?'

'Look, Maltby, people have been trying unsuccessfully for years to produce ball lightning in the laboratory. If the Russians can create plasma balls to order and get them inside aircraft hundreds of miles away they must be scientific geniuses. They deserve to inherit the Earth.'

Maltby hesitated a moment, then said: 'You know the name of Nicola Tesla?'

'Of course. I'm a physicist. The *tesla* is the international unit of magnetic field intensity.'

'What few scientists know,' Maltby continued, 'is that although Tesla's work was carried out nearly a century ago, many of his experiments with intense electromagnetic fields have never been repeated. He performed the most remarkable feats of electrical engineering, way ahead of his time, and he also carried out secret experiments with very high energy discharges – artificial lightning if you like. He believed he'd discovered a new type of force, capable of transmitting power directly from one place on Earth to another without wires or cables.'

Benson smirked. 'Surely you don't believe all that claptrap?'

'I don't believe Tesla's own explanation for his discoveries, but I think he may have found a way to control high-intensity electromagnetic fields and to manipulate them at a distance.'

'What's all this got to do with the Russians? Tesla was a Yugoslav.'

'In 1955 the Russian physicist Pjotr Kapitza, the man who won a Nobel prize for his work on superconductivity, published a remarkable paper on ball lightning. He tried to demonstrate that electromagnetic waves of the right frequency could become trapped between the clouds and the ground in a standing wave pattern. As more and more energy is funnelled into the field, so its intensity grows. At certain critical points – the antinodes of the wave – the strength could become great enough to ionise the air and create a plasma ball.'

Benson yawned.

'Of course,' Maltby said, 'I expect you know all this.'

'I don't see how Tesla and Kapitza tie in with a Russian threat. Just because Kapitza's Russian . . . '

'About four years ago the CIA received a tip-off that a Russian agent was planning to infiltrate a top secret defence establishment in Maryland working on DECEP.'

'What the hell's that?' asked Benson.

'DECEP: Destruction of Communication by Electromagnetic Pulses,' Maltby recited.

'You mean blowing the other side's circuits with a directed electromagnetic flash?'

'Precisely.'

'Well, well, what do you know?' Benson's voice was corrupt with sarcasm.

'About a month after the tip-off, a man was caught red-handed photographing an unpublished paper of Tesla's on directed electromagnetic beams. The paper had been secretly in the possession of the US government since the thirties, but it's only recently that defence scientists have taken it seriously. Under interrogation the agent admitted he'd been attempting to secure information about Tesla's secret experiments for use in the controlled plasma work at Novosibirsk, which is the leading Soviet centre for high-energy beam weapons, plasma weapons and DECEP research. And the director of the Novosibirsk lab is a certain Boris Vasiliev, former student of Pjotr Kapitza.'

Benson still looked sceptical. 'It's all pretty circumstantial, isn't it? Maybe the Russians are working on controlled plasmas. Perhaps they're even gullible enough to dabble in Tesla's discredited ideas. But that's still a long way from an explanation of these fireballs. For all we know, Soviet defence installations might be suffering precisely the same phenomena as NATO. After all, they would hardly advertise the fact, would they?'

'But you do agree that there is something going on?'

Benson sighed heavily. 'Look, it could simply be a freak spate of ball lightning events. You know, just like you get freak hailstones or tornados. There's no evidence that these fireballs are under any sort of control.'

'I agree,' said Maltby unexpectedly. 'That's my job. To find out whether these things are just some sort of natural quirk or something more threatening. Unfortunately the data's not very helpful. There doesn't seem to be any significant pattern in either space or time.

'Of course,' continued Maltby, 'there's a big selection effect because we only receive reports through restricted channels. As you say, none is forthcoming from the Eastern bloc. Nor are there many from over the ocean, or from relatively uninhabited regions like Antarctica or the Sahara.'

'What about time of day?' asked Benson.

'The same. No pattern.'

'Who's responsible for upgrading the data as new reports come in?'

'Wright-Patterson Air Force base at Dayton in Ohio is keeping an up-to-the-minute record. I've got direct access to the data base via LINKNET.' Maltby referred to the network of communication linkages between large US and European computer centres.

'I'll show you.' He handed Benson a piece of paper, a file of the latest fireball cases.

'Christ,' said Benson eventually. 'Are these all new?'

'The date is given in the right-hand column.'

'That's about five or six reports *a day*, just through military channels! Your friends must be going through some sort of mania.'

Maltby smiled. 'As I tried to say. This is a matter of national security, Professor.'

'What about altitude-dependence?'

'How do you mean?'

'Well,' explained Benson, 'according to this you've got three hundred and forty-eight reports in all with eighty-one coming from aircraft. Now the way I figure it, there are a whole lot more people down here than up there. Agreed?'

Maltby nodded.

'So the question is, statistically, why so many aircraft cases?'

Maltby didn't offer an opinion.

'The explanation is obvious, Maltby. There are clearly far more fireballs up there than down here.'

'You mean they are being activated high up in the air?'

'I mean they are much more likely to occur at high altitude. Just that.'

'Does that help?'

'Sure. What I would do is to pack a bunch of equipment inside one of those high-altitude experimental planes – the X whatever it is – and send it as high as it goes. See if one of these fireballs shows up. Shorten the odds considerably.'

Maltby nodded slowly. 'Okay. That's fundamental enough. I'll look into it.'

'Don't just look into, Maltby. Fix it. I'm interested. I want to know the answers.'

'I'll try my best,' said Maltby. 'Like you said, I'm working for you.'

The scratching from the tank became frenetic. 'One wonders,' said John Maltby, 'what is so attractive about the world outside the tank that they should crave for it.'

'Terrapins are creatures of instinct,' explained Tamsin. 'All that scrabbling is not part of a rational strategy.'

'Sounds like the M.o.D. I'm afraid I rather dropped you in it over this Benson matter, Tamsin.'

'Nothing changes, does it?' she replied, an image of an overturned punt flashing through her mind. 'Do I understand that he's now going to play ball? Or should I say fireball?'

'He's stopped ranting, if that's what you mean. Something's obviously convinced him there's a genuine puzzle. His natural scientific curiosity has conquered his cynicism – at least temporarily. Touchy people, these scientists,' said Maltby, and then added hurriedly, 'present company excepted, of course.'

'You know he actually witnessed a fireball personally?'

'Good Lord, no. When did this happen?'

'Yesterday. We were at a CND rally . . . ' Maltby grunted his disapproval, but she ignored him, ' . . . and there was some sort of riot, a gang of fascist thugs tried to break the meeting up. Anyway, in the middle of all this a bright yellow ball fell out of the sky. I thought it was going to drop right on top of us, but it veered away at the last minute. The whole episode was something of a nightmare.'

'I can imagine. Do you think the incident changed Benson's mind?'

'I don't know. He's such a strange man.'

'He's a slob.'

'No, John. That's too simplistic. Front-line scientific research imposes peculiar strains on people; it distorts their normal social behaviour. It's so competitive, yet so abstract. I'm convinced that beneath that abrasive exterior lies a subtle and sensitive personality.'

'Inside every physicist there's a human being struggling to get out?' Maltby eyed the latest futile endeavour in the glass tank. 'I can only hope he has more success than your pet reptiles.'

'He'd probably have been more cooperative if you hadn't worked for the M.o.D. He really is fanatically anti-military. He dismisses CND as a bunch of wimps.'

'I suppose it's understandable, given what happened to his wife.'

Tamsin's eyes widened. 'I didn't know he was married.'

'He's not. Didn't you know? His wife used to work for Delremo, the chemical giant that has all the big defence department contracts in the States. Apparently they were experimenting with nerve gas, and there was some sort of accident. Nobody really knows what happened. Anyway, some gas escaped and five workers died rather horribly. Katy Benson was one of them.'

8

THE SUMMONS FROM Sir William was for five-thirty and Maltby had a few minutes to kill. He sat with his feet on his desk staring at the ceiling, then reached for a book from the shelf behind him. It was heavy. Andrew Benson scowled at him from the dust-jacket, his hair tousled, standing arms folded in front of a scrawled blackboard, a clichéd picture of the academic in his lair. At least he could have smiled, Maltby thought, instead of glaring at the camera as if it were taking whatever was left of his soul.

Maltby slipped the dust-jacket off and read the blurb. It was almost meaningless to him. Maybe only a couple of dozen people in the world were qualified to read the book and fully understand it. Maltby looked at the photograph again. 'The loneliness of the long-distance genius,' he muttered. The more Benson discovered about his subject, the more people he left behind until ultimately he was talking only to himself. Maybe he could feel at home with only a couple of Americans, a European or two, a Japanese and a Russian.

On impulse he got to his feet, picked up two pins, crossed the room and pinned the dust-jacket on the noticeboard next to the door, then went back to his desk and rummaged in his drawer for his set of darts. He had kept them since his student days and they had won him a few quid. They were heavy, spring-loaded tungsten steel, the flights bearing the crest of his college. He weighed one in his hand for a moment then threw it at the photograph. It quivered in Benson's left eye and Maltby grinned. 'Come on, Benson,' he said. 'Come up with something, you bugger.'

The second dart thudded into the blackboard behind Benson's head and he was about to throw the third when the phone rang. It was Sir William's secretary saying that he was expected now and that he should meet Sir William in the car park. Maltby put down the phone, dragged on his jacket, went to the door, then flung the last dart. It zipped into Benson's right eye. 'Game shot,' Maltby said and went out, locking the door behind him.

Sir William was waiting for him in the back seat of his Bentley and nodded a greeting as Maltby sat next to him; a word to the driver and the car glided towards the ramp and the sunlight.

'Your tan has faded, Maltby,' Sir William said. 'A good sign,' He reached to his left, picked up a pile of newspapers and scattered them on the floor. Maltby looked at them. Each headline seemed to be personal affront, the tabloids shrill, the heavy papers muted, but all asking the same question, wanting to know what was happening.

'Not so good, Maltby,' Sir William said.

'No, sir.'

'I've read your memos. We don't seem to be getting very far, do we?'

'It's a new phenomenon, sir. New rules. No precedents.'

'And it's killing people.'

Maltby nodded and said nothing.

'I don't think this sunspot idea is catching on,' Sir William said, fluttering a hand at the newspapers.

'It's the best the Americans have come up with so far.'

'But perhaps not good enough?' The statement was a question and Maltby had no answer, and so he sat again in silence.

'And I'm seeing signs of panic, Maltby. Quiet, restrained panic, as panic in Whitehall always will be, but it is definitely panic.' He picked up a copy of the *Daily Star* and dropped it as if it were contaminated. 'And Washington,' he continued. 'It seems the President is becoming trigger-happy again, keen to play with his new toys.'

'Yes, sir. The problem is that the scientists over there are going for the mini-nuke theory . . . '

'Which, given the deafening silence from our Soviet friends, is quite a reasonable conclusion.'

'And frightening, sir.'

'Yes, Maltby. It is rather.'

The Bentley was making its way north towards the Bayswater Road and for a moment they sat looking at the rush-hour crowds.

'We're in a pretty pickle are we not, Maltby?'

'Every way we turn, sir.'

'Maybe God in His heaven has lost patience with us.'

'I wouldn't blame Him, sir.'

'But we can't assume such a scenario, can we?'

Maltby shook his head and looked out.

'And do you think your Professor can get us out of this pickle?'

'That's what I'm counting on.'

'He's an odd-bod, by the sound of it.'

Maltby grimaced. 'Malone says he suffers from the Oppenheimer syndrome. I would put it more simply. The man is an ostrich – an I.Q. in the thousands and a mental age of eight.'

Sir William nodded. 'Geniuses, like clerics, are not of this world, Maltby. You've done well to get him working for us.'

'Thank you, sir. The problem is that he doesn't believe in a threat.'

'Doesn't he now? A *naive* ostrich?'

'Perhaps.'

'No perhaps, Maltby.' He tapped him on the shoulder. 'But he will tell us what he comes up with, won't he? Won't go keeping it to himself?'

'I sincerely hope not, sir.'

'So do I Maltby, and it's up to you to see that he cooperates totally. Isn't it?'

'Yes, sir.'

'So you'll keep a close eye on him?'

'Indeed I will.'

'I mean, if he does discover that plasmas can be controlled, if he does manage to convince himself that these damned fireballs are a military threat, he won't run away and stick his head in a bucket of sand, now will he?'

'Hopefully not, if I have anything to do with it.'

Sir William turned and looked at Maltby for the first time. Maltby wanted to look away but he fought to hold the stare. 'We need more than hope, Maltby,' the old man said. 'You are not being paid just to hope.'

'I'm sure I can handle Professor Benson, sir.'

'That's the chap.' Sir William turned away and nodded. 'This young fellow Quenby is useful, is he?'

'Up to a point.'

'So you'll be travelling north again.'

'Yes, sir. I'm waiting for more data from Malone.'

'And the woman with the odd name?'

'She'll help all she can.'

'Good.'

The car had reached Kensington Palace Gardens and Sir William ordered the driver to take it slowly. As they passed the Russian Embassy, they looked out at a crowd of faces behind a police cordon. Maltby guessed a figure of two hundred, maybe more, angry faces and angry voices chorusing something, but he could hear nothing through the soundproofing.

'You can't blame them, can you Maltby?' Sir William said. 'I mean, if this damned thing is a natural phenomenon as your Benson thinks, it would be occurring over there, wouldn't it? They wouldn't be keeping silent, now would they?'

'I don't know, sir.'

'No. Nor do I.' He reached down, collected the newspapers and bundled them under his arm. 'Almost home,' he said. 'Going back or what, Maltby? Where can I drop you.'

'The nearest pub, sir.'

'Wise decision. But don't dull the brain, will you? You need to be bright-eyed and bushy-tailed.'

'Yes, sir.'

The Bentley stopped. Maltby got out and watched it pull away. Bright-eyed and bushy-tailed. Maltby had sensed the panic in Sir William. It was well-controlled, but it was definitely there all right. It made Maltby feel even more rattled. Bloody Benson. Why couldn't he have the feelings and reactions of normal people? As far as he could tell, Benson felt not the slightest flicker of anxiety about these fireballs.

Maltby needed that drink, badly.

The cleaners had opened the blinds again. Benson snapped them shut and switched on the television. Then he asked his secretary to go and fetch Nigel Quenby plus a mug of coffee. She replied that she was a university secretary, not a skivvy, so he swore at her.

Five minutes later Quenby came in, carrying the coffee.

'These fireballs, Nigel . . . '

'You can't get away from them it seems.'

'They intrigue me. A good plasma physicist ought to be able to figure out what, if anything, is going on. I thought we might give it a try.'

Quenby beamed at him. 'Great. Where do we start?'

Benson handed him a list of references. 'My guess is we're dealing with ball lightning or something closely related. Here is a list of publications. I want you to get over to the university library and check them out. Make photocopies of anything that looks worthwhile. And see if they have Barry's book.'

'Right.' Quenby took the sheet and turned to leave.

'Oh, and Nigel . . . '

'Yes?'

'The authorities think it's the Russians.'

'What? That's crap.'

'Quite. But there'll be a security lid on this little circus if we want access to M.o.D. data. So let's keep it low-key, okay?'

Quenby looked suitably conspiratorial, nodded, and left. Benson returned to his desk, picked up a picture of the train driver killed in the recent crash, and studied it contemplatively. Then he turned to Maltby's file. A passage had been highlighted in yellow.

'Plasma balls have been generated and sustained in laboratory conditions for about a second, after which instability sets in. Now it seems from eyewitness reports that much longer-lived plasmas containing considerably greater energy can be used effectively against military targets.'

'Military targets,' he grunted, glancing at the photograph of the dead driver. 'Percy was no military target.'

Benson had filled his shelves haphazardly with books, and he selected a few carefully. He'd already decided that there was no point in trying to scour the literature for a quick explanation of the recent fireball activity. First he had to build up an accurate picture of what was going on, then he needed to brush up on all the physics that might have a bearing on the subject. He worked for an hour, reading a standard research monograph on plasma confinement, until Quenby returned with a sheaf of photocopies. Benson flipped through them.

He got up from his desk and began pacing. 'What we have to discover, Nigel, is whether this recent spate of fireball reports involves some sort of ball lightning, right?'

'Right,' agreed Quenby, nodding enthusiastically. He knew Benson was really talking to himself, using the younger man as a kind of echo chamber, but he didn't object.

'If so, why the increase in number and severity?'

'If freak weather conditions . . .' Quenby stuttered, petering out in mid-sentence. Benson ignored him.

'We really need to know the weather details in each case.'

The television was showing a horror film, a semi-naked starlet running through woods, tripping over the compulsory root, breasts heaving, ready to be assaulted by whatever villain was behind her.

Benson closed his eyes and thought of danger. The problem with the ball lightning was that it was unlike the more common kind. Lightning conductors were no defence. If the public were to be protected, the first step would be to understand how the fireballs were being created and what their source of energy was.

On the television the starlet screamed. Benson opened his eyes, and turned off the soundtrack, then went to the blackboard. The only thing to do was to forget all that had been written and start from scratch, build up a theoretical picture from first principles.

He wiped the blackboard clean and chalked up the basic electromagnetic field equations that were ingrained in his brain. Then he drew a circle. The fireballs were said to be round so he would start with a spherically symmetric model.

After that, he'd try a toroidal structure.

That done, he sketched in a possible pattern of field lines, filling in the diagram with arrows and lines in a variety of colours. He stood back and gazed at the board, Quenby by his side.

'Looks like a map of the London Underground,' Quenby said.

Benson nodded. 'Now all we've got to do is solve the equations.'

'I suppose so.' Quenby knew there was little more he could do. Already Benson had gone way beyond him. Still, at least he could fetch the coffee.

Benson worked all day, breaking only for the occasional pace about the room. His secretary knocked twice and he ignored her. She slipped notes under the door. Quenby retrieved them. Benson ignored everything but the problem.

It was certainly a teaser. He went up blind alleys and back down. It began to take on the appearance of a Snakes and Ladders game, except that he couldn't find any ladders. The blackboard was a jungle of snakes.

That night he left by cab at one-thirty and was asleep as soon as he hit the hotel duvet.

Next day a picture began to emerge. Some of his formulae agreed with the work of two Italians a few years back. The outline of the properties of an electromagnetically-confined atmospheric plasma ball began to become apparent.

But the basic problem remained. How could so much energy be confined in such a stable fashion by electromagnetic fields alone?

The problem stared at him from the blackboard.

According to his model, the ball ought to disintegrate in less than a second, yet some of the fireballs were lasting for minutes.

The only answer was that the energy must be coming from outside the ball. He knew about the intense electric fields that could be generated naturally in the atmosphere, but how could the energy be concentrated and then sustained in the ball? And why did the thing come to life in the first place?

Benson turned to the board and methodically erased everything in sight. Then he set up a slightly modified set of equations, changing the boundary conditions to take into account a variety of external electric fields, both static and time-dependent. He soon discovered he could no longer solve the equations exactly, even for the cases of spherical or axial symmetry. He'd have to solve them in a numerical approximation, using the computer.

For the next two days Benson wrestled with the software. It only took him six hours to write the program, but another twenty for him and Quenby to de-bug it and start getting meaningful answers. He used the terminal in his room, totally absorbed and oblivious to the hubbub of the university.

The initial output from the machine looked disappointing. Then Benson changed a few of the parameters and started to get encouraging results. It began to seem as if a slowly varying electric field of the right frequency could drive a suitably confined plasma into a non-linear feedback loop, creating a type of mathematical behaviour known as a soliton. Benson knew little about solitons, so he spent another six hours in the library learning about them. By then he had become convinced he was on the right track. The fireballs were some sort of electromagnetic solitons driven by external electric fields of the sort associated with thunderstorms – but somehow time-dependent . . .

As Benson toiled on, thrashing out the details, his morale soared. He even caught himself humming a tune once or twice, something that hadn't happened since before . . . the troubles.

It was about midnight on the fifth day that Quenby discovered an error, an elementary matter. They'd overlooked a factor of 4π in a magnetic quantity when they'd converted the units they'd been employing to make use of an old textbook.

It changed everything.

Benson had all along been bothered about the peculiar way that the fireballs had entered buildings, even aircraft. An aircraft's surface is more or less a perfect conductor and would shield the interior from the external electric fields that Benson needed to power the fireball. He'd tried to get around this obstacle by using time-varying fields, creating a sort of waveguide effect that would propel the fireball down the aircraft's interior. The tricky thing had been to get enough power inside the aircraft without distorting the fireball's shape, or causing it to fall apart. His initial results indicated it might just be possible. Without the factor of 4π there was no hope.

Failure.

Exhausted and dejected, Benson reached for a video tape he'd obtained of George Todd's interview, slipped it into the recorder and stood back, watching and listening as the man told the story of the Alitalia crash once again. Benson watched it twice then turned back to the reference books.

' "The phenomenon has been observed within aircraft",' he read aloud. ' "See Jennison 1969 and 1971, and Uman 1968. The fact that ball lightning

68

has been observed within metal enclosures is a more serious problem since its existence within a metal enclosure is not compatible with an external energy source." '

It was the only stumbling-block. But it was fatal. Benson couldn't model a fireball that would invade an aircraft. Period.

What now?

Sleep.

Then?

He couldn't give up now. Not now. The fireball problem had got into his blood. He'd never rest till he solved it.

But he was stuck.

Help?

Perhaps. But who?

The car headlights reflected off the rain-soaked ground, dazzling her vision as Tamsin drove down the service road leading from the Biochemistry building. It was almost midsummer, and at these latitudes it never got fully dark, but the heavy storm-clouds had reduced the twilight to an eerie glow by ten in the evening.

She was tired. It had been a particularly trying day, working in the laboratory until seven and then waiting at the computer terminal for space. After a couple of hours in front of the screen, she'd encountered a bug in the program, and had to scrap the whole thing. Then she was forced to spend another forty minutes filling in a research grant application that would almost certainly be rejected.

She swung the car on to the main campus road, past the Physics block, peering into the gloom.

She almost ran him down. He stepped out looking the wrong way.

'You bloody fool, Andrew!' she shouted. 'Don't you know yet we drive on the left in this country?'

He looked exhausted. His eyes were sunken in their sockets, his hair was dishevelled and his shoulders stooped. He carried a battered briefcase under one arm.

'Get in!' she said. 'Before you kill yourself.'

They drove to his hotel in silence, the only sound being the splash of tyres in the roadside puddles. The streets were deserted.

'Have a drink with me, will you?' he said. 'I need to unwind.'

She hesitated. 'Alright. A quick one.'

Joe the barman looked at Benson with a frown, poured him a couple of bourbons and said nothing. They found a table in the corner of the bar. Benson raised his glass.

'To John Maltby,' he proclaimed. 'He's working for me, you know.'

'Really?' she said in a disinterested tone.

'Poor bugger.'

'Oh?'

'Can't be easy, working for a slob like me.'

'You're not a slob.'

Benson raised his eyebrows. 'Don't tell me I have a fan in the Biochemistry Department?'

Tamsin ignored the sarcasm. 'How's the project going?'

Benson scowled. 'Up and down. Mainly down.'

'I wish I could help,' she said mechanically.

'You can.'

'I can't imagine how.'

'Come to bed with me.'

Her lips tightened. 'You must be joking!'

He shrugged, drained his glass, and ordered another. 'To Pjotr Kapitza,' he said this time. 'A bloody sight better physicist than me.'

'I thought you were the best,' she replied.

'Kapitza's dead.'

'So you're on your own, is that it? The great Benson vs Mother Nature. Only so far she's winning.'

'That's about it.'

'Would you never consider collaborating? You know, two heads are better than one, and all that.'

'I've got Quenby.'

'Seriously. Is there no one?'

'Yes. Hendricks. You remember? He's the smart one with the dolly wife,' said Benson with heavy cynicism. Then after a pause: 'And poor old Burkov, I suppose.'

'Who?'

'Burkov. Leonid Burkov. A Russian . . . sorry, Georgian. We worked together once. Before the guys in jackboots came for him.'

'You mean he's in jail?'

'Yes. No. He's in some psychiatric place, or wherever it is they put people who don't toe the party line. Jesus, what a world.'

Tamsin was silent for a while. Then Benson got up to go. 'Well, I'm going to bed,' he announced, 'even if you're not coming with me.' Several guests turned to stare.

'You've forgotten your case,' she said, stooping to pick it up for him. A book fell out. *Astrophysical Plasmas* by Andrew Benson.

'Well, well, the great work.' She held it up briefly and flipped it open at the front. The page was blank except for the words: To Katy.

Tamsin stared at it for a moment, her mind turning somersaults.

He snatched the book rudely from her grasp and stuffed it into the case. 'I'll see you around,' he said, and left her sitting there.

9

Nathan Franks had always been considered to be a lucky photographer. Of course, he could take good pictures but so too could every one of his colleagues and rivals. He was also cunning, but not more than most. It was his luck that singled him out. He always seemed to be in the right place just before something was about to happen. It was his luck that had made him rich. Being born lucky was better than being born handsome.

The second week in June was his first vacation for two years and he was enjoying himself. After photography, his big love was skiing and you had to go high in June to find good snow, even in the Rockies. The way to do it was heli-skiing, just getting up there by chopper into the powder and coming down where no one had come before. He'd been to the French Alps and he had made two trips to Aspen, but once you'd done the powder, there was no way you would go back on the organized pistes. The way Nathan Franks had it figured, you may as well take up bowls.

That morning he'd almost killed himself, coming too close to a gully he hadn't seen. Now he was relaxing in Harry's Bar next to the heli-port, six thousand feet up. He had adrenalin in his bloodstream, high-quality oxygen in his lungs and he was about to pour brandy down his throat when the phone rang. Harry answered it and went white.

Nathan went over to him and asked what was wrong. It was a full minute after he had hung up that Harry could speak and what he had to say had Nathan reaching for his camera.

'Hey Harry, lend me some shoes.'

'Why?'

'I need shoes. I can't walk in these things.' He pointed to his three-hundred-dollar ski boots.

'What size are you?'

'Don't matter. Just give me something for my feet. Quick.'

Harry dug out a pair of sneakers from behind the bar. Nathan dragged off his boots, slipped into the sneakers and was out of the door fast, leaving his brandy on the counter. Harry reached for it. He needed it. Unless his cousin had gone crazy, then some kind of war was about to start. But it made no sense, why would anyone want to bomb a place like Patterson Creek?

A young pilot named McGovern was topping up the tank of his helicopter when Franks arrived, panting, grabbing him by the arm.

'You ready to go?' Franks asked.

'Sure. But where are your boots, man? And your skis? You gonna run down the mountain?'

'I want you to take me down,' Franks said. 'You know Patterson Creek.'

'Yeh. But I only do the mountain. That's what I'm paid for.'

'You got the range for Patterson Creek?'

'I guess so, but . . . '

Then Franks produced a business card, scribbled on it and handed it over.

'This is my IOU. It'll be backed by my paper.'

McGovern whistled. 'I should clear this with the boss.'

'No time, McGovern. Let's go.'

'I don't have enough gas to get back.'

'So?'

For ten seconds, McGovern thought about it, in which time Franks was already in the passenger seat, his belt buckled, testing out his camera and checking how many rolls of film he had. Today was lucky. He'd been taking pictures of the mountain. Yesterday he'd left the camera in the hotel.

'Okay,' McGovern said, then eased himself into the chopper and switched on the ignition. The little machine rose and swung away, south and east deep into the valleys following the old Indian trail over the ridges. As they crested the fourth they saw smoke and both men gasped as one.

Franks leant out, felt the wind in his hair and the comforting feel of the viewfinder at his left eye. All he could think about right then was how much time he had over the rest of the pack. McGovern stared bug-eyed at the smoke, trying to calculate the height of it and what could have caused it and thanking God it wasn't in the shape of a mushroom.

He checked his altimeter. He was flying at five hundred feet. In a couple of

73

minutes they would be in the thick of it.

'Whaddya want me to do?' he yelled, but there was no reply. He glanced to his left and saw the photographer leaning half-way out of the chopper, held in by his seat belt, taking snaps like some kind of stunt man. He wondered what was so wrong with taking them through the perspex shield, but then he, Jack McGovern, was just a chopper pilot, not a hot-shot news photographer.

Now he could smell the smoke and the controls began to take on a life of their own, the chopper bucking in sudden turbulence. Then Franks was beside him, yelling in his ear, telling him to get right in close.

'Can't,' he yelled back.

'Do it for chrissakes.'

McGovern shook his head and pointed. Ahead, two Army helicopters had arrived from nowhere and were signalling.

'Chinooks,' he said.

'Ignore them,' shouted Franks.

'It's the goddam military. They're signalling us down.'

'Ignore them.'

'Not for two thousand bucks I won't.'

'I'll double it.'

'Not for double, not for treble, I ain't gonna end up on the front page of your newspaper.'

'What can they do?' Franks yelled. 'Shoot us down?'

'That's just what they'd do. Then you'd be in your own paper for sure, in the obituary columns.'

'They wouldn't.'

But McGovern had banked away and was losing height.

'Get as close as you can and set me down,' Franks was saying.

'You bet. We're almost out of gas.'

There was the choice of a narrow strip of blue road or the cornfields. If he chose the corn maybe Franks would have to pay compensation to the farmer. McGovern was still thinking rationally, as if what had happened in front of him didn't make any difference, as if there would be anyone claiming compensation, as if there wasn't a crater ahead which was God knows how many yards wide.

Franks was out and running before the chopper had settled, stumbling in the foot-high corn, arms thrashing, trying to run. When he reached the road, he sprinted towards the smoke, trying to gauge the extent of the damage, his mind full of questions. Then, in the smoke he saw a police car, a big Buick. State troopers. He stopped, took a couple of shots then moved forward slowly. There was no one around, just the car blocking the road, the driver's door open. He could hear the rasp of the radio. He went right up to it, his eyes stinging from the smoke, ducked into the car and stuck his ear to the radio. It was blurred by static. He heard only a phrase or two, but it was enough. Then a voice behind made him jump.

'What do you think did this?' It was McGovern. He was staring ahead and trembling as if in shock.

'Who knows, but this place is crawling with cops and they're not going to take any notice of press cards. We'll come back if we can, but right now you got to get me to a place called Pacatello. You know it?'

'Sure. Just down the road.'

'Know the hospital?'

'Sure.'

'Enough gas?'

'Just about.'

'Come on then . . .'

Five minutes later the chopper put down in the car park of the Pacatello supermarket. The hospital was three hundred yards down the road, a big place on four levels. Franks headed towards it, leaving McGovern to go looking for gas. He walked slowly, took a couple of shots of the main gate and the sign announcing it as the County Hospital. A group of people stood by the gate talking to two men in uniform. Franks waited until they had turned away, deep in conversation, and slipped past them unnoticed and up the short gravel drive to the main entrance. Two cops were on the door. He turned left, following the arrows towards casualty. In the ambulance park, the vehicles were parked at random. Franks counted five. He tapped the bonnet of the nearest. It was warm. There was a uniformed security man at the double doors. The place was sealed tight but Franks knew hospitals. He'd staked them out many times. He knew his way in. He'd even got into Bellevue once. There was always a laundry door somewhere.

Five minutes later he found it and was inside.

The place was in chaos. He saw a doctor run full pelt along a corridor. He stepped back to let a trolley pass and glimpsed an old, white, wrinkled face that looked dead. Then he checked the signs, followed the arrow towards Reception, turned a corner and found himself in the main hallway. At the reception desk, a crowd of people clamoured at three clerks. Behind the clerks stood a State trooper. The phones would be ringing off the walls by now and he wondered how his colleagues would be getting on dealing with the hospital Secretary. They would be getting stalled, there would be sweet nothing coming out of this place. But Nathan Franks was on the inside, his camera folded flat inside his parka. In the old days, when he started, it was a problem to hide a good camera, but not anymore.

A few minutes later on the first floor, he found what he was looking for. The locker room was empty and his luck was holding. He closed the door behind him and tried each locker. The third was open. He pulled out a white coat and slipped off his parka. The coat was on the small side but no one would notice. He looked at himself in the mirror and unclipped the identity tag from the left lapel: Dr M.L. Harris. The coat smelled of morphine and he wondered what Dr Harris's speciality was. Maybe Dr Harris was female. He slipped the tag into his pocket and checked the locker. There was a bonus. A stethoscope. It was corny but there was something of the ham actor in Nathan Franks' make-up. He slipped it round his neck, picked up his parka, stuffed it behind the radiator, then stepped out into the corridor.

No one acknowledged him as he made his way around the hospital, neither staff nor patients. He knew the protection of the uniform. People accepted what they wanted to see. He felt invisible and now that he was invisible, he knew where to go next.

The staff canteen was busy. He got in line, bought a coffee and looked around. Three nurses were sitting together in the far corner and from where he stood, he could see they were deep in conversation, hands fluttering, heads together like little birds. There was a space at the table next to them. His luck held. They were talking about the disaster. He did not even have to drink his coffee. He had hardly sat down before he was up and away again, heading for Intensive Care.

On the way upstairs, following the signs, he tapped the camera in his pocket. He had set it for the gloom of the hospital ward and he would just have to trust to luck again, for he would have only one chance. There could not be a second attempt.

He stopped for a moment at the door he wanted. There was a porthole at eye-level. He looked through and saw a nurse sitting at a desk. Behind her was a glass door. It was opaque. He would need to run the gauntlet of the nurse. Now Nathan Franks began to sweat. He was very close, but the nurse was a big, powerful woman. He did not want anything to go wrong now. The last thing he needed was to ooze any sign of suspicion.

He pushed the door open and strode in. The nurse looked up and nodded to him. He stopped by her desk and glanced at the glass door.

'Are the survivors in there, nurse?'

She frowned. 'Pardon me,' she said.

'From Patterson Creek.'

'No.' Her frown deepened and she pointed to the ceiling with her pen. 'They've been moved to Isolation.'

76

'Okay, thanks.' He turned and walked out. The nurse watched him go, then got to her feet. There was something odd about him. No doctor would use the word 'survivor'. It was out of place; patients, yes; casualties, yes; survivors, never; and he wasn't wearing a name-tag. She moved to the door and peered through the porthole. The man was walking too fast. She noticed his shoes and his trouser cuffs: strange rubber trousers, like ski pants, and they were wet, the sneakers thick with mud. The pep talk half an hour ago from Matron leapt into her mind. The press would be arriving, they'd been told. On no account was anyone to speak to them.

She went back to her desk and snatched at the phone.

Nathan Franks ran up the stairs, bumped into a nurse and apologized. Why Isolation? Isolation meant something nasty. He felt tense and excited. Lucky Nathan Franks. All his nerve ends jangled and told him that he was on to something here. And the only one on the inside.

The door was signposted but he could have guessed anyway. A fat cop stood outside, chewing gum, a pistol and a bleeper on his belt. Franks slowed up, trying to look relaxed and stopped in front of him. He smelt the peppermint on the man's breath and said, 'Excuse me, officer.'

'Doctor,' said the cop.

He stepped aside and Franks went past him into a small reception area. Through a glass door he could see four beds, and he counted ten doctors and nurses. He moved the five paces to the door, his camera out now, adjusting the lens, so single-minded and tunnel-visioned that he did not see the international warning sign on the wall. He drew breath, pushed open the door and stepped inside, the camera on motor-drive, catching the expressions of surprise and anger, and the little girl crying, and an old man lying, mouth open like a corpse, and three nurses round a cot. He wanted to get a picture of the baby but there were too many bodies in the way, so he turned away playing the percentages, getting out before someone grabbed hold of him and maybe tried to do nasty things to his camera.

He went through the reception area fast, hearing the first shouts of outrage behind him. At the door the cop had his back to him, struggling to get his bleeper out of his belt. It was stuck. Franks' legendary luck was holding, and he had reached the stairs before the cop realized he had gone. He was moving fast now, as fast as he could without attracting attention, out towards the fresh air and the nearest telephone.

The battering on his door was insistent. Benson fought against it for as long as he could, then stumbled to the door, furious, and pulled it open.

His secretary stepped back a pace, her eyes flitting involuntarily up and down him, taking in the stubble, the half-closed eyes, the crumpled clothes. She could tell he'd slept all night in his office.

'Whassit?' he mumbled.

'Sorry, Prof,' she said. 'I know you told me that you weren't to be disturbed.'

'That's right.' Benson blinked, looked down at himself and rubbed his hands together, shivering.

'Well, as you're here, come in then.' He pulled the door wide open and stepped back but she shook her head.

'It's just that it's the Vice-Chancellor's summer party this evening.'

Benson gaped at her.

'It's compulsory.'

'Bullshit.'

'Miss it at your peril,' she warned.

Benson softened a shade. 'Okay. Thanks for telling me.'

'It was Dr Bright, really,' she explained. 'She rang me up and said I'd better let you know.'

'Oh did she.'

'You didn't get my notes? I put them under the door.'

He shook his head.

'And I've got five days' mail for you.'

Benson was fully awake now. He looked down at himself and shivered again.

'So you'll be going then?'

'I'll think about it. I wouldn't want to put my career in jeopardy.'

'Right then.'

She turned and went back down the corridor. He watched her go, then closed the door, leant against it and began to laugh. Miss it at your peril. Only the British could throw a party and make it compulsory to attend. No wonder they were going down the drain. Still, Tamsin would be there. Maybe a break would unblock him. Maybe what he needed was a couple of hours away from the problem.

The weird sub-arctic twilight bathed the desolate landscape in a surreal glow. Forests and lakes stretched as far as the eye could see. The top of the wooden observation tower gave a commanding view of the surrounding countryside, and it was just possible to make out the lights of Lämpsa far to the south.

'What a God-forsaken place,' mumbled Maltby.

'But discreet,' replied the British army Captain, his eyes never leaving the image intensifier. After a pause he said: 'I can see the Landrover now.'

Maltby relayed the information over the transceiver. 'I hope to God they keep between the red flags,' he said, pacing up and down the platform in the confined space. The Captain shifted his position slightly. 'Stop worrying. The Finnish authorities assure us it's been done this way several times before.'

About a mile to the east the Landrover came to a stop at the appointed spot in a clearing.

'What's happening?' demanded Maltby.

'Nothing,' replied the Captain. 'They're waiting.' A gentle breeze stirred the silent forest around them. Maltby slapped sharply at his face. 'Bloody mosquitoes!'

A full five minutes passed, then an unmarked black saloon car emerged from a forest track, made its way slowly into the clearing and stopped about twenty yards from the Landrover. Neither vehicle used lights.

'They're here,' announced the Captain, his trained eyes searching the clearing for any hint of a double-cross. But he saw only the edge of the deserted forest in the amplified half-light of the viewer.

'Contact,' said Maltby into the transceiver, and resumed his anxious pacing.

The Captain could make out two figures climbing from the saloon, a tall soldier in combat uniform and a small stooped man in ill-fitting civilian clothes. The driver remained behind the wheel.

Simultaneously a man climbed from the passenger seat of the Landrover. He was carrying a suitcase and a briefcase and he walked confidently and quickly towards the black car, giving the little man only the merest glance as they crossed.

The little man stumbled. No one moved to assist him. He recovered, walked on shakily to the Landrover and climbed inside. At the black car, the soldier held the rear door open for the man with the suitcase, and climbed into the back seat after him. The car then reversed slowly into the forest. A full minute elapsed before the Landrover started to move, carefully performing a three-point turn. It then made its way slowly westward between the flags until it disappeared from the Captain's vision.

'Done,' said the Captain, looking up at Maltby. The man from the Ministry nodded and spoke briefly into the transceiver.

There was a pale flash from the south and presently a low rumble of thunder rolled across the forest. Maltby gazed at the sky nervously. 'Let's get out of here,' he said.

It was a beautiful summer evening, with strong clear sunlight shafting through the elm trees. The party was being held in the garden at the Vice-Chancellor's residence just outside the town. Benson ambled aimlessly around the lawn, admiring the rhododendrons that flanked it and filled the air with the scent of their flowers. The scene was pervaded by the tinkle of glasses and the soft buzz of polite conversation.

Several of the guests eyed Benson suspiciously. 'He might have troubled to shave for the occasion,' someone muttered. 'He's suffering from cultural shock, poor chap,' remarked another. 'Let's go and talk to him.' But the Vice-Chancellor pre-empted them.

'Good of you to come, Professor Benson,' enthused the VC. 'You've met my wife Hilda, haven't you?' Benson nodded at her and tried to think of something to say.

'How are you settling in?' the woman enquired, in an exaggerated upper-class English accent.

'I like it here,' replied Benson simply.

'The weather's a bit different from California, I imagine.'

'I hadn't noticed.'

Benson spotted Tamsin arrive out of the corner of his eye. She was wearing a cream blouse and blue slacks and looked stunning. She came straight over to them.

'Ah!' said the VC. 'Do you know Dr Bright, one of our . . . er, bright young biochemists, if you'll excuse the pun, Tamsin.'

'We've met,' she said, then leaning towards Benson: 'John Maltby wants to see you. Now.'

'Tell him to go screw himself,' hissed Benson. The Vice-Chancellor and his wife both gaped and turned in search of other guests.

'Must you be so offensive!' barked Tamsin. She fumbled in the pocket of her slacks and withdrew a sheet of paper. 'He told me to give you this.'

Benson glanced at the sheet, then looked up sharply. 'Where did he get this?' he demanded. Tamsin shrugged.

He looked again at the piece of paper, his eyes flitting over the familiar equations. At the bottom of the page a formula was highlighted in a box. Benson's brain raced as he checked that the formula really did fit the equations. It did. There was no doubt. One of the toughest problems of his career – finding an exact solution to Einstein's field equations for a triaxial neutron star – lay solved before him.

But it couldn't be . . .

They drove in the little Fiat through the soft evening sunshine at top speed along country lanes, out on to the fells beyond the town. After a few miles they turned up a farm track, crossed a cattle grid, and descended into a valley. A small stone cottage lay hidden among a copse of pine trees. A police car was parked in front. Tamsin pulled up behind it. Maltby came out of the cottage.

'I hope you'll excuse my little melodrama, Professor, but there's someone I'd rather like you to meet.'

They'd climbed from the car just as an unkempt and haggard old man stepped out of the cottage doorway. 'Hello, Andrew,' he said, in a thick Russian accent.

Benson gasped. 'But it's not possible . . . they destroyed your mind!'

'Almost. But not quite.'

Benson stared in astonishment at his old friend's appearance. Burkov looked years older. He was nearly bald and his face was discoloured by red patches. The clothes looked odd, loose-fitting as if they belonged to someone much bigger. Only the voice was the same as Benson remembered, deep and melodious as if the man were perpetually on the verge of laughter.

'You like my solution to our old problem, hey?'

Benson grabbed the old man, held him in a hug, feeling him wobble like jelly as if there were no bones in him.

'Careful, Andrew,' he wheezed. 'You squash me.'

'You look terrible, Leonid. What did the bastards do to you?'

'It was not pleasant,' the Russian said and smiled, his eyes vanishing in folds of skin.

He stood back and stared into the old man's face, thinking of the last time they met, five, six years ago at a seminar in Prague. Leonid was slim then, with a full head of hair and cheekbones that made women whimper, yet here was this little, bald, fat man and all that remained of him was his smile: Leonid Burkov, the greatest astrophysicist of his generation, now a trembling testimony to man's inhumanity to man.

Burkov smiled at Tamsin, and shambled back inside the cottage. He gently lowered himself into a chair, then looked up at Benson.

'Do you know what I feel like, Andrew?'

Benson grinned at him, remembering his friend's bizarre taste in drink. 'Not a brandy and Babycham?'

'You got it,' said the Russian and began to laugh, and Benson saw that there wasn't a tooth left in his head . . .

'It's what they call a "safe house",' explained Tamsin when the others had left. 'There's a housekeeper who's SIS, and a permanent but discreet police presence outside. The exchange has been kept under wraps on both sides.'

'Exchange?'

'They swapped Leonid for some spy.'

'Oh.'

'It was all very sudden,' Burkov explained. 'One moment I was at home, the

81

next I was being driven to some remote spot near the Finnish frontier. It wasn't an order, you understand. They asked me if I would like a little trip to England. I didn't know why, not until your Mister Maltby met me and told me about these fireballs.' He shrugged. 'Interesting phenomenon, ridiculous conclusion.'

'Quite,' said Benson nodding vigorously, delighted to be talking at last to someone who spoke the same language.

'And so, here I am.' He laughed, a wheezing sound, his shoulders shaking, laughing till he began to cough. When he recovered, he wiped his eyes and ordered another drink. 'Your friend Maltby doesn't seem to like you much,' he said.

'I'd be worried about myself if he did,' Benson replied.

'He said you were interested in the phenomenon but that you had certain reservations. He said that you were like a lot of academic people. He said you were somewhat cloistered.'

'Cloistered?'

'Yes. From that word, I deduced that you had been telling him to sod off.'

Benson grinned and reached out, clasping Burkov's hands. They were cold and flabby and Benson felt a surge of affection for him and disgust at what had been done to him.

Burkov smiled. 'So what made you change your mind?'

'I got curious.'

Burkov nodded. 'This is a beautiful place, isn't it?' he said, looking out of the window at the sunset over the fells. 'It certainly beats the *psikhushka*.'

'The what?'

Benson had never heard the word. And so Burkov explained.

'It began not long after the last time we met – remember it was in Prague, the seminar on pulsars. We had been discussing for days. It was an interesting meeting. We could think of nothing else at that time. We never discussed politics in those days, did we? Politics were irrelevant. They were for other people. It was another part of the brain, nothing to do with us. How humanity organized its affairs socially or economically, whether it be the East or the West, always seemed sublimely unimportant to us. You have a saying about living in ivory towers. I suppose we did. We saw things differently from other people. Other people are concerned with what goes on around them, not what is happening inside their heads. And to think that sometimes we felt superior . . .

'I knew that the security people disapproved of me. It was all noted down; what I drank, who my friends were, even my liking for what they called reactionary music. So absurd. So irrelevant.

'Anyway, it was Galina who got me involved, indirectly of course. You know that she has always been political and for years I patronized her, patted her on the head, indulged her sometimes, said there-there. Occasionally I would even listen to what she had to say, but when the others came, the others from the Democratic Movement, I always made an excuse and went to my study. They were so emotional, you see. Not one of them could sustain a logical argument for long. They always lapsed into emotion, forever losing themselves in slogans and anecdotes.

'I paid no attention until the day two men came to my laboratory and talked about Galina. They said she was being stupid and could get into trouble. They mentioned what they called her anti-Soviet writings. You know, the *samizdat*. But soon it became clear that they were not interested in my wife. She posed no threat to them. It was me they were after. It would be something of a coup to them if I were to denounce Galina's politics. As a good Marxist, they said I should be pleased to do what they asked. And it is to my eternal shame that, at first, I agreed in my mind to do it, once I'd explained to Galina of course. If it made them happy, if it stopped them pestering me, then I would sign whatever they wanted me to sign. As I said, in those days, politics seemed so petty. It was all a charade played by stunted intellects. What difference, in the end, would politics make to the great scheme of things? You remember at that time we were on the verge of producing a fully relativistic treatment of the galaxy clustering problem?

'I went home that night and told Galina what had happened. I tried to reason with her. I told her about the scene at the end of *Casablanca* when Humphrey Bogart tells Ingrid Bergman that the problems of little people ain't worth a hill of beans in this big world. I liked that. Hill of beans. But Galina would not listen. She said that if I did what they asked, I would be betraying her. I tried to explain again, that it was just a silly, infantile game but she would not listen. We fought. At least, she fought and I escaped to my study. She shouted through the keyhole, poor Galina. The next day the others came to me and resorted to kindergarten threats if I did not sign. I was getting attacked on all sides. It would have been easy to sign but in the end I didn't. Some kind of primitive stubbornness stopped me.

'Finally, when they had given up on me, they reached for their lawbooks and the psychiatrists. I told them that my work was more important than their meaningless little games but they did not listen. My work suffered. I could not concentrate. I wrote to the Head of the Academy but my letters were not answered. I phoned but never got past the switchboard.

'Then they came for me, in the afternoon, not like the movies with the knock on the door in the middle of the night. They said I was acting irrationally. You know the logic. If the social system is perfect, anyone who criticizes it or, in my case, fails to denounce those who criticize it, must be abnormal.

'Eventually a panel of psychiatrists found that I was schizophrenic with traces of paranoia, and I was sent off to be cured. Later I was charged in my absence with conducting anti-Soviet conversations. They produced an *agent provocateur* from the Democratic Movement who said I spent hours in discussion with Galina and others at my home. But you know all this. I know you were one of those who signed a letter of protest on my behalf and I thank you for that.

'At first when I was waiting to go to the hospital – the *psikhushka* – I was more annoyed than frightened. I didn't believe the stories I'd heard. Then when I saw the place, I knew that the word hospital was a misnomer. Hospitals don't have high walls and barbed wire. Hospitals don't have guards with guns or wild dogs to keep the patients in. Hospitals don't have convicted criminals as orderlies. They don't make use of your bladder as a weapon. . . I must explain this last point. Visits to the lavatory have to be earned. The orderlies are in complete control. They use lavatory visits as a form of currency. They like to be bribed. If you are not a good patient, they take away your privileges. You have to piss and shit where you lie. It is not pleasant.

'Most of the inmates are common criminals. Plus those who have tried to cross the border; then there are the politicals. I was a political. After a while, small, seemingly trivial things took on immense importance, like the period of time you are allowed to take your mattress into the yard and beat the fleas out of it. The mattress becomes very important and if you miss the chance of beating it for whatever reason – maybe you are too ill or there's a punishment mark against you – then you can become desperate and you fall into the trap of despair, which they want because it makes their job a lot easier.

'And it is difficult to fight them because of the drugs. They used sodium amobarbital which affects the central nervous system, a kind of truth drug. And haloperidol which induces convulsions and was used as a punishment. And trifluoperazine which is a sedative. A combination of these stops you functioning. After a while you can't eat or read or even move around. But sulphur is the worst. Sulphur hurts. It raises the temperature to forty degrees Celsius and gives you piles. You can't stand walking around and it's agony to lie down. Sometimes they strap you to the bed. Sulphur was the worst. It was the main punishment drug. Do you know that you can hear the needle go in? I don't know if it's real or a hallucination, but the effect and the memory of it is the same. You could feel it creep into your vein like fire then spread throughout your body. No, it was not pleasant.

84

'They had no mirrors in the *psikhushka* and now I think it was a blunder. You could see your body deteriorate of course. You could see it becoming flabby and the skin flaking. And you knew when your teeth began to crumble, but you couldn't see your face. And then when Galina visited, I understood. When I saw the reaction of my wife trying to hide the horror at the sight of me . . . then I understood. Later she told me that my bloated face, my rash from the erisypelas were bad enough to see, but what was worse was the fact that there was no expression in my eyes. They were dull and lifeless. But Galina was strong. Seeing my condition made her fight all the harder for my release, which was fortunate because in the last year I could do little for myself. I couldn't find the words to attack them. Even now it is sometimes a struggle. I come to a simple word, like, for example, window, and I can't think of it. Since the *psikhushka*, life is a constant crossword puzzle.

'And so their prophecy becomes self-fulfilling. They say you are schizophrenic, then give you drugs which produce the symptoms of schizophrenia and say told-you-so. Then they tell you that as soon as you admit you are ill, you have taken the first step towards becoming well. I think I agreed to that at one point. I don't know. I can't remember. I certainly thought of suicide a lot, but then they would have won. Suicide justifies all they are doing, proves that you have been crazy all along, and so I fought the urge. I won that one.

'Meanwhile, Galina was writing letters to everyone. The International Court of Justice was involved. Amnesty International, and of course all my colleagues all over the world. Did I thank you for that?

'Eventually all the pressure paid off. I don't remember much. All I know was that one moment I was in my cell and the next I was back home in Georgia. Sometimes in my mind I was back in my cell but that was hallucinations. For months, time was all in a mess. Even now I get flashbacks, but when they happen, I know it's a dream, which makes it acceptable.'

He paused at last and Benson took hold of his hands again. 'I wrote to you in Georgia about a year ago. Word of your release got out through Amnesty. I suppose you didn't get the letter.'

'Of course not. They wouldn't let me travel either, not until now. It was a kind of house arrest, I suppose, but at least it was better than the *psikhushka*.'

Benson slowly shook his head. 'I don't know how you are still sane,' he said.

'How do you know I am?' said Burkov, and began to wheeze again with laughter.

At midnight, Tamsin dropped Benson off at the hotel. He could hardly remember even mentioning Burkov to her. He smiled. Burkov was a gift; even a mentally-impaired Burkov was a delight to have around. They had decided on the ground rules. They would make use of whatever evidence Maltby gave them and together they would solve the fireball problem. There would be a great joy in presenting the results to Maltby, to show him that it was something natural and not the work of the Kremlin. He was looking forward to that day.

'Thank you, Tamsin,' he said simply, and kissed her full on the mouth. She didn't resist and he didn't exploit it. Perhaps that would come. He'd had more than enough joy for one day.

10

Dan McGuire floored the gas pedal and swung on to the fast lane of the Arlington freeway. Being an Air Force test pilot entitled you to some privileges, but unpunctuality was not counted among them. He drove fast, but easy, his bulky body moulded to the line of the sedan as though he were part of the design. That's how he saw himself, man welded to machine – a subtle empathy with technology that distinguishes an outstanding pilot from merely a good one. In the X-17 he regarded the plane as an extension of his own frame – his own psyche: mind and body tuned finely to every stress, every minute force.

With Dan's elbow resting on the open window, the air-conditioner was fighting a losing battle against the 90°F waves of hot, humid air that flooded into the automobile. But McGuire didn't mind the heat; he had been raised in Atlanta. The son of a trucker, Dan had spent much of his youth helping his father load and unload giant Dodge transporters. Mostly old McGuire had hauled lumber or tobacco, and the occasional livestock. It was just a small outfit, but profitable. Most of all Dan had liked to ride in the cab with his father, high above the road atop the monstrous machine. He could still feel the throb of the giant engines and smell the burnt oil and pungent diesel from the exhaust.

The thrill of manipulable power had never left Dan and, when he signed up for the Air Force at eighteen, he knew his calling in life. It took another seven years before he made it to the top – the supreme aeronautical technology – the

X-17 experimental plane. Piloting the X-17 rocket plane, McGuire had flown higher and faster than any existing aircraft. Of course, the Space Program had long since made such records meaningless, but to McGuire space flight was reserved for pansies.

'I fly my plane,' he assured his buddies. 'No sitting back on my ass, listening to mission control.' And at 115,000 ft and 4,000 m.p.h., flying a plane was no easy task.

Andrews Air Force base occupies a huge airfield located about ten miles from Washington. McGuire operated both out of Andrews and Wright-Patterson at Dayton, Ohio, but X-17 flights were not a weekly joy-ride. The plane itself had to be carried aloft strapped to a huge B-52 bomber, like a baby monkey clinging to its mother's belly. The rocket motors consumed fuel at such a prodigious rate that flights of only a few minutes duration were practicable. McGuire had last flown the son-of-a-bitch the previous March, and was not expecting another flight until October.

It had been with uncharacteristic short notice that McGuire was ordered to report to his commanding officer, a smooth Texan by the name of Lennox.

He entered the door of the top security building and perched himself on the corner of the desk belonging to Lennox's secretary.

'Hi, Cindy. What's new?'

Cindy, twenty-two, blonde, spotty and toothy, blushed a little.

'Captain Lennox is with someone at the moment, but I'll tell him you are here.' She spoke briefly through the intercom.

'I see you fixed your hair different,' said Dan. Cindy blushed some more.

'The Captain says for you to go right in, sir.'

Dan gave her a wink, sauntered over to the door, knocked and entered. Inside he found Lennox chatting to a heavily-built, perspiring, middle-aged man with sparse hair and a baggy suit. Lennox introduced him as Malone.

'We have a job for you, Daniel,' announced Lennox.

At 80,000 ft the horizon is nearly four hundred miles away, but being night all Dan could discern amid the inky blackness of the eastern seaboard was the delicate tracery of lights from a dozen major industrial cities. The sky above was still blacker, except towards the north where, even at midnight, the glow of summer twilight persisted. The X-17 shuddered and jerked as Dan eased the titanic rocket motors up to full thrust. He savoured the feel of the g-forces in his back as the craft roared upwards at an angle of nearly sixty degrees, clawing through the thin air, climbing at a phenomenal rate.

The altimeter clocked up thousands of feet like his sedan clocked up tenths of a mile – ninety-three, ninety-four . . . so tuned to the machine were his perceptions that he could even sense the minutely altered trim caused by the instrument reorganization that had been necessary to accommodate Malone's equipment.

Dan stared out at the darkness around him. The red-hot nose of the rocket plane glowed dully in the night air. Behind, the two wings – scarcely more than diminutive fins for a craft which was more a rocket than a plane – were quite invisible in the darkness.

Fifteen miles below, Malone and Lennox anxiously watched the progress of the X-17, on a radar screen at Andrews Field.

Malone's equipment was monitored automatically from the control tower, and the raw data fed directly into a computer in Washington. McGuire communicated only sporadically, offering in laconic tones technical information about the plane's handling characteristics. When the craft passed 98,000 ft the pilot gave a sharp cry. Out of the corner of his eye, Dan had momentarily spotted a luminous white ball which shot past in the slip-stream. He banked the aircraft slowly, but the object, whatever it was, would already have been miles behind. At 105,000 ft McGuire began to level the plane's trajectory. With the nose tipped forward, his body felt almost weightless as the upward acceleration slackened. The nose seemed to glow more brightly now as he watched, taking on a strange sort of luminosity which he had never encountered before. The fabric of the plane seemed to have two distinct colours, the familiar deep red of heated metal, but now augmented by a sort of brilliant orange blob. Consternated, McGuire watched the blob grow in size and begin to protrude from the front of the plane. After a few seconds it swelled up into a hemisphere about one foot in diameter and began to slide menacingly up the nose of the craft, towards the forward observation port. Horrified, he watched the ball fill the small window in front of his face. For an instant Dan could see a turmoil of fiery activity – and then it exploded.

At 4,000 m.p.h. an exploding window eighteen inches from one's face has a devastating effect. McGuire's head vanished, and the delicate equipment packed behind his body disintegrated. The pilotless craft lurched violently to starboard and slowly rolled over.

On the ground, Malone heard the intercom go dead and watched the radar trace uncomprehendingly as the plane began to plummet earthwards. Lennox punched several buttons furiously and rushed from the control room. Three minutes later the X-17 hit a plastics factory in Harrisburg and blasted a crater thirty-five feet deep.

The first thing Burkov did on entering Benson's office was to open the blinds.

'It's not a pretty view,' said Benson.

'Any view is pretty,' Burkov said as the blind rasped up to the ceiling. Then he looked out. 'I see what you mean.'

'And it's raining.'

Burkov stood hands on hips, gazing out. 'It's not exactly Pasadena but it's better than working in a dungeon.' Then he turned and smiled. 'Okay, show me the fireballs.'

It did not take him long to fill Burkov in on the work he had done. He showed him the file, the computer print-out and the scrawls on the blackboard. Burkov said nothing, asked no questions, just silently took it all in.

Finally he showed him his attempt to construct a theoretical model of the fireball's structure.

Burkov nodded and ran his finger along the blackboard.

'It looks impressive,' Benson said. 'The only problem is . . . it won't work.'

'Too little energy?' Burkov asked. 'Stability problems?'

'Right. And the difficulty of getting the balls to go inside conducting cavities.'

Burkov nodded again, then made a slow circuit of the room. Silence for a full minute, then he smiled. 'You remember our work on neutron stars?'

'Sure.'

'There too we had a puzzle about the energy source, about stability and the right boundary conditions, didn't we?'

Benson nodded.

'How did we tackle that problem?' Burkov asked.

'Went back to basics,' Benson said. 'Forgot all our preconceptions. I remember you saying: "Let's take nothing for granted. Let's go back and list all conceivable possibilities." '

'So. Let's do it.'

'Okay. We start with the source of energy. It's got to be some form of electromagnetic field. The question is where can . . . '

'Why?' The word zipped through Benson's concentration. He blinked. 'Well, surely we're dealing with an electromagnetic phenomenon here,' he said. 'What other conceivable energy source can there be?'

'Energy can come in many forms, Andrew. Just because effects of the fireball are electromagnetic, doesn't have to mean that the source is also.' He ambled up to the blackboard, broke a piece of chalk and licked it. 'Okay,' he said. 'What have we got?'

He wrote: gravitation.

Then: electromagnetism, nuclear, chemical, mechanical.

Then he scribbled a longer list, sub-dividing the five categories into their different forms.

Benson moved behind him and peered over his shoulder.

'We can rule out gravitation straight away,' he said. 'Too little mass.'

'Agreed.'

'And these things can hardly be mechanical.'

Burkov grinned at him and Benson continued. 'That leaves nuclear and electromagnetic. My guess is that chemical energy would be both inadequate and unstable. These guys pack a pretty hefty punch.'

'And nuclear? Surely not.'

'The temperature's too low,' agreed Burkov.

The Russian stood silently for a moment, then tapped the blackboard with his chalk. 'Suppose – just suppose – that the energy source resides within the balls after all. How does that affect the entropy balance?'

'Good question,' said Benson.

For two hours they worked on the thermodynamics of the fireball, absorbed in the mathematics. It was just like the old days, Benson going off in new directions, Burkov gently steering him in the most fruitful one. Working with Burkov, he was constructing an entirely new picture – a fresh approach – to the fireball's structure, using the ideas of heat-flow and radiative balance in place of the field theory treatment.

The conclusion was that the fireball's energy was too great to be electromagnetic. It *had* to be something else.

But what?

In frustration Benson chalked up an unfinished equation for energy on the blackboard: $E = ?$

Then he slumped into his swivel chair and stared morosely at the board.

'What would Einstein have written in ?' he said.

Burkov answered by chalking up: mc^2, and they both laughed heartily.

The phone rang. Benson's secretary said she had a Mr Maltby on the line. Benson raised his eyebrows. 'Shall I tell him to piss off, Leonid?' Then he jumped, startled, as he felt the Russian's clammy hand on his arm, the grip vice-like in spite of Burkov's frail condition.

'Remember the poet Donne,' he breathed into Benson's face. ' "No man is an island." What right have you to ignore the rest of the world?'

Benson was taken aback and stammered an apology. 'Put him through,' he told his secretary.

'There's someone from Washington I'd like you to speak to,' explained Maltby. 'I'm going to patch him through.' There was a series of clicks, then a voice said: 'Dr Benson? My name's Malone. Sam Malone. Maltby tells me you're working for him.'

'He's working for me.'

'As you wish. I'm the front man for an outfit called C7 we've set up to look into this fireball business. It's being headed by Hendricks. You know him?'

'Sure.'

'First off, would you consider joining us?'

'Work with that shit!' Benson expostulated.

'It's the reply I expected. Anyway, I thought you'd like to know we ran that little experiment you suggested.'

'Experiment?'

'With the rocket plane. Hunting for fireballs at high altitude.'

'Oh yeah. Any luck?'

'We found one. Only it got too close. It got *inside* the aircraft. The wreckage was spread all over half of Pennsylvania.'

'Oh. Too bad.'

'Yeah. Especially for the pilot. I'll send over the data we got, for what it's worth. But that's not all.'

'Oh?'

'We lost Patterson Creek too.'

'What?'

'Patterson Creek. A little township in Idaho.'

'Lost? What do you mean lost?'

'Lost. Annihilated. Wiped out by a huge fireball yesterday evening.'

'Jesus.'

'Four survivors only, 'cept they won't last long. They're dying, Benson, in a very characteristic way. Of radiation sickness . . . '

The phone went dead but Benson just stood there in stunned silence, holding the handset.

'Bad news?' asked Burkov.

'You could say that.'

11

BENSON COULDN'T SLEEP. The damned fireballs were getting to him. Malone's bombshell about the radiation had completely thrown him.

He kicked off his bedclothes and paced the bedroom in the dark, going over and over the same old reasoning. Glowing balls meant electromagnetic energy, confined in some way. Benson reckoned that he knew as much as anybody about such phenomena. He also knew that by no stretch of the imagination could the confining fields be strong enough to produce dangerous radiation.

Yet something kept nagging at him, deep in his subconscious, a half-forgotten association. Fireballs and radiation. Radiation and fireballs. What was it?

Benson stared disconsolately from the hotel window into the empty street. A prowling cat scurried across the road and vaulted a low fence.

Suddenly he had an idea.

Quickly he dressed, grabbed his briefcase, phoned for a cab and headed for the Department. It was deserted, plunged in darkness. The night security guard nodded briefly as Benson used his own key to gain access to the building. He didn't stop at his room, but went instead directly to the Physics library, again using his key to enter.

Benson switched on the lights and blinked in the fluorescent glare.

Quickly he sought out the computer terminal that stored the library's data base, sat down and flicked the screen into life. He tapped out a few simple instructions and sat back to wait.

The program was a straightforward key-word search routine. It identified and displayed all published research papers with the specified words in the title. Benson had specified two words: 'fireball' and 'radiation'.

Simple.

Benson cursed. The screen began filling with hundreds of references having titles like 'Prompt radiation from nuclear fireballs'.

He wasn't interested in H-bombs.

How to narrow the search?

He tried 'ball lightning' in place of 'fireball'. The effect was the opposite. After half a minute the computer told him it had no listing.

Benson rubbed his eyes and sighed.

Then he remembered that the data base was restricted to post-1980 publications. Perhaps there was something before that?

A few more instructions hooked the library computer on to a national network and thence to the National Library data base. The machine demanded a grant number to pay for the search.

Benson gave it.

Seconds later eight references appeared on the screen. Benson's pulse quickened.

His eyes flicked down the list. One reference instantly caught his attention: 'Gamma radiation from ball lightning'. A paper in the journal *Nature*, 1972.

Benson strode between the journal stacks until he reached *Nature*, and peered at the volume numbers. The relevant volume sat innocently in its place. He pulled it out, fumbled for the page. The article was there.

Benson rapidly scanned the contents, getting the gist. Then the vital phrase leapt out the page: 'confirming the antimatter theory of Ashby and Whitehead'. His brain circuits finally connected.

Antimatter.

The idea of antimatter, Benson recalled, went back to the early 1930s, when Paul Dirac found some unexplained solutions to his equation for electrons. At first Dirac thought the solutions were trying to describe protons, but it soon emerged that they represented something totally new – a hitherto unknown subatomic particle – like the electron, but with opposite properties. A sort of mirror image of the electron. An anti-electron.

A year or two later, Carl Anderson discovered Dirac's anti-electrons, or positrons as they became known, in cosmic rays.

That was only the beginning. It turned out that every known particle possessed its own antiparticle – antiprotons, antineutrons, antineutrinos, and so on.

That much was accepted science.

The theory being discussed in the paper before him went beyond that. Way beyond . . .

Burkov was far from pleased at being woken before 6 a.m., but Benson's voice sounded insistent, almost shrill, over the telephone.

'Leonid, I think I've cracked it'.

The Russian grunted sleepily.

'Listen, Leonid. Can you come over here right away?'

'Where's "here"?'

'The Department.'

'At six in the morning?'

The phone went dead.

An hour later they sat in Benson's room sipping some vending-machine liquid slanderously designated coffee.

'Hold on, hold on, my friend,' pleaded Burkov, arresting Benson's frenetic monologue.

'Let's take it from the beginning. My brain's a little slow this early in the morning.'

Benson consciously calmed his excitement.

'Now,' said the Russian. 'Everybody knows about antiparticles. We all learn about them at school. Particle physicists play with them every day. But they are merely subatomic particles. These fireballs . . . '

'I'm not talking about subatomic particles,' cut in Benson, 'but whole chunks – well, micron-sized fragments – of antimatter.'

'That's absurd!'

'Why?'

'Because, my dear Andrew, antiparticles are highly unstable. As soon as they encounter any matter, then bang!' Burkov flung his arms expressively. 'Mutual annihilation. So how can whole chunks of the stuff be simply floating around in the atmosphere?'

Benson grimaced with exasperation. He stared at Burkov pointedly as though he was a simple child.

'Fact,' said Benson, enumerating on his fingers. 'Every known type of particle has its antiparticle.' Burkov nodded gravely.

'Fact. Antiprotons, antineutrons and antielectrons exist, and could in principle unite to form anti-atoms.'

'In principle, my friend, in principle.'

'Fact. Anti-atoms in large quantities could make up bulk antimatter that would look identical to ordinary matter. Indeed, the laws of physics are symmetric between matter and antimatter. They do not distinguish . . . '

'Wrong.' This time Burkov interrupted. 'The grand unified theories . . . '

'Got nowhere,' countered Benson.

'A matter of opinion.' Burkov looked doubtful. 'The proton decay experiments . . . Who knows?'

'OK, Leonid. Let that one pass. Do you remember this?'

Benson held up a slim book. It had the title *Worlds–Antiworlds*.

'Indeed, my friend. By a famous Nobel prize-winner, Hannes Alfvèn.'

'Then you'll know,' continued Benson, 'his theory that the universe contains equal quantities of matter and antimatter. Some galaxies, like ours, are made of matter, others antimatter. We can't tell just by looking.'

The Russian looked incredulous. 'Surely you're not suggesting that these fireballs are coming from another galaxy?'

'No, of course I'm not. I'm just establishing the fact that the idea of antimatter existing in bulk is not merely a flight of fancy, but a respectable scientific theory of long standing.'

Burkov seemed unconvinced. 'But I thought these matter-antimatter cosmologies were knocked on the head in the 1970s. Nobody could explain how the two got separated after the big bang.'

Benson was out of his depth here. He was trained as a plasma physicist. While he'd done some good work in astrophysics, cosmology was not his field. And Burkov knew more particle physics than he.

He paused, then grabbed the phone, dialling mechanically. A sleepy voice answered.

'Hi, Ben. It's Andy. Andy Benson.'

'Christ, Andy,' came the reply. 'I just got to sleep.'

'Sorry, Ben. I forgot you Berkeley guys turned in early.'

'I thought you went to England after all that business with Hendricks.'

'I did. Here I am.'

'So what's new?'

'I just need a quick professional opinion, off the top of your head.'

'Oh, yeah? At this time of night?'

'It's urgent, Ben.'

'How's it urgent?'

Benson didn't answer, but just pressed on.

'What's the current status of matter-antimatter symmetric cosmologies?'

'Oh hell, Andy. I don't know. It was a popular idea in the 1960s I guess. Some French guy called Omnès made a big deal over it. There was always trouble over the gamma ray background.'

'Oh?'

'Yeah. You see, even in space things keep bumping into each other. Whole

96

galaxies sometimes. Any contact between matter and antimatter would cause wholesale annihilation with a huge output of gamma rays. Averaged over the whole universe this would produce a pretty intense flux that would certainly be detected.'

'Surely if the matter and antimatter were well enough separated annihilation would be pretty negligible?'

'Sure, Andy. But how did they get separated? You'd expect everything to come out of the big bang mixed up together.'

'I guess so. What about these grand unified theories?'

'That was the last nail in the coffin. Before that nobody knew how to make matter without antimatter. The grand unified theories broke the symmetry and predicted that the big bang would cough out a slight excess of matter. Then as the universe cooled down, any antimatter would have annihilated into gamma rays, and the gamma rays ended up as the microwave background we all know and love.'

'Is that it?' asked Benson.

'That's never it, Andy. The grand unified theories hit a dead end really. They were great on paper, and explained a lot. But nobody ever got any convincing experimental evidence that they were on the right track.'

'You mean the matter-antimatter theory isn't totally sunk?'

'It's sure keeping a low profile.'

'Thanks, Ben. How's the family?'

'Asleep, Andy.'

'Oh, yeah. Sure, Ben. Well, thanks pal. See you around.'

Benson turned to Burkov.

'That was Schumacher. He isn't wild about antimatter cosmologies, but doesn't write them off completely. Says the grand unified theories are pretty, but unproven.'

Burkov shrugged. 'So, I let you have your own way. I still can't see what all this has to do with fireballs.'

'The problem all along has been to understand how these things can confine so much energy electromagnetically, right? No matter how you model the field configuration you simply can't make the balls energetic enough and still remain stable.'

Burkov nodded.

'Another problem with the electromagnetic model is how in the world the fireballs can get inside buildings, let alone aircraft. They're pretty well perfect bloody conductors.'

Benson paused a moment. 'But the thing that really convinced me the balls couldn't be electromagnetically-powered was the radiation. There's no way you can get that level of activity in an atmospheric plasma. There had to be some source of energy far in excess of any electromagnetic arrangement.'

'And you hit upon the idea of antimatter to power the fireballs?'

'It wasn't my idea, Leonid. A couple of English guys called Ashby and Whitehead suggested antimatter as an explanation for ball lightning back in the 1970s.'

Burkov stilled looked extremely sceptical.

'But it's crazy, Andrew. Even if – and it's a big if – there exists antimatter in quantity out there in some other galaxy, first, how has it got here? Second, why doesn't it just annihilate as soon as it touches the atmosphere. How can it survive down at ground level?'

'I don't know the answer to the first question yet, but I have some ideas about the second.'

Benson went to the blackboard and began drawing a diagram.

'This is the form of the potential between hydrogen molecules. Now suppose one of the molecules was anti-hydrogen. That would alter the exchange term, right? And you'd probably get something like this.' Benson drew another diagram.

Burkov studied it for a moment and said: 'You mean there'd be a repulsion?'

'Only a fraction of an electron volt perhaps. I still have to do a proper calculation. And this is only for hydrogen. We'd need to look at lots of other cases. Iron, for example. We've no idea what elements this antimatter might contain.'

'Let me see if I've got this straight,' said Burkov. 'You're claiming that a lump of antimatter can remain relatively stable in the Earth's atmosphere because it's shielded from the surrounding matter by a small electromagnetic potential barrier.'

'Yup. Of course it'd only work for a tiny mass. But then you only need a minute amount of antimatter to deliver a huge quantity of energy.'

Burkov stared at the board thoughtfully for while.

'What would trigger the annihilation in the end?'

Benson shrugged. 'It wouldn't need much. A thunderstorm perhaps. Or impact with a solid object. Possibly even the electric field of a metallic structure, such as an aircraft or a radio aerial. Anything really.'

'That would certainly explain why the fireballs tend to appear near military installations,' conceded the Russian.

'It would also explain the altitude effect,' said Benson. 'If these granules of antimatter are coming from space you'd expect most of them to annihilate in the upper atmosphere. Only a tiny fraction would reach ground level.'

Burkov crumpled his plastic cup and stroked his chin for while.

98

'But why now? Why have these things suddenly turned up out of the blue – literally?'

'I don't know, Leonid. But if I'm right it'd be important to find out whether the Earth can expect to intersect substantially more quantities of antimatter. The destructive power could be unthinkable.'

There was an anxious silence as both men dwelt on the unpleasant consequences.

'At least it puts paid to the Red Menace theory,' said Burkov brightly. 'That's one up the arse for your Mr Maltby. If he believes you.'

'He'll believe me,' said Benson grimly.

The flight to London was almost empty. Fear of the fireballs had hit the airlines badly. Benson thumbed mournfully through a newspaper, its pages full of alarm. Shrill headlines told a story of a world thrown into panic by the fireball menace. The Patterson Creek catastrophe occupied the centre spread, illustrated by lurid photographs, including some taken inside a nearby hospital where the survivors were dying of radiation sickness. The piece was accompanied by the inevitable scare-line: LONDON NEXT?

The radiation hazard had found its way into the newspapers too, fuelling the speculation that the fireballs were mini-nukes and the Russians were responsible. 'A Time For Resolve' thundered the editorial. The sunspot cover-story had obviously fallen apart. In an official statement, a White House spokesman openly accused the Soviet Union of using covert means to sow the seeds of panic in the West. For their part, the Soviets denounced the President as a warmonger, he was using the fireballs as a pretext for stepping up military pressure on the Warsaw pact.

Benson flung the paper down in despair.

'Hello,' said a little voice. A small boy peered at him over the seat in front. 'Hi.'

The boy disappeared and Benson heard his mother telling him to sit still and stop annoying the other passengers. The boy transferred his attention to the window, and began studying the clouds. 'Shall we see God, Mum?' he whispered.

'Shhh,' the woman replied.

'Shall we Mum?'

'Be quiet will you.'

The face appeared again over the seat. 'Will we see God, Mister?'

Benson smiled and envied the boy's simple innocence. 'Maybe,' he replied. 'Just keep looking.'

The captain announced their descent to Heathrow. Benson tried to doze, but he felt too edgy. Then he heard the little boy say: 'What's that light Mum?'

'Where?' asked the woman sharply, straining to look out of the window.

'Look, that yellow light. Over there!'

Other passengers had heard the exchange and were anxiously gazing from the windows. Benson felt his pulse quicken. He glanced out of the window but saw nothing unusual. They were descending slowly over central London on the approach to the airport.

'There! Look!' he heard someone cry. 'It's one of them fireballs!'

Within seconds the plane was in uproar. Passengers were standing. A woman screamed in panic. Two stewardesses rushed along the cabin, trying to calm nerves. The situation was like crying 'Fire!' in a theatre, only worse. In this case there was no exit. Benson's mouth went dry and an image of McGuire flashed through his mind, confronted by a fireball in the confined space of his cockpit.

A metallic voice filled the cabin. 'This is the captain speaking. Please do not be alarmed, there is no danger. Some of you may be able to see another aircraft approaching from the south with its landing lights switched on. It is visible from the left-hand side of the aircraft as a bright yellow glow just below the cloud-base. We are about to land at Heathrow. Please ensure that you have your seat belts on and your seats are in the upright position ready for landing.'

Benson spurned a taxi and took the tube into London, clutching his briefcase containing the neatly-bound report on the antimatter theory. It was raining again. He walked from the tube station to the address Maltby had given, which turned out to be an anonymous-looking building in a sidestreet off Whitehall. There was no obvious indication that this was part of the Ministry of Defence. It was late afternoon.

The reception area was painted dull brown. Benson gave his name to a dull-eyed official who reached for a telephone, and paced up and down while he waited. Presently the man said: 'Mr Maltby will meet you as soon as he can in The Feathers, sir.'

'The Feathers?'

'The pub across the road.' He gestured in the general direction of Trafalgar Square.

'I see.'

A pub? Benson hadn't expected to confront Maltby in a pub.

The Feathers was a diminutive watering-hole frequented by the well-connected, already over-full with men in pin-striped suits and American tourists. Benson ordered an orange juice; he wanted to keep a clear head. There were no seats left, so he stood against a wall festooned with old photographs and assorted Victoriana.

A full half-hour passed before Maltby finally appeared. 'Well, well, well,' he said. 'So the mountain comes to Muhammad.'

'We can't talk here,' complained Benson, ' in this crowd.'

'I have a car outside.'

They exited to find a chauffeur-driven black Rover parked defiantly on the double yellow lines. Benson and Maltby climbed into the rear. A soundproof glass screen separated them from the uniformed driver.

'I have an appointment in Pimlico,' Maltby explained, as they pulled out into the traffic. 'Now shoot.'

Benson reached into his briefcase and withdrew the folder, but made no attempt to hand it over. 'Have you heard of antimatter, Maltby?'

Maltby stared at him for a moment. 'Vaguely. I've read a bit of science fiction. Something to do with positive electrons isn't it?'

'More or less, except it's science fact.'

'What's this got to do with the fireballs?'

'The point about antimatter is that it's the source of enormous energy; one gram of the stuff would supply all of London's power requirements for a whole week. It makes nuclear power seem primitive. I'm convinced that antimatter is the power source of the fireballs.'

Maltby looked at Benson with a mixture of scepticism and consternation. 'You're saying these balls are made of antimatter?'

'No!' Benson rolled his eyes. 'It would take only the tiniest speck of antimatter to supply the energy of a fireball the size of a football. That's how they get inside aircraft, don't you see. Just a microscopic grain of antimatter dust, yet all that energy released in a halo around it.'

Maltby still seemed confused.

'Here,' said Benson, handing over the file. 'The complete theory.'

There was a few moments silence while Maltby scanned the contents of the file, pausing to frown occasionally. Eventually he shut the folder and looked up.

'So,' he said. 'They're manufacturing the stuff are they?'

Benson gaped in surprise, and Maltby smiled at him.

'The ultimate weapon, eh?'

'What?' rasped Benson hoarsely. 'You're mad, Maltby. Insane. I've come all the way down here to tell you the fireballs have a natural origin, and you immediately assume the Russians are behind it. Is there no limit to your stupidity!'

'Well where are you suggesting this antimatter is coming from?'

'From space, of course.'

Maltby's eyes widened a fraction and a half-smile appeared on his lips. 'Oh, really, Professor, surely you don't expect me . . . '

'Let me out!' Benson groped for the door-handle.

'Very well, old chap.' Maltby tapped on the glass partition and gesticulated at the driver. 'I confess I had expected something better from you Benson, especially after all the trouble we went to in getting your friend Burkov out. Perhaps you've been working too hard. Why not take a rest, eh?'

The car pulled in to the kerb and Benson leapt out, slamming the door. Maltby unwound the window. 'Send me your expenses will you, there's a good chap.'

Benson rounded on the seated civil servant. 'I hope the next fireball takes out you and your whole fucking Ministry, mister!' he flared.

'No chance, Benson. Haven't you heard? The fireballs have gone away. No reports at all now for the past forty-eight hours. Ciao!'

'The supercilious bastard! I'd like to wring his bloody neck!' Benson raged.

'That would do no good at all, my friend,' replied Burkov. 'Remember, you are dealing with a bureaucrat, not another scientist. They think differently. Believe me, I know. I am Georgian.'

The two men dwelt on this in silence for a while, staring gloomily at Benson's blackboard decorated in a riot of mathematical symbols. Eventually Burkov turned a quizzical eye on his comrade. 'So, the fireballs have gone. What now?'

'I'm taking a break, Leonid. I've put up with so much bullshit since arriving in this dump, I need to get away for a while. There's an astrophysics conference coming up next week in Trieste. I thought I'd go.'

'And then? Are you really going to settle in Milchester. Become an English academic?'

'There's nothing else.'

'That I cannot believe. You are the best.'

'Tell that to the National Science Foundation.'

'And what of this young lady who always drives the car? Is she your mistress?'

'She doesn't think so.'

The old Russian leaned forward and looked at Benson gravely. 'We have a saying in Russia. Don't feed the sheep before lighting the fire.'

Benson blinked uncomprehendingly at this cryptic maxim. 'What are you going to do, Leonid? I guess they'll give you political asylum or whatever. You could get a university appointment anywhere.'

Burkov sighed deeply and spread his hands out. 'I'm in no hurry to go anywhere. After all those years in the *psikhushka* there is much I wish to catch up on. Tchaikovsky, for instance. Besides, my guardians are still edgy about the KGB. There are worse places to be confined than Lanbrock Moor; in summer at least.' He looked at his watch. 'Ah! Five-thirty already. The driver will be impatient. My housekeeper has planned a special meal for today. Roast beef with something called Yorkshire pudding. Do you know this thing?'

'Yes. It's crap.'

'My dear friend. You cannot know, you cannot know. See you pal.'

Benson sat for an hour, deep in thought. Then he picked up the phone and called the Biochemistry Department.

'It's me.'

'Hello Andrew,' she replied. 'I hear the fireballs have gone.'

'So they say. Tamsin, how do you fancy a vacation?'

'With you? You think I'm a masochist?'

'Listen. There's an astrophysics meeting in Trieste next week. I was planning to do a bit of touring afterwards, take in a few crumbling ruins and all that. I'd really like to have you along.'

'Oh, Andrew. I don't really think . . . '

'Say you'll think about it.'

'Alright . . . well . . . yes.'

'Yes you'll think about it, or yes you'll come?'

'Yes I'll come. I must be mad.'

'Tamsin, that's great! Now for the bad news.'

'Oh no.'

'You're driving.'

'Bastard!'

They took the midnight ferry from Dover and drove through the following day as far as Switzerland. Benson directed Tamsin to a small hotel just outside Lausanne. They checked in to a twin-bedded room, and then found a restaurant overlooking the lake. Afterwards, with darkness falling, they walked arm in arm along the lakeside.

'I guess that's where the airliner crashed,' said Benson, looking out across the water.

Tamsin shivered. 'Thank God it's all over. Will you publish your theory when the fuss has died down?'

'What's the point? No one would believe it.'

'It's still of some scientific interest, isn't it?'

Benson shrugged and changed the subject. 'Let's buy a cuckoo clock. As a memento.'

She smiled. 'At this time of night?'

103

'There's a little place up here that stays open.' He indicated a narrow passageway between some old houses.

'How do you know? Have you been here before?' she asked.

'Yes. I came on my . . . ' he broke off.

'Honeymoon?' she finished for him.

His face looked bleak. 'Yes.'

They walked slowly in silence for a while.

'Andrew,' she said softly. 'What was she like – your wife?'

For a moment she thought he wasn't going to answer. Presently he said: 'She was five-foot-two with long red hair and the finest collection of sea shells in California. People found her attractive. I thought she was a goddess.'

They stopped and gazed silently across the lake. A warm breeze ruffled the inky surface of the water, fragmenting the reflection of the crescent moon into a myriad dancing slivers. Somewhere in the distance a church clock chimed. She touched his hand gently and said: 'Take me to bed.'

The Eighth European Symposium on Relativistic Astrophysics was held at the International Centre for Theoretical Physics at Miramare, about five miles west of Trieste. Accommodation was at the nearby Lido Hotel. Drinks were free at the reception.

Benson shuffled around awkwardly, trying to avoid at least half the participants. At each conference it got worse. There were people he knew and didn't want to engage in conversation, and there were those he vaguely recognized but wasn't sure about. In the end he was reduced to wandering around with an inane sort of half-smile on his face, which, with a bit of wishful thinking, could be interpreted as a luke-warm greeting. Or maybe he just looked pickled.

He spotted a tall, dark-haired woman in green pressing resolutely towards him through the throng. He tried to back away on to the balcony. Virginia Wetherell was more than he could take at that time of the evening.

'Andrew Benson, you old bastard!' she bellowed, drawing even more attention. 'Fancy seeing you here. I thought you'd disappeared into a black hole somewhere in Europe. I've been looking out for your obituary.'

'Hello, Virginia.'

'Where are you working? What happened at Caltech?'

Benson looked around in panic for a means of escape. His heart leapt as he saw Tamsin working her way towards him.

'I'm at Milchester.'

'Where?'

'The University of Milchester. In England.'

The woman frowned deeply. 'Why, for Christ's sake? What's there?'

Benson sensed Tamsin at his elbow. 'It's got an excellent Physics Department,' she said. 'Didn't you know?'

Virginia turned to Tamsin with raised eyebrows.

'This is . . . er, Dr Tamsin Bright, Virginia. She's a biochemist. From Milchester.'

'Oh,' she said, in a tone of faint surprise. 'Not really your scene this, is it?'

'Not really,' replied Tamsin, smiling sweetly.

Virginia melted into the crowd. Benson kissed Tamsin lightly on the forehead. 'Let's get out of here,' he said.

The conference was arranged around plenary sessions in the morning and shorter parallel sessions on more specialist topics after lunch. Benson soon tired of the review talks, and tended to sleep through the specialist sessions. He found it hard to muster any enthusiasm for his subject, and avoided getting drawn into any detailed discussions with the other participants. After a while, the others got the message, and Benson was left alone, a surly, disinterested figure.

Tamsin spent each day sightseeing or lazing on the little beach near the hotel. In the evenings they drove into town to try out different restaurants. Tamsin turned out to be something of a connoisseur of Italian food.

By the fourth day Benson was willing to pack up and go. He arranged to meet Tamsin after the final session. 'It's a talk on gamma ray astronomy by George Harrison,' he explained. 'An old friend. He'd notice if I opted out. God knows I've got precious few friends left.'

Benson filed into the lecture theatre with the other participants and found a seat near the back for a quick exit when Harrison was through. The lights dimmed and a slide appeared on the screen over Harrison's head. 'There are twelve reasons why it's a good idea to study cosmic gamma rays,' the speaker began. Benson yawned and started counting prime numbers. It was a mental game he reserved for the boredom of the lecture room.

Harrison droned on about some satellite project he'd been involved in – something by the name of GANU or JAMU or whatever. Anyway, Harrison seemed very paternalistic about it. The data looked good. Plenty to keep the theorists busy.

Slide after slide came up on the screen. The room seemed oppressively stuffy and hot. Benson had reached 3979 and was nearly asleep when suddenly Harrison made a remark that jolted him out of his reverie.

'. . . annihilation of positrons to produce this intense burst of gamma rays,' Harrison was explaining, '. . . quite without precedent. We recorded the

105

single event at 14.24 GMT on 14 February. You can see here.' Harrison prodded at the screen with a ten-foot cane. Benson peered intently.

'The leading burst here,' continued the speaker, 'is followed over the next few minutes by these secondary peaks.' Harrison indicated a graph showing a huge spike followed by a series of erratic bumps.

'The event was also recorded by the Japanese satellite ISPEG, which enables us to get a fairly accurate fix of the sky coordinates.' Harrison wrote the coordinates down on a blackboard and Benson made a note of them on the back of an envelope extracted from his trouser pocket.

'It's difficult to categorize an event of this sort,' Harrison went on. 'The intensity of gamma radiation is so enormous that I can only think of describing it as a gamma ray explosion produced by positron annihilation in some extragalactic object. But what the source of the antimatter can be I wouldn't hazard a guess.'

The lecture broke up, and Benson slipped out to find Tamsin. He walked down to the hotel deep in thought. Gamma ray explosion. Antimatter annihilation on 14 February . . . just before the fireballs started. But it didn't make sense; there couldn't be a connection. Harrison's satellite had been scanning the very depths of the universe. They were studying gamma ray sources millions of light years away in space . . .

'Hi. Have you forgotten what I look like?' It was Tamsin. He'd walked right past her.

'Oh, sorry. I was thinking.'

'So I see. Anything interesting in Harrison's talk?'

'No.' He smiled at her. 'Let's go.'

They checked out of the Lido and headed for Venice. The drive was a long one, and Benson spent most of it staring thoughtfully out of the window. Tamsin gave up trying to make conversation. By the time they reached the city and found a suitable hotel it was dark.

They ate in a little bistro near the Grand Canal, and wandered, holding hands, round the narrow streets, surrounded by decaying elegance. Reaching St Mark's Square, they crossed to the waterfront and gazed out across the Adriatic. The Cipriani château on the island of Gindecca looked as though it were from a fairy tale in the bright moonlight.

Tamsin sighed. 'Isn't it enchanting, Andrew?'

'Mmmm.'

She looked up at him. 'What's on your mind?'

'Oh, nothing really. Just something that Harrison said.'

'About gamma ray astronomy? I thought you only went to the lecture out of politeness.'

'I did.'

'It's not connected with the fireballs, is it?'

'Whatever makes you say that?'

'I know you better than you think, Andrew.'

'It's hard to see how gamma ray astronomy can possibly have any link with the fireballs.'

'But still you're puzzled?'

He stooped down, picked up a stone and threw it into the dark water. They watched it disappear with a plop. A noisy crowd of tourists bustled past, laughing and jostling. When they had gone Benson said: 'It seems that a couple of weeks before the fireballs began there was a huge pulse of gamma radiation picked up by a couple of satellites. The data indicates it could have been produced by antimatter annihilation.'

'A coincidence?' ventured Tamsin.

'Must be. These gamma ray sources are thousands, even millions of light years out in space.'

Tamsin pulled him closer. 'Look, Andrew, the fireballs are a thing of the past. You're getting obsessed. Let them go. We're supposed to be on vacation, remember?'

He smiled at her. 'Sure.'

Tamsin breathed in the warm Adriatic air contentedly. 'This is beautiful. Look at the moon, Andrew. It must be full.'

The moonlight bathed the whole city in a silvery glow, and picked out the phosphorescence of a distant ship's wake. Benson looked up at the moon, and in an instant something clicked inside his brain.

'Is anything wrong, Andrew?' He seemed transfixed, staring at the moon. 'Andrew!'

He looked down at her, wide-eyed. 'Oh God, Tamsin. I think I know what happened.'

'What are you talking about?'

'Come on,' he said. 'I've got to find a phone.'

'Why, for God's sake? What's the matter?'

Benson pulled away. 'No time to explain,' he said, and started to run.

12

'MY GOD,' SAID Burkov as he entered Benson's office. 'You look awful.'

Benson sat slumped behind his desk, unshaven and dishevelled, with red rims around his eyes. Three discarded plastic coffee mugs littered the desk top amid a disorderly heap of papers.

'I've been up all night,' replied Benson, 'waiting for the first flight back from Italy.'

'And what, if I may be so bold as to ask, has happened to the young lady?'

'Tamsin? Oh, she's driving on to Rome, or Naples, or somewhere. Did you check out the things I asked about when I phoned, Leonid?'

Burkov pulled up a chair and sat opposite Benson. 'It took me half the night. My SIS minder was most suspicious.' Burkov handed Benson a sheet of paper. 'Here.'

Benson studied the figures written on the sheet and nodded gravely.

'Would you mind telling me what's going on, Andrew?'

'When I was in Italy I dropped in on the Eighth European Symposium on Relativistic Astrophysics in Trieste. For old time's sake. Yesterday Harrison gave a lecture on gamma ray astronomy – some new satellite or other. Anyway, I was nearly dozing off when suddenly he started talking about positron annihilation. Apparently they're all baffled by a weird event recorded last 14 February that produced a huge burst of 511 keV gammas . . . ' Benson referred to the characteristic energy of gamma rays from the annihilation of positrons. 'The main burst was followed by some secondary activity, more or less random.' He groped in his pocket and took out the crumpled envelope on which he'd sketched the data. Burkov eyed it silently.

'14 February was just a week or two before the fireballs started, according to Maltby's crowd. I kept getting this feeling that there must be a connection, yet it seemed crazy. Gamma ray sources are way out there in the galaxy. I knew the coordinates Harrison gave corresponded to somewhere in the direction of the constellation Virgo. It meant nothing. Until last night, that is.'

'What happened last night?' queried Burkov. 'If it isn't indelicate to ask.'

'Tamsin and I were in Venice looking at the moon.'

'Very romantic. And?'

'The moon, Leonid. That's the connection.'

'What?' The Russian looked perplexed.

'The gamma rays. Don't you see – they came from the moon! It was in Virgo on 14 February. That's why I wanted you to check the lunar tables.'

'You're saying there's antimatter on the moon? That's ridiculous.'

'I'm saying that antimatter *hit* the moon – on 14 February.'

Burkov still looked confused. 'Didn't Harrison spot the lunar connection?'

'Nah!' Benson waved a hand dismissively. 'He's a cosmologist. They ignore everything this side of Andromeda.' He got up from behind the desk and began pacing the office. 'Let me tell you my theory, Leonid. I'm now convinced that the fireballs were caused by antimatter dust from space. The problem all along was explaining the origin of that dust. The mistake we made was in assuming the antimatter was always in that form.

'Suppose, however, that some antimatter enters the solar system not as a dust cloud, but in a more integrated form.'

'A rock?'

'Perhaps. Maybe it originated as a single chunk of material but became fragmented as it passed through interstellar space. After all, any time it hit a micrometeorite of matter there would have been a hell of a bang.'

Burkov looked incredulous. 'A *rock* of antimatter – flying through interstellar space? I don't understand, Andrew. Where could such a rock come from?'

'From another galaxy, of course.'

'What!'

'I know it's gone out of fashion, Leonid, but we can't be sure all galaxies are made of matter. For all we know there could be antimatter galaxies too. They'd look identical. We wouldn't know. And there are bound to be occasions when debris gets flung out – even whole stars.'

Burkov remained incredulous.

'Anyway, it was just bad luck that as this flotilla of antimatter debris was sweeping through the solar system the moon got in the way. It's my guess that the stuff struck the moon with a glancing blow. The resulting explosion would have vaporized most of the antimatter, but some of it survived, mixed in with splashed-off moon rock. In particular, fragments near the periphery would have been blown back into space by the explosion before they had a chance to annihilate fully. The violence would have altered the incoming trajectory drastically, trapping the remaining debris in orbit around the Earth-Moon system.'

Benson paused, looking at his companion for some reaction. The Russian just sat there, looking pale. Then he said: 'There's a way of checking.'

'Moonquakes?'

Burkov nodded.

'I've done it. I telexed Goddard as soon as I got back.' Benson picked up the telex reply, printed out on computer paper, and handed it to Burkov.

'Confirm violent seismic activity 2-14 vicinity crater Vestine. Will fax details re main event and splashback soonest. Event accompanied by prominent plume from moon's limb much reported in press at time,' he read aloud.

The Russian looked up at Benson. 'A plume? Reported in the press?'

'It was. I checked the London *Times* – the main library keep back-issues. They carried a short piece on 17 February. They talk about a volcanic eruption.'

'So the gamma ray burst, the moonquake and this . . . eruption, all coincide?'

'That's about it.'

'And nobody else has spotted the connection?'

'Not as far as I know.'

Burkov remained silent for a while, thinking deeply. Finally he said: 'If you're right Andrew, and this antimatter is really trapped in orbit around the Earth – and I have to confess the evidence is pointing that way – you know what it means, don't you?'

'Yes,' said Benson. 'They'll be back. Some day soon, bigger and nastier fireballs.'

It took another day for the full impact of Benson's discovery to sink in. Then two things assumed paramount importance. First, they had to work out the eccentric orbit of the remaining antimatter debris. Next they needed an estimate of the total quantity of material involved. The fear was that the fireballs to date had been caused by the Earth merely brushing the edge of a highly diffuse antimatter dust cloud. If the stuff came nearer on each pass, the consequences didn't bear thinking about.

On the practical front Benson fixed with his secretary Sally to get a couple of camp-beds, so that they could sleep over in his office if necessary. This suggestion met with strenuous objections from Burkov's SIS minder, who insisted on remaining outside the Physics Building in an unmarked blue Rover at all times that Burkov was there. Nor was Burkov's appearance in the West something which Benson wished to advertise at that time. The last thing he wanted was for the press to come sniffing round them when they were trying to work. Already Quenby and Stratton were getting curious about the peculiar-looking Russian who kept popping in and out of the Department at odd hours. Benson gave them some cock-and-bull story about an old colleague from California, and fended Quenby off by setting him an outrageously difficult field theory problem that would keep him busy for months if necessary. Then they got to work in earnest. They set about finding the answers to the orbit and mass-estimation problems with single-minded dedication, rarely stepping outside Benson's office.

The obvious way to tackle the first question was to analyse the accumulated fireball data to see if there was any sign of periodic behaviour. The trouble was that the rate of reports was not a very precise indicator of the actual incidence of fireballs, being distorted by factors such as media hype and national security procedures. Certainly the abrupt cessation of fireballs that had occurred the previous month was unprecedented.

Benson and Burkov worked doggedly at the computer terminal, manipulating the data and trying to drag out any sort of systematic trend. The basic technique was to use Fourier analysis, a means of breaking down a distribution into components of different periodicity. But however the data were organized, no particular period stood out prominently.

After many hours of exhausting and concentrated work they were forced to admit defeat.

'We're getting nowhere,' said Benson, crashing dejectedly into his swivel chair. 'If this stuff's orbiting the Earth there's got to be a periodicity. But where is it?'

Burkov sat drumming his fingers, his frail features looking even more drawn and haggard from the lack of sleep and dreadful sense of responsibility that suddenly lay upon them.

'Perhaps we are rushing at this, Andrew. Let's think calmly for a while.'

He poured two more coffees and they sat sipping in silence for a moment, before the Russian resumed.

111

'We are supposed to be physicists, yes?'

Benson shrugged, said nothing.

'So let us think like physicists and not computer witches.'

'Wizards.'

'Yes, wizards. Now, we are agreed that the antimatter is spread out in a swarm or cloud and is following an eccentric orbit that brings it very close to the Earth on each pass. Right?'

'Right,' agreed Benson.

'So what happens when the stuff arrives?'

'We get fireballs.'

'We get fireballs,' repeated the Russian. 'But not just like that. The dust somehow remains stable for a while, filtering slowly down to ground level, before something like an electric field or a thunderstorm sets it off. Then bang.'

Benson nodded wearily. 'Except that the larger particles probably go bang as soon as they hit the atmosphere. What about the big one that took out Patterson Creek. How did that reach ground level intact?'

They thought about that one for a while.

'There could be a sort of shielding effect,' suggested Burkov. 'As the surface material starts to annihilate, it will radiate strongly and force the surrounding air molecules away. Once it hits a solid object, though, the whole thing explodes in one go.'

'Maybe.'

'But most of the data here refers to the early fireball incidents – the small ones. So let's restrict attention to the fine dust. What can we say about its behaviour? How long would it take to drift down to the ground?'

'Who knows? A few days, I guess. It'd depend on the size of the grains, and the weather patterns.'

Burkov nodded. 'So a sudden injection of antimatter grains into the upper atmosphere wouldn't lead to an abrupt spate of fireballs. The effect at ground level would be considerably spread out in time.'

'Uh-uh. Which is why our graph here is all smeared out.'

'So, the rate of fireball reports is not, after all, an accurate indicator of the time of encounter of the Earth with the orbitary debris.'

'Agreed,' said Benson slowly. 'Unless . . . '

'Unless we filter out all the ground level reports and restrict the analysis to the aircraft cases,' interjected Burkov eagerly.

Without further discussion they quickly instructed the computer to reorganize the data, retaining only the high-altitude cases. Then they fed this data into the Fourier analysis program. Seconds later the screen filled with symbols.

The 36-day cycle was unmistakable.

Benson gave a whoop of delight.

'Christ, Leonid, when's the next fireball cycle going to start?'

'The next injection of antimatter is due, let me see, about the middle of next week. Allow three, maybe four, days for it to drift down; I'd say we'll be getting reports by the middle of July.'

'I'd like to see Maltby's face.'

'What about a celebration bacon sandwich?' suggested Burkov.

'Though we don't really have much to celebrate, do we?'

'I guess not.'

'Afterwards, some sleep.'

'Yes, sleep.'

Both men crashed out on the camp-beds and slept through the rest of the day. They rose that evening, feeling stale and depressed by the dead weight of anxiety over the impending fireball threat, a threat that they alone appreciated.

The most urgent priority now lay in trying to estimate the total mass of antimatter in orbit around the Earth.

'The orbital characteristics are no help at all,' said Benson morosely. 'The only handle we've got on the mass is the gamma ray data. We can make a guestimate of the total energy release from the lunar impact.'

'That's no use without knowing the velocity of impact,' replied the Russian.

'Let's say ten kilometres per second.'

'Why?'

Benson shrugged. 'Typical relative stellar speed in the spiral arms of the galaxy.'

'Suppose the antimatter is extragalactic? Isn't that more likely?'

'Then the speed would be higher.'

'That's one hell of a speed.'

'Yeah. You'd expect the stuff to go splat on impact, not slop around all over the solar system.'

'Must've been grazing incidence – just glanced the moon's surface.'

'Maybe.'

'Let's model it that way anyway,' suggested Burkov. 'The splashback data from Goddard ought to help confirm it.'

They worked on all through the next night, alternating between a jumble of

113

equations on the blackboard and the computer on Benson's desk. Twice they had to get distant colleagues out of bed with guarded queries about the gamma ray satellite data, so they could relate the intensity of the bursts to the energy released when the antimatter hit the moon.

Although the data they had to go on was desperately fragmentary, it soon became clear that the total mass of antimatter debris in orbit must be greatly in excess of the quantity that had already fallen to Earth. The awful truth began to dawn on them that the fireball threat might now be of colossal proportions.

'What we've had already is just a side-show,' said Benson. 'The main action is yet to come. I don't need to tell you what would happen if even a pea-sized particle of antimatter drops on central Europe.'

'World War Three.'

'And how. You can be sure if the antimatter doesn't get you the superpowers will. Shit. What a stupid way for *homo sapiens* to go.'

'Maybe we did our sums wrong, Andrew? We should try to get some sort of independent check on the amount of this stuff up there.'

'Yeah. But how?'

'If the mass of debris is big enough wouldn't we be able to see it? Through a telescope I mean?'

'Hell, Leonid, I don't know. Presumably nobody has or we'd know about it.'

'Would we? What would it look like through a telescope?'

'A cloud, I guess. Some sort of comet perhaps.'

'Who'd know about that?'

'A lot of comets are found by amateur astronomers. I suppose the Royal Astronomical Society would know.'

Benson phoned the RAS and asked for the Secretary. After a moment or two he was connected.

'This is Professor Andrew Benson here. I'm trying to find out if there have been any new comets discovered recently. I want to give a lecture on comets.'

'You obviously don't read the newspapers, Professor.'

'Oh?'

'Try today's *Times*. That gives all the details we've got at the moment.'

The secretary hung up.

Benson punched telephone buttons furiously.

'Sally. Get me today's *Times*.'

'But, Professor Benson, I'm just leaving for my . . .'

'Get it. Now!'

He slammed down the receiver.

114

Ten minutes later Sally knocked uncertainly at the door and peered tentatively into the room. It looked like a pigsty. Papers and books lay scattered across the floor, a pile of discarded plastic cups had been built into a facsimile of the leaning Tower of Pisa and a half-eaten bacon sandwich was stuffed into the in-tray along with a heap of orange peel. The place stank like a tramp's den.

The two occupants were no less offensive. Benson's face was covered by several days' growth of beard and his eyes were hideously bloodshot. The Russian looked to be at death's door, an already abused body now positively cadaverous, his clothes unkempt and creased.

The girl regarded Benson wide-eyed as he snatched the newspaper from her.

'Er, Professor . . . ' she stammered. 'I'll be away for a couple of weeks. In Greece.'

'Why?' said Benson, uncomprehendingly.

'Holiday.'

Benson just stared at her blankly, and she retreated through the door, relieved to get away from whatever insanity was taking place.

Benson hastily spread the newspaper on the floor and scanned the columns while Burkov looked on expectantly. They soon found it.

'Schoolboy discovers mystery object in space,' proclaimed the headline. Benson read out the report:

'A 17-year-old Southampton schoolboy could go down in history as the discoverer of a new type of astronomical object. Mark Stanhope, a keen amateur astronomer and pupil of St Cedric's Comprehensive School, Southampton, was observing the Crab Nebula through his home-made 12-inch reflector when he spotted an unusual patch of light.

' "I checked in my star atlas, and soon realized there were no galaxies in that position," explained Mr Stanhope. "I thought it must be a comet. But then I noticed the twinkling . . . " '

Benson stopped and the two men stared at each other in stunned silence, instantly aware of the implication.

Benson resumed the report in subdued tone.

' "At the centre of a wispy patch of luminosity there seemed to be a flickering light."

'A spokesman at the Royal Greenwich Observatory said last night that due to adverse weather conditions they had not yet confirmed Mr Stanhope's observations. However he did admit that it would be most unlikely that a comet would display the flickering phenomenon described by the schoolboy.

'Mr Stanhope, who is sitting his A levels next year . . . '

115

Benson broke off, stood up and stared grimly out of the window. It was raining again.

'A flickering light source in the middle can only mean a large solid object,' he said.

'I agree,' responded the Russian huskily.

'Irregular in shape, and tumbling over and over, the sunlight reflecting haphazardly off its uneven surfaces.'

'A cloud of debris, it seems, and in the middle a rock.'

'A bloody great rock.'

'Of antimatter.'

'Jesus Christ.'

Both men fell silent at the enormity of the discovery.

Presently Benson said: 'Well, at least it confirms our theory. Obviously the rock didn't break up completely when it hit the moon. I wonder how big it is?'

'For it to be visible at that distance in a 12-inch telescope it would have to be at least a hundred metres across,' ventured Burkov.

'Ten million tonnes of antimatter,' muttered Benson, incredulously. 'And it only needs one tonne to devastate the whole planet.'

'We don't know that the rock is going to collide with the Earth. Until now we seem to have brushed only the tail of the debris.'

'But with each cycle it's getting closer.'

'So far, yes. However, we need to work out the exact orbit before we can be sure that trend will continue. My guess is that the dust is spread out over many thousands of kilometres, so we can't deduce much about the orbit of the rock itself from the fireball data.'

Benson rubbed his eyes, suddenly overcome by fatigue and despondency. 'How easy will it be to calculate the orbit, Leonid?'

The Russian thought for a moment.

'From the 36-day cycle we know that the orbit goes out beyond the moon, so it will involve the gravitational fields of the Earth, sun and moon together. It could be very complicated. We'd need several days at least of careful observations, and then a good computer programme.'

'We don't have those resources here,' said Benson. 'We'd have to get assistance from elsewhere.'

'Now the story's broken maybe the professional astronomers will get on to it anyway.'

'You don't think they'll make the fireball connection do you?'

'It would be most unlikely. They wouldn't have the data to spot the 36-day cycle, even if anyone suspected a link.'

'So what do we do now? Go and plead with Maltby?'

116

'I think not, my friend. He'd only dismiss the discovery of the rock as a coincidence. Our evidence is still too fragmentary.'

'But we can't just sit here and ignore the fact that a few thousand miles up there enough antimatter to disintegrate a planet is careering around in an eccentric orbit.'

'At this stage we won't get anywhere working through government channels, I fear. They are fools, East and West. Their minds are too narrow. We will have to follow the route we both know well. Treat the problem as a straight scientific one and use our influence in the scientific community. It is not, after all, inconsiderable.'

'Yours isn't, Leonid. I've cocked up my career, don't forget.'

The Russian smiled thinly. 'I'm sure you can still pull a few ropes.'

'Strings.'

'Yes, strings.'

Benson turned wearily to the telephone, consulted a notebook, and rang a number in Arizona. 'I'll try Ed Tarling at Kit Peak. He owes me one.'

After a few minutes Benson was connected with Tarling. He cut short the pleasantries.

'Ed, I need your help urgently.'

'Sure,' came the reply. 'Just so long as you don't want me to interrupt my observing schedule. We got this really good photometric data on M46 . . . '

'Ed, this is really important. It could be a major discovery.'

'Oh, yeah? Don't say those Limeys have retrained you as an observational astronomer?'

'Seriously, Ed. I've been doing some theoretical work with Leonid Burkov.'

'No shit? I thought Burkov was zonked out.'

'He's right here.'

'Jesus. How is he?'

'Recovering.'

'Yeah? So what's this big theory, Andy?'

'Have you heard the report about this English school kid finding a mystery object?'

'Eh? Come on Andy, cut the crap. We're serious astronomers over here.'

'I'm *being* serious. Leonid and I predicted its existence.'

'What is this, some sort of leg-pull?'

'Look, Ed, we're both pretty tired and we need your help to clinch this. It could be a big thing for all of us. Please stop buggering me around.'

Benson gave the astronomer a quick rundown on the newspaper report and made a few vague remarks about rogue asteroids and some new project they were supposedly working on to test gravitational effects in the solar system.

When he'd finished Tarling said. 'I don't believe a word of it. But anyway, what do you want me to do?'

'Get the orbit for us.'

'Christ, Andy, what do you think I'm doing for a living? Running a cosmic circus? We only get three hundred hours observing time this season. You can't expect me to start making unscheduled runs on expensive equipment like this.'

'You don't need to use the big telescope, Ed. Get one of your graduate students to handle this on the 50-inch.'

'It's hard enough keeping those lazy bastards on the main project.'

'Then it'll be a bit of light relief for them. I bet they'd jump at the chance to be in on something new.'

There was a few moments' silence, then a long sigh.

'I guess I owe you one, Andy.'

'So you'll do it?'

'Leave it with me. No promises mind.'

'Thanks pal. There's one more thing.'

'Oh Christ, what now?'

'Have you got the software to work out the orbit?'

'Not here. We can do it back at LA on the network.'

'That's great. I really appreciate your help, Ed.'

'Yeah. Well, I'll let you know.'

'And, Ed. This could be really big, so let's keep it in the family, eh?'

'Whatever you say. Bye.'

Benson turned to Burkov. 'He'll do it,' he said. But the Russian had fallen asleep.

When Tarling phoned back three days later his mood was markedly different.

'Say Andy, you really started something over here. I got a couple of students going bananas over that mystery object of yours. What did you say it was? A rogue asteroid? Sure doesn't look like an asteroid. Not that I'd know one if I saw one. I leave all that solar system stuff to those wankers at the Smithsonian. But this mother's got a tail. Like a comet only it isn't a comet 'cos the tail's *bent*. Would you belive that? It's shaped like a boomerang! When J first . . . '

'Ed. What's the orbit?' Benson cut Tarling short. The crucial thing was the orbit.

'Oh, er . . . we just did that. It's real close. Within the moon's orbit for half the time. Very eccentric. In fact it'll only just miss us next time around.'

'You're sure of that Ed? It will miss?'

'No, I'm not sure. I think it'll miss by twenty thousand miles. But that's bloody close for an asteroid, or whatever it is. You know, you're right, pal. This could be something big. How the hell did you and Burkov *predict* such a weirdo?'

'It's a long story. Look, we have to be sure about the orbit, and one pass may not be enough. We need to do a complete extrapolation on this one.'

'Afraid it's gonna hit us, are you? Quite a bang if it does. What with all that fireball business, then a big meteor impact. Christ. Could be serious.'

You don't know just how serious, thought Benson.

'When can we get a long-term projection, Ed?'

'It'll take a few more days' observation if you want to go to two periods. The orbit's pretty messy. Don't you think we'd better announce this? Get some confirmation on the orbit?'

'No, Ed. No announcements,' said Benson sharply.

'It's your baby I guess. But if there is some danger, don't you think . . . '

'We'll handle it this end.'

'OK. Whatever you say. What d'you want me to do?'

'Can you let us run the orbital analysis from here?'

'I guess so. You can patch into the LA net through London or Edinburgh, I think. We can keep sending the data down the line from here.'

'Thanks.'

'You sure we shouldn't go public? Some other guy might be checking out that newspaper report.'

'I doubt it. Let's keep it low-key till we're sure, Ed.'

'Right. Oh, best wishes to Burkov.'

Benson and Burkov had wisely used the three-day lull to catch up on lost sleep, clean up the office and themselves, and double-check their calculations. Neither man had any doubts now about the basic correctness of their theory. With the fireball menace apparently over, the subject was slowly disappearing from the headlines. No further contact with Maltby or Malone had been received or initiated. Everything now hinged on the improved orbital data. If future gravitational perturbations were going to swing the antimatter away from the Earth again, then the threat would recede.

On the other hand . . .

For two days they worked on the orbital problem, linked to the big University of California computer on an approved scientific network. Progress was slow. But each new set of observational data improved the accuracy of their extrapolation.

The anxiety was wearing both of them down and Burkov had to take long rests at his country retreat. Benson had taken to drinking heavily and ate little. His colleagues at the University had obviously written him off as insane. The blinds stayed shut and the door locked. But no one bothered him.

He'd set up the orbital analysis to give a predicted 'perigee', a technical term referring to the distance of closest approach of the rock with the Earth. Everything depended on the perigee being as large as possible. At the outset the error bars were too large to have any confidence in the computation, but as more and more data got fed into the computer from Kit Peak so the errors shrank, and Benson's hopes shrank with them.

The probable range of values for the perigee steadily converged on zero.

The rock was going to hit the Earth in 10 days time.

13

THEY WALKED IN silence for an hour on the fells beyond the city, lost in the horror of what they had discovered. Finally Burkov stopped, exhausted, and sat on a dry-stone wall, trembling, wheezing that he was tired out.

Benson looked around him, for the first time aware of his surroundings and the time of day. It was early evening. He sniffed and smelt gorse. The city was hidden in the valley. It was as if they had walked away from mankind and arrived at some place that existed before the Earth was polluted by humanity.

'Almost makes you glad to be alive,' he said.

Burkov looked up at him. 'The problem is, Maltby's obviously useless. Maybe Malone would listen. Of course, we could go the traditional route, deliver a lecture, publish a paper.'

'Lecture to whom, publish in what? By that time we'll all be blown to atoms,' said Benson.

Burkov shook his head. 'We've got to think,' he said, and in that moment, Benson's frustration turned to anger. He reached down and pulled the old man to his feet, squeezing his shoulder, hurting him.

'Why bother, Leonid? We're at the terminal stage. We're the last witnesses. How the hell can we stop ten million tonnes of rock? Even if we could figure out a way it'd need global resources. That's a joke! The West thinks it's the Russians. The Russians think it's the West. So to hell with them all. You and I can sit back and watch mankind disappear up its own foolishness. We're buggered my friend, and that's a fact.'

121

'Nice speech. Now let me go. You hurt.'

Benson dropped his hands and stepped back.

'Think about it.'

They stared intently at one another, two men with such wildly different backgrounds and life-styles, united by science and now by a shared secret of horrendous proportions.

'What is there worth saving?' cried Benson.

The Russian smiled weakly and said, 'Me.'

The odd sight of a dishevelled old man riding piggy-back on a tunelessly whistling hiker drew stares of astonishment from the locals. Benson was still whistling as they strode into town. They stopped at the first pub they saw and Burkov slid off.

'I'm thirsty,' he said.

'You're thirsty?' said Benson. 'You're buying.'

It was a small place, just three tables, one occupied by two old men. A fat barman polished glasses. It had been passed over by the designers from the breweries. If it were not for a youth in denims playing a fruit-machine, the bar could have been nineteenth-century.

Burkov ordered two beers and Benson nodded to the old men who grinned at him awkwardly.

Burkov sat down. The place was silent except for the warbling of the fruit-machine and the occasional rat-a-tat when the youth won a few coins.

'So,' said Burkov. 'What are our possibilities?' He took a long pull from his glass, then he began tracing a pattern on the table. 'Let us assume that Whitehall and Washington are out. We've had it with them.'

Benson nodded, only half listening. He was, in his mind, back in his room, staring at the mathematics scrawled on the blackboard, going over the equations, double-checking for mistakes.

'. . . and we've agreed,' Burkov continued, 'that there is no time to go through the normal procedure . . .'

Benson closed his eyes, the better to visualize the blackboard, then twitched, startled, as the fruit-machine clattered like a machine gun and the youth whooped. It went on for half a minute then the youth collected his money, and danced to the bar, ordered a beer, and sat perched on a stool, grinning, feet tapping to imaginary music, fingers snapping. The fruit-machine was playing a few bars of a tune called 'Congratulations'.

'Conclusion,' said Burkov. 'We go to Moscow.'

The song of the fruit-machine ended.

'Moscow?' Benson repeated, the word echoing in the sudden silence. The youth glanced at him, then back at the barman.

'Not Moscow itself,' Burkov said. 'Not geographically. By proxy, so to speak.'

'The Embassy?'

Burkov smiled. 'Finally my friend, you are listening to me.'

They sat for a while in silence, Benson thinking, trying to work out the consequences of Burkov's suggestion. The thought of the Russian Embassy made him shiver, the idea that once in, he would not get out, or if he did, he would be branded as a spy or something, for surely MI5 or someone would keep a check on anyone trying to enter . . . Then he thought of Burkov.

'You would go there, after what they've done to you?'

'They let me out. They don't want me back. They would do me no more harm.'

'But would they listen? Have you any credibility with them.'

Burkov shrugged. 'How do I know? Like you I am a scientist. Unworldly. Cloistered. I don't know how these things work. I can't even get through a le Carré book.'

Benson grinned and patted the old man on the arm. Time for another beer, then home. At the bar he was aware that the place was suddenly quieter. Then he realized; the youth had gone; must have tiptoed out.

For half an hour they mulled over the limited possibilities, morose and anxious. Benson recalled once reading a paper on bar conversation. The favourite topic after sex and football was saving the world. Now here they were, a decrepit Russian and a disgraced American scientist, playing the part for real. He grinned in spite of himself.

It was getting dark as they left. The street was deserted and Burkov was tired. He needed a cab. There was a bus-stop a few hundred yards away but it was anybody's guess how long they'd have to wait. Then they noticed the blue saloon parked opposite. A thickset man sat reading a paper in the driver's seat. The minder. Benson had forgotten. The stupid idiot must have been trailing them across the fells.

He walked over and tapped on the window. The man wound it down. 'Can you give us a lift back? Your protégé is on his last legs.'

The minder twisted round and looked at Burkov. Then he unlocked the rear door and the two scientists climbed in. 'The SIS at your service,' he said, and drove off.

The following day they stood in Benson's office and made up their minds. They would contact the Russians. Tell them everything. Then they'd go and see Maltby and spell it out. Once the fireballs returned, they would have to be taken seriously.

'Haven't we forgotten something, Leonid?' said Andrew. 'Your minder. We can't just go to the Soviet Embassy with him in tow. They wouldn't let us.'

'We'll have to shake him off somehow,' replied the Russian.

Benson thought for a moment, then picked up the phone. The familiar voice had a strange effect on him. 'Tamsin, it's Andrew,' he said simply. 'We need your help.'

'Aren't you going to ask if I had a good holiday in spite of your abrupt departure?'

'I'm glad you're back.'

'So I can help, is that it?' She sounded distinctly frosty.

'Listen, Tamsin. I'm sorry about Italy, but we've stumbled on something big – and unpleasant. Can you get over here right away? I'll explain everything.'

The two men watched Tamsin go steadily paler as they related the discovery of the lunar connection, the antimatter stream in orbit, and then the existence of the rock and its scheduled encounter with planet Earth.

'So you want to contact the Russians to see if they'll help stop the rock,' she concluded.

'It's probably a forlorn hope,' responded Benson. 'But, yes, something like that. Maltby's useless. The Russians may be our only chance.'

'I don't see how I can be of any help.'

'I want you to drive us to London; to the Embassy.'

'Is that all?'

'Sure.'

She looked uneasy. 'Shouldn't we clear it with John Maltby first? I mean, involving the Russians . . . '

'There's no time for diplomatic niceties. We're heading for global disaster. We need some drastic action.'

'Okay. When shall we go?.

'Now. Bring your car to the service entrance at the back of the building.'

'Why the service entrance?'

'I need to stop by the computer room,' he lied. 'The service entrance is nearer.'

The little red Fiat was waiting as they slipped out the rear of the Physics building. Benson glanced up and down the service road briefly, and saw no sign of anyone. They piled into the car, Benson in front next to Tamsin, Burkov in the back clutching a briefcase.

They drove for about an hour, finally getting on to the M1 motorway. As

124

they sped down the southbound carriageway, Benson went over and over the whole fireball saga: the antimatter, the lunar collision, the discovery of the rock, the computations. It all fitted – too damn well. He looked out at the passing cars, the green fields beyond, the occasional houses. The over-whelming *normality* of it all contrasted ludicrously with the stupendous threat that faced them. In a month, thought Benson grimly, none of this may exist. All those people out there are going about their daily lives blissfully ignorant of the threat that lies literally over their heads . . .

'We're being followed.' Tamsin's voice jolted Benson out of his deliber-ations. He turned round. A blue saloon was keeping pace about a hundred yards behind. He swore under his breath.

'You're sharp,' he told her. 'It must be Leonid's minder. We'll have to lose him.'

She turned and glared at Benson. 'So that's why we left from the back of the building. All that rubbish about the computer room was just to keep me in the dark. You've got a bloody nerve involving me in this. We could all end up in jail.'

'We'll all end up vaporized if something isn't done!' he flared. 'For God's sake Tamsin, it's too serious to start worrying about national security and all that crap!'

'Alright! Alright! Don't hassle me. We'll wait till we get to London, then I'll try and give him the slip in the suburbs. I'll take a roundabout route through the East End. It should be nearly dark by the time we get there.'

They drove on in silence, Tamsin checking the rear-view mirror regularly. The blue saloon stuck to them like glue. Eventually they reached the end of the motorway and joined the dense suburban traffic. Once or twice Tamsin thought she'd thrown the minder off, but he always reappeared on their tail, following every twist and turn. Benson became edgy.

'We can't just drive up to the Soviet Embassy and walk in. Maltby's guy is bound to make a scene. Can't you skip a red light or something?'

'And kill us all?'

He turned round. The blue saloon was there, two cars back. They were passing through a run-down part of the city, with dismal terraced houses interspersed among derelict warehouses and dirty factories.

'Do you know where you're going?' he asked.

'I used to live round here as a child.'

'No kidding? In this dump.'

'It wasn't so bad then. It's been hard hit by the recession. The rich have moved out, leaving mostly immigrants and the unemployed. No wonder the crime's uncontrollable.'

'Inner city decay. The same the world over.'

Suddenly the car lurched. Benson hung on to the door handle, and Burkov sprawled across the rear seat. Tamsin had swung into a narrow street between two warehouses, and was accelerating frantically. They took the next bend at thirty and roared down a cobbled street lined with trucks. In the half-light Benson could just make out a pair of massive steel gates at the end of the street.

'It's a dead end!' he cried, turning sharply to see the blue saloon appear at the intersection behind them.

'Hold on!' shouted Tamsin as they sped towards the gates. Suddenly she swung the wheel to the right, and they shot through a hidden opening at the end of a warehouse. A filthy canal lay to their left, the bankside strewn with old timbers and discarded household furniture. They bumped and lurched crazily along the broken concrete track paralleling the canal, narrowly avoiding potholes and abandoned cars. The engine screamed as Tamsin slammed the car into a low gear and swung right again.

They turned into an open area where a warehouse had been demolished, the ground being left rough to serve as a temporary lorry park. The little Fiat careered across the bumpy surface, hurling its occupants around. For a moment Benson was convinced the car was out of control, but Tamsin hung on to the wheel grimly, working the gears in furious succession.

Eventually they exited on to a regular highway, empty of cars. Tamsin took that street and the next at seventy, then slowed, turned left over a railway bridge, and after a hundred yards or so she pulled off the road into a pub car park. She chose a parking spot right at the end, out of sight of the road, behind a large truck, and switched off the engine. They all sat in silence for a moment.

'I take back all I've ever said about women drivers,' said Benson. 'Leonid, are you alright?'

The Russian looked distinctly ill, but nodded.

'No sign of our friend,' remarked Tamsin. 'I suggest we stop for a drink.'

'I certainly need one after that,' replied Benson.

They found a spare table in a seedy-looking bar patronized by youths wearing leather clothes and shabby-looking old men with red faces and empty eyes. Benson ignored their stares as they sat with their drinks, planning the next move.

'There's no point in going to the Embassy at this time of the evening,' said Benson. 'Our best bet is to find a cheap hotel somewhere, and phone ahead to make an appointment.'

'What are we going to tell them, Andrew?' asked Burkov. 'That we want to enlist their help to avert the end of the world?'

'You speak to them, Leonid. Say you've been held against your will by the

126

British and you want to return to Russia. Tell them you've got important information to impart, military secrets or something. Anything really, just so long as it gets us inside the Embassy.'

They finished their drinks and got up to leave. Eyes followed them as they passed through the bar and out into the car park. It was completely dark now, and the sky was overcast again. Benson peered through the gloom for signs of the blue saloon, but the car park was almost empty. They kept to the shadow as they made their way towards the large truck.

Benson heard a slight rustling sound and spun round. A street light dazzled him; the back of the pub was in inky darkness. Suddenly there came a high-pitched cackle, then another and another.

'Run for the car!' shouted Benson, but it was too late. Half a dozen youths, almost invisible in their black leather, surged out of the shadows and surrounded them.

'Look what we've got 'ere,' said the leader. 'A bunch of toffs.'

'They'd better 'ave plenty of money,' said a second.

Benson's pulse raced. 'Look, you can have all our money if you'll let us leave quietly,' he said, trying to sound reasonable. 'We've got important business . . .' He realized his mistake. There was a sharp click, and he saw the glint of a knife blade in front of his face.

'D'ya 'ear that? 'e says they're important people.' The leader's face was inches away from Benson's, and he could make out the snarling animal features in the darkness. 'Important to who?' The youth spat out the words in a guttural voice tinged with pure hatred. Benson recoiled in revulsion. 'Not to us, you ain't.'

Tamsin let out a sharp gasp.

'The bird's got nice tits,' sniggered one of the others. Benson watched in disbelief as a skin-headed youth clasped Tamsin by the hair and began groping her freely.

'Get 'er clothes off,' gloated another, his voice distorted by alcohol.

'No! Please!' she screamed, as hands clawed at her.

The leader turned away from Benson briefly to leer at the spectacle. In that instant Benson lifted his foot and crashed it into the youth's back, sending him sprawling against the group crowding around Tamsin. There followed a screech of obscenities, and then a roar of pain as Burkov waded into the mêlée wielding a heavy wooden stick that he'd picked up from the ground.

'Animals!' screamed the Russian in rage, flailing about him mercilessly.

Benson made a grab for Tamsin, and tore her free, pounding his fist in fear and loathing into the face of the youth holding her hair. 'Get to the car!' he bellowed. 'Run!'

A boot thumped into his thigh and sent him crashing down. He felt a sharp stab of pain as someone kicked him in the stomach, then the ribs. Through a haze of nausea he could just make out the pathetic figure of Burkov, his legs buckling, going down amid a rain of blows.

Suddenly the whole insane panorama was frozen in blinding white light as Tamsin drove straight at them, headlamps ablaze. She screeched to a halt inches from Burkov's crumpled form, and leant on the horn. The air was filled with a banshee blare, and the youths scattered.

Benson coughed in agony, forced himself on to his hands and knees and crawled over to his fallen comrade. Burkov lay twitching, a thin stream of blood trickling from his mouth. He mumbled something in Russian.

'Leonid!' choked Benson.

The Russian opened his eyes and stared straight at Benson. 'You'll have to save the world without me, Andrew,' he said, and went limp.

14

Tamsin's shrieks pierced the very depths of his soul. He gazed despairingly at her naked body spreadeagled on the ground, pinned down by lust-crazed punks, grinning contemptuously at him. Beside them sat Leonid, blankly staring at the rape and singing softly in Russian.

She turned to look at him, pleading for help, but he couldn't move. Someone was holding his arms. He cried out, but the grip only got stronger.

'For God's sake try to keep still!' he heard her say.

'What?'

'Keep still. You'll injure yourself.'

Benson squinted and stared uncomprehendingly at the nurse as she tried to force him to lie flat. His whole body was bathed in pain.

Then he remembered. The car park, the leather-clad louts, Tamsin being mauled and Leonid . . .

'Burkov!' he shouted, then winced at the pain in his chest. 'Where's Leonid?'

'All in good time, Professor Benson. Now try to relax. You've had a bad time.' The nurse was a pretty brunette with a fierce gaze and a no-nonsense manner.

'Where am I? I've got to reach . . . '

'You're in hospital, and you're not going anywhere.'

Benson glanced around the room. It was spartan, ten-by-ten with white walls, a tiled floor, a hanging cupboard, and devoid of furniture save for his

129

bed, a small cabinet and a trolley covered with medical gear. A single bright lamp burned fiercely above the bed. A normal hospital room.

But was it? Something was wrong, and in his hazy state it took Benson a while to figure out what it was. There were bars at the window.

He tried to sit up. 'There was a woman with me,' he said. 'Is she alright?'

The nurse looked at him sternly. 'She's under sedation. She'll be fine. Now keep still while I give you something.' She pushed him flat again and took his arm. He felt the sharp prick of a needle.

'I don't want anything! Don't you understand, there's not much time left! I have to get out of here! I . . . '

The nurse turned away, and without another word she left the room. As she closed the door Benson heard a key turn in the lock. This isn't a hospital, he thought. It's a prison. And then he lapsed back into unconsciousness.

When he woke again, he was alone. He had no what time it was; his watch had been removed. His chest ached dreadfully, and he had difficulty moving one leg, but otherwise his injuries didn't seem too serious.

He lay for a long time slowly reconstructing the events of the last day or two, and trying to make sense of his present predicament. He looked around for a bell or alarm of some sort, but saw nothing. Nor was there any sign of his personal belongings. No sounds reached his ears from outside. Eventually he tried to get out of bed. Shakily he stood by the bedside, and hobbled a few steps around the tiny room. Carefully he exercised all his muscles. Not too bad, he thought.

Suddenly the door opened. A white-coated man of about forty stood in the doorway. Benson took him to be a doctor.

'Get back in bed immediately!' he commanded. 'You're in no fit state to wander about.'

'Isn't that up to me to decide?'

The man grasped Benson's shoulder. Benson flung him off, and made his own way back to the bed.

'I demand to know where I am, and what has happened to my friends,' he snapped.

'You're in no position to demand anything.'

'Why am I locked in?'

'This is a high-security hospital,' replied the doctor. 'You're being kept here for your own good.'

'You can't lock me up against my will. This is supposed to be a free country.'

'Not for law-breakers, Professor.'

'I haven't broken any laws!' protested Benson.

'Abducting a foreign national under the protection of the British government, evading an official bodyguard, conspiracy to commit treason . . . not to mention causing an affray. I'd say that was pretty serious law-breaking.'

'Abduction! Treason! Are you mad? Listen, I've got some information of the greatest importance and urgency. I *must* contact the authorities immediately.' Benson felt too weak to fight.

'We are the authorities.'

'Oh Jesus. Will you get me John Maltby? He works for the Ministry of Defence.'

'He's already here,' said a familiar voice. Benson turned to see Maltby standing in the doorway. 'Well, Professor, what have we been up to, eh? Playing at spies? It all went rather wrong, didn't it. Especially for your poor Russian comrade.'

Benson stared at Maltby. 'He's dead, isn't he.' It was a statement, not a question.

'Yes.' Maltby crossed to the bed. 'Very regrettable, I'd say. After all we did for him. I hope your conscience doesn't keep you awake too much.'

'It wasn't my fault! We were attacked.'

'Not your fault? You mean it wasn't your idea to make a dash for the Russian Embassy?'

'No. As it happens it was Leonid's. How did you know we were heading there?'

'Tamsin has told me everything.'

'So you know about the fireballs returning, and the lunar connection, and the orbiting . . . '

Maltby held up a hand in protest. 'Spare me all that poppycock, Benson.'

'It's true, damn you! I've got the data to prove it! Don't you realize, man, there's going to be a disaster. We haven't got much time. We'll have to involve the Russians, mobilize every resource! I'll explain . . . '

'He's becoming hysterical. Give him another shot,' said Maltby softly to the doctor.

The man grasped Benson's arm and brandished a syringe.

'You're not listening to me! Maltby! For God's sake see reason!'

Benson struggled desperately to evade the needle, but was easily overcome by the strength of the two men. In scarcely half a minute the room began to swim before his eyes and then fade away.

When he came to next time Benson simply lay there in cold anger. He thought of Leonid and all he'd been through and the orbiting antimatter and how they'd slowly pieced the whole horrific story together. He thought of his despair at attempting to avert the impact of the rock, and the little Russian's plea that he at least was worth saving.

How ironical! Burkov must have spent years in rooms like this, being pumped full of chemicals every time he betrayed a spark of independence. And what had been achieved in their great crusade to save the planet? He'd got Burkov killed anyway, and now he, Benson, was incarcerated in the very sort of institution that Burkov had escaped from. The little man's last words kept going through Benson's head. 'You'll have to save the world without me, Andrew.' Well a fat lot of good he was doing!

At that moment his mind was made up. He slipped out of bed and looked through the bars at the window. With something of a shock he saw that the hospital was in the countryside, a converted mansion set among extensive grounds. On the lawn below uniformed guards patrolled with dogs.

Benson turned away and began examining the room. He looked under the bed and in the small cabinet. Then he began sorting through the things on the trolley. Nothing. Finally he opened the cupboard. It was empty, save for a few hangers. He started to close the door, then changed his mind. Extracting a wooden hanger he scrutinized the wire hook. It passed through a hole in the curved wood and was fixed with a stud. Benson stood firmly on the wooden section and wiggled the metal back and forth until the stud snapped off. Then he pulled the wire free. Selecting a suitable section of the concrete wall, he then speedily filed the jagged end of the wire to form a sharp spike. He tested it gingerly against the skin of his forearm. Satisfied, he climbed back into bed, and put the spike beneath the pillow.

Benson lay for another hour or two. Nothing disturbed the eerie silence. He began to feel hungry. He contemplated shouting for food, but decided against it. Better not to let them know he was feeling better.

Another hour passed. Then a key turned in the lock and the nurse entered, carrying a tray.

'I've brought you some food,' she said simply, placing the tray on the cabinet beside the bed. Benson moaned fitfully. The nurse bent forward and looked at him with professional appraisal. He waited till her head was low enough and then he sprang.

Flinging the bedclothes aside he hooked an arm round the back of the girl's head and rammed her face down against the bedclothes. She squeaked a muffled cry of alarm. Summoning all his strength, Benson rolled round on top of her, using his weight to overcome her struggling. He forced his left hand under her face, covering her mouth, and pulled her head back so she could breathe again. Simultaneously he extracted the spike from beneath the pillow and pressed the point against the flesh of her throat.

'Keep still!' he rasped in her ear. 'Or I'll stick this through your windpipe. It may not be much of a weapon, but I can keep on stabbing till I pierce something vital!' The girl's struggling abruptly stopped. 'Now, how do I get out of this place?' He slipped his hand off her mouth but kept a firm grasp on her chin, forcing her head back and keeping the pressure on the spike.

'You're mad!' she hissed through clenched teeth.

'That's right, sweetheart. Mad as a hatter. What's the sentence for murder in this country? About the same as treason? I've got nothing to lose, baby. You'd better believe it! Now answer my question, before I start losing my patience!'

To Benson's intense relief the girl made no attempt to resist. 'You can't escape from here. It's a high-security hospital. There are guards everywhere.'

'What's in the corridor outside?'

'Other wards.'

'And guards? Remote surveillance?'

'No, not here.'

'You'd better be right!' He prodded her throat with the spike to reinforce the message.

'Believe me!' she hissed. 'No guards, no cameras.'

'I need a white coat. Where can we get one?'

'There's a linen cupboard at the end of the corridor.'

'Take me there. And remember, any tricks and you get it right through the windpipe!' Benson tried to sound menacing, but his heart was pounding uncontrollably and his voice seemed remote, unreal. He only hoped the nurse would interpret the shaking as a sign of mania rather than the effects of weakness.

Together they shuffled into the corridor. It was deserted. Benson looked for wall-mounted cameras in the harsh glare of the overhead strip-lights, but none was visible. Slowly they made their way to the end of the corridor, Benson with his hand clamped firmly over the girl's mouth and the spike at her throat. Her breaths came in sharp gasps. He noticed that his limp was bad, but not hopeless.

The linen cupboard door was unlocked. Benson pushed the nurse inside and made her switch on the light. The cupboard turned out to be a small room equipped with steel-frame shelving stacked with bedding, bandages and clothing. The room smelt musty, and Benson began to feel faint. He'd have to hurry before his strength failed him.

He forced the girl over to a shelf of bandages. 'Tie your ankles together with those,' he instructed, transferring the spike to the side of her neck. The girl did as she was told, finishing with a double reef knot. Only then did Benson relax his grip on her. He seized a second roll of bandage, and quickly tied the girl's wrists behind her back, then he tied the wrists to part of the steel frame for good measure. Satisfied, he bent over her and pressed the spike once more into the middle of the terrified girl's throat until he felt the skin puncture. A thin trickle of blood ran down her neck. 'I want some answers, lady, and I want them quickly. Do you understand?' The girl stared at him wide-eyed and tried to nod without impaling her larynx.

'Good,' hissed Benson as savagely as he could. 'Where did you get the food?'

'The kitchen is in corridor 3,' she croaked, her eyes never leaving his face. 'If you follow this corridor down, it turns through a right angle and eventually joins corridor 3. There's a locked gate and a guard at the T junction. Turn left. The kitchen is a few yards down on the right.'

'Cameras?'

'Above the gate.'

'Your name?'

'Grey. Nurse Grey.'

Benson stared into the girl's face. 'How do I know you're telling me the truth?' he demanded.

'Please!' she squealed. 'I am, I am!'

He took the spike away, and opened another roll of bandage. Then he wound it round and round the girl's face to make a gag, taking care to let her breathe properly.

Rapidly he searched the small room until he located a white coat which he slipped on over his pyjamas. He found a pair of black cleaner's shoes in a corner and tried them for size. Too small, but he could just about walk in them. His appearance wouldn't stand up to close scrutiny, but it would have to do for now. Finally he helped himself to a couple more rolls of bandages and looked down at the young nurse, helplessly tethered, her eyes fearful. An image flickered through his brain of Tamsin overpowered by a group of punks.

'I'm sorry to frighten you,' he said lamely, and slipped out into the corridor.

The harsh lighting and complete absence of sound combined with his hazy mental state conspired to give Benson's surroundings a surrealistic quality. It seemed as though the bend in the corridor would never come. When he reached it he peered round the corner cautiously. It was as the nurse had described. He could see the iron-barred gate at the T junction about fifty feet away. A guard sat on a stool on the far side, reading a newspaper. Above him a camera monitored the long corridor.

Benson stopped and considered his next move. Somehow he had to get through the gate. What then? One step at at time, he decided. He drew a deep breath and stepped around the corner. The guard remained immobile, engrossed in his newspaper. Benson tried to act as though he were in a hurry, concealing his limp as best as possible. When he'd gone thirty feet or so the guard looked up.

'Quickly!' shouted Benson at the guard. 'It's Nurse Grey. She's had an accident!' He beckoned frantically, and retreated round the corner to his cell, leaving the door ajar. He prayed that the guard wouldn't notice his pyjama trousers flapping, or pause to question his identity. Relieved, he heard the guard unlock the gate and run down the corridor towards him. A moment later he burst into the room. Benson was waiting; he hit the guard squarely in the jaw. The man crumpled to the floor, out cold.

Benson knew he had only a few minutes before the security guards manning the TV monitors got curious and came to investigate. Quickly he stripped off the man's clothes and put them on, discarding the pyjamas. Then he donned the white coat once more, over the guard's uniform. Nothing fitted properly, but he would get by at a glance. He felt inside the jacket pocket, and was pleased to discover a wallet complete with credit cards and money.

Using the bandages he bound and gagged the unconscious guard, then slipped the man's gun into the oversized pocket of the white coat. Returning to the corridor he closed the cell door and hurried off towards the open gate. The camera lens stared accusingly at him. Benson kept his head low; at any moment he expected a sharp-eyed security operator to recognize him and activate the alarms.

He passed through the gate without incident, closing it gently behind him. The sound of voices came from the direction of the kitchen. Benson pressed on. He could hear the clink of crockery and the whirr of utensils. He came to a pair of large double doors and stopped. The kitchen. What now?

Before he had time to think the doors swung open and he nearly collided with an orderly reversing out with a meal-laden trolley.

'Watch out mate!' cried the orderly.

'Sorry,' muttered Benson. The orderly looked at him oddly for a moment, then sauntered off up the corridor, pushing the trolley ahead of him and humming furiously.

Benson barged through the swing doors without further ado. The kitchen area was L-shaped with white walls and stainless steel work surfaces. Steam rose from several large vats, and four huge ovens were mounted against the far wall. Men dressed in fawn overalls milled around. He could hear the clamour from a service hatch out of sight around the corner.

'Who gave Nurse Grey that meal?' he bellowed. A dozen pair of eyes turned towards him. Nobody said a word. God, thought Benson, his nerve failing. Suppose nobody answers me?

'I may be new here, but when I order a gluten-free meal for one of my patients I expect to get one!' he shouted as convincingly as he could. 'Who's responsible?'

'Nobody said nothin' about a gluten-free meal.'

Benson swung round. A burly man of about fifty with a bushy beard and angry red eyes had emerged from a small office. He was dressed in a dark suit. Benson took him to be the catering manager.

'You in charge here?' Benson demanded.

'Who are you?' countered the big man, suspiciously.

Benson started to panic. He had to keep the initiative. He looked around desperately for a means of escape. Next to the man's office was a large door with glass panels. A store. A light shone from the far side.

'Come with me, you idiot!' Benson snapped at the man. 'I'll have to show you myself.' He walked over to the store, the big man on his heels, protesting with a liberal use of obscenities. Benson was banking on the combination of shock and confusion to carry off the charade. It worked.

Once inside the store Benson rounded on the officer and rammed the gun barrel against the side of his face. 'Not a sound!' he hissed. 'Or I'll blow your brains out!' The man's eyes widened in fear, but he made no attempt to cry out.

'Where's the service entrance?'

The officer's eyes flicked to the left. At the far end of the store was a service lift with a grille gate. Benson transferred the gun to the man's back and prodded him towards it. He pulled back the grille with his free hand and pushed the man inside. Then he closed the grille again and pressed the button for the ground floor. Nothing happened. Benson swallowed hard. At any moment someone might enter the store and see them in the lift. He pressed the button again, and there was a sharp clonk. The lift started to descend slowly.

Benson held the gun to the man's head again. 'What's on the ground floor? Tell me quickly!'

'Vehicle entrance,' said the man, his voice unexpectedly shaky.

'Guarded?'

'The guard is outside. There's a folding door across the entrance.'

The lift jolted to a halt. They were in a small dimly-lit loading bay. Two blue vans were parked against a concrete plinth. Large crates and piles of boxes lay stacked against the walls. There was no sign of life. Benson prodded the man out of the lift with the gun.

'How do the doors open?'

'A red button on the wall over there.' The man nodded to the right of the leading van.

'Can you drive these vans?'

'No.'

'Liar!' Benson jabbed the gun into the back of the man's neck.

'Yes!'

'Keys?'

'In the ignition.'

'Get in.'

They climbed into the van nearest the entrance. Benson crouched down behind the driver's seat, out of sight.

'When we go through the doors I want you to keep on driving until we reach the main exit, do you understand?' The man nodded. 'Any tricks and I'll shoot you without hesitation! Now punch that button.'

The man leaned out of the cab and pressed the red button. There was a whirring sound, and the doors began to roll back. Daylight flooded in. Benson could see the main drive, lined by trees as far as a huge pair of wrought iron gates, about two hundred yards away.

'Let's go!'

The officer started up the van and pulled out of the loading bay. Nobody challenged them as they headed down the drive.

'When we reach the gates act normally. If they start to argue tell them there's an emergency. Say there's been an outbreak of salmonella poisoning and that you're personally taking food supplies to the laboratory.'

The van slowed to a halt. A uniformed guard with a dog approached the driver's window. Benson shrank back behind the seat, well concealed in the van's gloomy interior. The driver held up a pass; nothing was said. Benson held his breath and waited.

The gates opened. The van drove through.

At that instant the air was filled with the shriek of sirens. Benson swore viciously.

'Keep going!' he shouted. 'Faster!'

The van accelerated. Benson saw that they were in a winding country lane, lined by woods dense with overgrowth. He glanced back. No vehicle followed them.

'Faster!'

The van careered down the lane, its tyres squealing at the bends. After about a mile Benson told the man to stop.

'Get out,' he ordered. The man obeyed without a word, getting down from the cab on to the road. Benson kept the gun levelled on him through the open door as he climbed into the driver's seat. 'Thanks for the lift,' he said cheerily, and drove off.

After another hundred yards Benson reached a crossroads. A signpost indicated places like Little This and Nether That – tiny English villages with absurd names. There was no traffic along the narrow lanes. Benson picked a road at random and drove on, eventually coming to a collection of cottages and an old stone church. The road forked. Another signpost said Bedford. Benson followed it.

In a mile he reached the main road and joined the flow of traffic, relishing the anonymity. Only at that stage did he start to relax. Suddenly he found himself laughing hysterically. He'd never really believed he could carry it off! But the luck of the damned combined with the desperation of someone with nothing to lose had won out. It was only then that he noticed how tired he felt, how his hands were shaking.

He parked the van in a side street in Bedford, discarded the white coat and the gun and walked towards the town centre. After a few minutes he spotted what he wanted – a run-down second-hand shop. For a few pounds he purchased a faded grey raincoat that nicely concealed his ill-fitting guard's suit. Then he made his way to the station.

Benson had already decided that there was no point in trying to make it to the Russian Embassy directly. The British security people would be waiting. In any case he had nothing to show the Soviets. He had no idea what had become of the briefcase full of data that Burkov had brought along. His only hope of convincing the Russian authorities was to present documentary evidence. That meant he'd have to return to Milchester, to his office. In any case, thought Benson, his own office would be the last place Maltby and his heavy mob would expect to find him.

15

It was dark by the time Benson reached Milchester. The meal on the train had given him much-needed strength, and the journey provided the opportunity to think through his next move. He had little doubt that there would be a general alert out for him. Escaping from Her Majesty's custody was not an offence to be taken lightly. He'd have to be extra cautious.

He melted into the crowd at Milchester station and climbed into a cab. Rather than going directly to the Physics building, he got the driver to drop him off just beyond the campus, and then he walked back, approaching the building from the rear. The car park was empty and no vehicles were parked in the service road. The building was in complete darkness, and as far as he could see the place was deserted.

Making his way round to the main entrance, Benson rapped on the glass door. The night porter sat watching TV behind his desk. He looked up, then came over to open the door.

'Sorry,' said Benson. 'Forgot my key.'

The porter ambled back to his desk with a grunt and resumed his seat in front of the television.

'Anyone asking for me?'

'Nope.'

'Could I borrow your master-key, please – to unlock my room?'

The porter gave him his God-save-us-from-all-academics look and handed Benson a key.

'Thanks.'

He took the stairs to the second floor. The corridor was in darkness. Groping his way to his office, Benson unlocked the door, crossed the room and closed the blinds. Then he turned on the TV, sound down, to provide illumination. He didn't want anyone to notice a light on in his room.

The room was as he left it. Hastily he began collecting together papers, files, computer print-out – anything that would lend credence to his story. Then he switched on the computer terminal on his desk and tapped in a few commands. He needed the latest orbital data from Kit Peak. An error message appeared on the screen. He cursed and tried again. The same words.

Irritably he called up a standard matrix inversion program, and was instantly invited to specify his input. Evidently the network was functioning properly. What was the problem? He tried accessing the Kit Peak data one more time. Nothing.

Grabbing the phone in frustration, he direct-dialled Tarling.

'Dr Tarling is on leave sir,' said a cheery female voice.

'Where?'

'I'm afraid I can't tell you that. May I have your name please?'

'No you may not.'

Benson slammed down the phone and stared fiercely at the computer screen. At that moment the light came on and a voice said: 'So the fugitive returns to his lair. Just as we thought.'

Swinging round in his chair Benson's heart sank as Maltby entered the room accompanied by two very large policemen in uniform. He closed his eyes and sighed deeply in defeat. Maltby wandered around the office, picking over the various papers that Benson had assembled. 'Thinking of going over to our Soviet friends, are we?' he said smiling. 'No confidence in Western democracy, eh?'

'That's rich! You talk about democracy after locking me up in that prison camp!' bellowed Benson. 'You bastards are all the same, East and West.'

'Tut, tut, Professor. Strong words.'

'I demand to see a lawyer.'

'That won't be necessary.'

'It's my right, damn you!'

'We're dropping all charges.'

'What? You mean I'm free to go?'

'In a manner of speaking.'

'What does that mean?'

'It seems we owe you an apology, Professor Benson.'

'I don't understand.'

140

Maltby frowned. Then he crossed to the television and turned up the sound. Benson looked at the screen. It showed a chemical plant or factory ablaze. ' . . . believed dead,' said the commentary, 'and in Spain at least fifty people are reported injured following a fireball explosion close to a naval base. And back home the Prime Minister, in emergency session . . . '

Maltby switched the set off. 'You were right, Benson. The fireballs are back with a vengeance.'

They drove for two hours at high speed in the police car, blue light flashing, taking the motorway south. Eventually they turned off on a country road. After a few miles the car slowed to a halt at a road-block. Benson could see soldiers with rifles.

'Martial law?' he asked.

'Not yet. But soon I think,' replied Maltby.

In the distance they could just make out the shape of a huge vehicle lumbering up a hill, accompanied by motorcycle outriders. Cruise missiles – being deployed. Benson's stomach turned over.

'You still think it's the Russians, don't you?'

'Well, it certainly isn't the Salvation Army.'

Benson knew it was futile to argue. Shortly the road ahead was clear and the police car was waved through the checkpoint. A mile further on they passed the remains of what had once been a peace camp. It was deserted, the inhabitants no doubt rounded up and in jail. Turning a bend they came to the entrance of the US military base. Soldiers with guns at the ready converged on the car. Passes were scrutinized carefully, and then the barrier was raised and the police car allowed through.

'You should feel at home again, Professor,' said Maltby. 'A little piece of England that is forever America.'

The car drew up outside a concrete bunker. As they stepped out a jet screamed along the nearby runway and lifted abruptly into the air. Benson watched it depart with deepening unease.

Maltby led the way into the command centre, deep underground. They were accompanied by two American soldiers in full uniform. They passed through a series of steel doors, and finally came to what for all the world looked like a university seminar room – without the windows. There was a large table, a screen, a dozen chairs and a coffee machine. Five men sat in deep conversation.

One of the men, a large, balding American with huge hands, rose to his feet as they entered, and squinted at them.

'You Benson?' asked the man.

141

'Yes. Who are you?'

'Malone.'

Benson cast his eyes around the room. The walls were covered in maps. On the table several large black and white photographs lay scattered. He stiffened as he recognized what they were.

Maltby spotted his reaction. 'You see, Benson, you're not the only one to have discovered the significance of this thing in the sky.'

Benson recalled the erased computer data and Tarling's abrupt disappearance. Suddenly it all became clear to him. The military were moving in on his act now, putting it under wraps. Malone's next remark was predictable.

'We hope you're ready to cooperate with us now, Professor.'

'On whose terms?' said Benson warily.

'Mutually acceptable terms, of course.'

Benson looked at Maltby, who just smiled. Malone resumed: 'You recognize this?' He held up a large black-and-white photograph showing a smudge of light surrounding a dense bright spot.

'Of course', replied Benson.

'It was picked up by our survey equipment a couple of weeks ago. We christened it the Unknown.'

'A bit dramatic isn't it?'

Malone shrugged. 'At first we were disturbed but not alarmed. Then some clever ass at Wright-Patterson found a link with the fireballs. Something to do with the periodicity of the orbit. Now we're worried, Professor. Very worried.'

'So you did a bit of computer hacking and discovered I'd made the same connection?'

'Yup.'

'I trust that Tarling is being well cared for?'

'A much needed holiday in Hawaii. Special holiday camp.'

'What do you want me to do? You seem to have all the answers.'

'One or two of our scientists at Wright-Patterson are persuaded that your antimatter theory is worth checking out, crazy as it might seem at first sight.'

Benson said nothing. One of the army types blew his nose noisily.

'But we still have to convince the President and his top aides. In particular we have to swing the Chief of Defence Staff if we're to get the resources to combat this thing.'

'What's that go to do with me?'

'I've set up a meeting with the Chief at the Pentagon for tomorrow afternoon. I want you to accompany me and back me up on the technical side.'

Benson stood impassively, weighing up the new developments in his mind.

His natural antagonism towards the military and his pique at being plucked out of circulation were tempered by the relief that at last the authorities were beginning to see reason, accepting his basic hypothesis. He knew time was getting short, he couldn't ignore the desperate situation. Perhaps with the full resources of the US military at his disposal *something* could be done. But he wasn't going to give in easily. These bastards had given him the run around for weeks.

'Why should I help?'

'Your country is in grave peril.'

'Don't give me that patriotic crap!'

'Then as a gesture to the memory of your friend Burkov. It's what he would have wanted.'

Benson had to admit that was true. He chewed his lip. Several pairs of eyes stared at him expectantly.

'OK Malone. I'll see this Defence guy tomorrow and we'll show him the evidence. Then we'll see what he's prepared to give us to tackle this problem. But there's a condition.'

'Oh?'

'I want Dr Bright along.'

Malone frowned. 'Who?'

'Dr Bright's at Milchester University,' explained Maltby. 'She's a bio-chemist.'

'Why do we need a biochemist for chrissakes?' spluttered Malone.

'Because she's a friend of mine, right,' said Benson.

Malone raised his eyes.

'Besides, she has a right to come. She's been in on this thing from the start. I don't see why she should be pushed out now.'

'Anything you say, Benson.'

'I'll fix it,' said Maltby, making for the door.

'Hang on, Maltby,' interjected Benson. 'None of your abduction tactics, understand. If she doesn't want to come, then she doesn't come.'

'Oh, she'll come,' said Maltby.

And he left.

The US Chief of Defence Staff was Bud Zweiger. It wasn't that he'd picked up the nickname Bud. His parents had actually christened him that.

Bud liked the name Bud, and even the President called him Bud. Everyone else called him 'Sir', including his 32-year-old stepson.

Zweiger was thin, wiry and rather vacant-looking. But he wouldn't have made it to Chief if he hadn't in fact been reasonably quick-witted and learned to recognize an enemy threat when he saw one. Since the fireball scare, Bud had caught the President's paranoia about the Red Menace, and fully supported his superior's continuation of the State of Alert. War fever had gripped the Western world, and Bud was determined that if the holocaust was coming he for one wasn't going to be caught with his pants down.

Not that it mattered much. However the nuclear arsenals were unleashed the general effect would be the same. But Bud was a professional soldier. He wouldn't like to screw up the high point of his career, even if it was the end of it – and everything else. It would be a good clean annihilation so long as Bud was in command.

And the papers arrayed before him on his oversized desk convinced Zweiger that annihilation had been brought one step nearer.

'You're quite sure it's not one of ours, Major?'

Malone contrasted Zweiger sharply in appearance. Overweight and balding, his intelligent eyes darted nervously back and forth like a sparrow suspecting an imminent pounce from a cat.

'Out of the question, sir,' replied Malone to Zweiger's query. 'We keep tabs on all our hardware, and the European junk, right down to the last can of beans.'

'So it's got to be Soviet? What are the bastards up to now?'

Benson, silent until now, almost exploded. He tried to butt in, but Malone waved him to be quiet.

Zweiger stared uncomprehendingly at the stack of survey photographs and the meaningless pages of technical data.

'Hell, Major,' he continued, 'I can't understand all this garbage. Just spell it out for me.'

'These are regular survey plates, sir, from eight of our satellite tracking stations.' The Major showed Zweiger the stations marked on a map. Then he pointed to a faint irregular white line against a uniform background of black on one of the photographs. 'This is the track of the Unknown. It's on a really weird orbit, sir, that takes it out beyond the moon.'

'Sounds like a Soviet planetary probe that's gone haywire.'

'Negative, sir. They'd have no reason to keep a scientific mission secret.'

Zweiger regarded the Major sceptically. He didn't trust the Russians to play anything straight.

'Are you saying that this new satellite represents a threat to our security? That we should destroy the fucker?'

'It's not my place to recommend strategic responses, sir. But I do consider this object hostile, though I confess we are completely ignorant of its mode of operation.'

144

'You mean it's a Soviet secret weapon?'

Benson rolled his eyes, but Malone still ignored him.

'I mean that we have evidence – statistical evidence – that this object is associated with the fireballs,' he said.

'What!' Zweiger thumped his desk and gaped at Malone, looking rather like a stranded cod-fish. The Major pulled some more papers from his briefcase and spread them out. Then he said: 'The orbital period of the object is 36-days. Here is an analysis of all fireball reports from the military over the last four months, and these are the aircraft cases alone.'

Malone traced his finger over a graph of peaks and troughs.

'If you look at the scale here, sir, you'll see these have a 36-day periodicity. Too much of a coincidence, don't you think?'

Zweiger stared intently at the papers, mentally going over a checklist of procedures. The Soviets must be mad to think they'd get away with it. He'd known it was them behind the fireballs all along. Now they had some hard evidence, they could act.

'Major, how is this thing producing the fireballs for chrissakes?'

'We don't know for sure, sir. But the main satellite seems to be spewing out a huge cloud of gas or dust or something, over thousands of miles. It's my guess that this material is reaching Earth and somehow giving rise to the fireballs.'

'How?'

'That's where Dr Benson here can help, sir.'

Zweiger eyed Benson coolly. 'Oh?'

Malone cleared his throat and explained about the work Benson had done with Burkov in England, how they had been studying the fireballs at the instigation of the British Ministry of Defence and independently discovered the 36-day periodicity. He left out Burkov's murder, not to mention his Russian origin and the fact that Benson's relations with the Ministry of Defence were strained, to say the least.

When Malone had finished Benson went straight in. 'You can forget the Soviets, Mr Zweiger. They're not responsible for either the fireballs or this object in space.'

Zweiger turned a bright shade of pink, and rose visibly in his chair. 'Now just a minute, who the hell . . .'

'I know what's causing the fireballs,' Benson cut in.

Zweiger's jaw sagged, but Benson didn't give him time to speak.

'It's antimatter.'

'Anti – what?'

'Antimatter.'

Zweiger just blinked, so Benson gave him the details, the bare essentials, enough he hoped to make a convincing case. When Benson got to the bit about the explosive power of antimatter Zweiger's eyes widened noticeably; here was something the man could appreciate.

When Benson had finished, Zweiger regarded him sceptically.

'Why should I believe all this fanciful crap?'

'Because this cycle of fireballs is the last, Mr Zweiger. Then we take a direct hit. And if I'm right, the bang is going to make your precious nuclear weapons seem like firecrackers. It'll be total annihilation – and I mean *total*.'

Zweiger paused for a moment, uncertain. Then he turned to Malone.

'Is this right, Major? That the Unknown will hit Earth?'

'Unless it changes course, yes.'

'You make it sound as though it's out of control.'

'We just don't know enough about it, sir.'

'Could the Russians have put such a thing up as part of their SDI programme, and then lost control of it? Released these bloody fireballs by mistake?'

Malone shrugged.

'You're thinking with your arse, Zweiger!' shrieked Benson, thumping his fist on the Chief's desk. Zweiger turned deathly pale. Nobody, *but nobody*, ever spoke to him that way.

'This . . . this, *Unknown*, as you fondly call it, is as big as a supertanker,' Benson continued, unabashed. 'Do you suppose the Russians could have launched such a thing? Well, do you?'

Zweiger didn't say whether he did or he didn't. He just sat stunned, fixing Benson with a look of utter astonishment.

Malone quickly intervened. 'This is a technical point, sir. We know the Unknown is big, but the size doesn't necessarily mean mass. The Soviets could have launched a regular craft, and then deployed extensive membranes to cover a large surface area. Perhaps for solar cells, who knows? Until we can get a good look at this thing it's anybody's guess how heavy it is.'

Zweiger tore his gaze away from Benson and looked at the other man. 'What do we know about their recent launch schedules, Major?' he said huskily.

'Well that's very significant, sir. You see, the Russians unexpectedly launched a very large deep-space probe from their military cosmodrome in Baikonur on 12 February. That was just two weeks before the first reliable fireball reports. The mission was kept top secret.'

'Did they, by God!' replied Zweiger. 'And where was it heading?'

'We couldn't track it all the way, sir,' Malone answered. And then he looked squarely at Benson. 'But our best estimate is that it was heading for the moon.'

Malone's flat statement exploded in Benson's mind like a bombshell. The moon! All along the lunar connection had been the key element in his theory about the fireballs. Now here was Malone announcing that the Russians sent a probe to the moon at the very time the antimatter arrived. It was too much of a coincidence, but what the hell did it mean?

'And that's not all, sir,' continued Malone. 'A couple of days afterwards – about the time their probe would have arrived in fact – a massive explosion was detected on or near the lunar surface. A huge plume of material was observed in the vicinity of the crater. It even got reported in the newspapers at the time. And the same day our seismic instruments on the moon recorded a moonquake in about that area.'

And an unprecedented burst of gamma radiation, thought Benson, *but leave that out.*

It was enough for Zweiger. 'It all adds up, Major,' he concluded. 'I'd better apprise the President.' He began enumerating the points on his fingers. 'The Russians launch a secret military probe to the moon. Large membranes are deployed to provide massive solar power. An outburst, either planned or accidental, occurs, and material is released. The whole system takes up an Earth-intersecting orbit and, by some as yet unknown mechanism possibly involving the controlled use of this anti-stuff, fireballs are created in the Earth's atmosphere.' He sat back and whistled. 'The sons of bitches.'

Benson closed his eyes, aghast, and swore. Zweiger leapt to his feet.

'Okay Benson, get the hell out of here. We're grateful for your scientific opinion I'm sure. Now we have military matters to discuss. My assistant will escort you from the building. Good day.'

Crushed, Benson turned, and without another word left the room. The two men watched him go. When the door had closed Zweiger said: 'That guy's a slob, Malone. I don't want to see him again, right.' Zweiger's tone abruptly changed as he dismissed Benson and his abstract ideas from his thinking, and turned to more pragmatic matters, things he was used to dealing with. Like the Russian threat.

'What we have to decide then, Major, is whether this satanic device has gone out of control. According to our intelligence the Soviets are getting their fair share of fireballs too. Of course it could be a screen – those guys would stop at nothing. If we're taking most of our hits on military targets, that'd give the bastards one hell of a head start when it came to a first strike. And meanwhile the civilian strikes are causing such panic we've got all our forces stretched just keeping law and order! Jesus! And the main action's yet to come. When this mother impacts the Earth you can bet we'll really get some fireballs where we don't want them! When did you say it's going to hit?'

'Next Friday,' replied Malone. 'Friday the thirteenth.'

'I'd lay short odds that the Soviets have got that pencilled in for a first strike! Tell me, Major, should we nuke the Unknown right away? Screw up their plans a bit?'

'I wouldn't recommend that, sir.' Malone seemed hesitant.

'Why not, for chrissakes?'

'If your basic premiss is correct and the Russians are in control of this thing, they wouldn't let the main craft smash back to Earth unless it had already completed its function. In which case going for the Unknown is a waste of resources and will only serve to alert them. On the other hand, if it's out of control, blowing it to bits might make matters worse – otherwise *they'd* blow it up, wouldn't they? Either way it's pointless.'

'But suppose that's precisely what they *want* us to believe? Maybe they'll change its orbit at the last minute, and deal out a really bad dose of fireballs to go with their first strike?'

'Then we can hit it when it changes course.'

'I still favour nuking it right away.'

Malone looked uncomfortable. 'There's another reason I'd advise against that, sir.'

'Oh?'

'There's just a chance that Benson might be right, that this object might be some sort of antimatter debris from outside the galaxy.'

'What? That bastard's crazy! You're not seriously suggesting there's anything in his ridiculous theory, are you? I mean, Christ!'

'I grant you it's pretty way-out, sir, but just *suppose* it were correct. The effect of hitting it with a full nuclear payload would be catastrophic. You wouldn't just get the nuclear blast, you'd get wholesale annihilation of the entire payload with an attendant energy release the equivalent of thousands of nuclear explosions. The Unknown would be smeared over the whole sky, and we'd never stop the stuff coming straight at us. And when what's left hits . . .'

'You're not making sense, Major! If this thing's made entirely of antimatter as you're suggesting, what difference will it make whether it hits us in one piece or many?'

'If it is a rock of antimatter, then we have only one hope. That's to try and deflect it away from Earth.'

Zweiger looked exasperated. 'And how do we do that, for God's sake?'

'We'd have to hit it with tiny pellets of matter, precisely aimed, to produce controlled small-scale explosions. It'd be a pretty dicey affair, but it's all we can come up with.'

'This is insanity, Malone. How can we set up something like that by Friday the thirteenth?'

Malone looked distinctly uncomfortable. 'Our only chance is to use the KEW.'

The KEW was the simplest form of Star Wars defence. It consisted of an orbiting space platform from which pellets were fired with extreme accuracy at enemy missiles. They destroyed the missiles by brute force – the crude effect of very high energy impact. The system was designed for use in all-out nuclear war, so it had a one-time capability only.

Zweiger gaped in incredulity. 'You *are* mad, Malone. The President would never squander a key element in our defence on the very eve of an expected Soviet strike just in case that crackpot Benson turned out to be right after all.'

'You could always hit the Soviets first . . . save the KEW for the Unknown.'

Zweiger smiled wryly at the Major. 'We'd still need the KEW to knock out their retaliatory strike.'

'Would you at least consider, sir, putting it to the President that he holds open the option for now of using the KEW against the Unknown – pending further investigation?'

'Investigation?'

'Yes, sir. There's one way we can check out Benson's theory, but we'd need Presidential approval. If we could send a small probe to the Unknown, get close enough in to obtain good images, we'd be able to see whether it's a rock or a spacecraft.'

'Do we have the capability to launch such a probe right away?'

'No, sir. But we do have the hardware in space at the moment. It would be feasible to make the orbital corrections to intercept the Unknown as it comes in at us.'

'What hardware, Major?'

'There are two options. We could redirect a weather satellite. The trouble is, the optical resolution would be poor. That wouldn't matter so much if we could get right up to the Unknown, but it only needs the satellite to touch a speck of the surrounding antimatter and it'd be instantly decommissioned. The best bet is to use a high resolution spy satellite.'

'You ask for a lot, Major.'

'I know, sir.'

The two men sat in silence for a while as Zweiger thought it through. Then he said: 'Okay Malone, I'll discuss your proposal with our Chief Scientific Adviser; see what *he* thinks about this guy Benson. I don't want to trouble the President until we're sure. He's got his hands full enough at the moment trying

149

to hold the country together. Now you get off to your little bolt-hole. I'll get back to you as soon as we reach a decision.'

'Thank you, sir,' said Malone.

Zweiger waited till the Major had gone, then he picked up the phone. 'Get me Stanley Hendricks.'

The wail of sirens merged into a chilling cacophony. From her hotel window Tamsin could see columns of smoke across the city, though whether started by fireballs or rioters she had no idea. It didn't really seem to matter.

'It's all coming apart, isn't it?' she said.

Benson joined her by the window. They looked down into the street below. It had been sealed off by State troopers behind steel barricades to protect the hotel for VIPs – foreign diplomats, essential government employees, scientists. As they watched, a roaming mob appeared on the next block, perhaps forty or fifty youths on the rampage. A single car remained parked on the block. It was soon overturned and set ablaze. Then the mob began smashing the large plate-glass windows of the stores, helping themselves to things they couldn't possibly transport away – an absurd orgy of greed. Suddenly a volley of shots rang out; the State troopers were firing randomly into the crowd of looters. The mob scattered. Several lay bleeding on the street. Nobody made any attempt to attend to them.

Tamsin turned away from the window in disgust. If it was like this in Washington, God knew what was happening in Los Angeles or Liverpool or Lanchow. She switched on the television, searching with difficulty for a channel with any reception. Since the latest wave of fireballs had begun, many of the stations had been knocked out, their transmitters proving particularly attractive for the exploding balls of plasma. Eventually she found a station still functioning. Programme schedules had been ditched in favour of continuous news interspersed with government entreaties for people to stay calm, remain indoors and await instructions. If Washington was anything to go by those entreaties were proving spectacularly ineffective.

The newscaster had long abandoned any sort of coherent presentation, as news of disaster upon disaster came in thick and fast: towns blasted, forests, oil refineries, factories set ablaze, aircraft grounded, food distribution failing, riots, murders, rapes . . . Armed conflict raged in dozens of the world's trouble spots as fanatics took advantage of the universal chaos to settle old scores. All over the world, it seemed, civilization was breaking down. Except perhaps in the Eastern bloc? Nobody knew; East and West had sealed each other off.

And amid the mayhem and confusion both sides prepared inexorably for war. Forces were placed on full alert, martial law was declared, missiles primed, submarines sent to their battle stations.

Tamsin stared mesmerized at the screen, the scenes of torment and destruction washing over her. Abruptly the picture disappeared. She swore viciously and switched the set off.

'Why bother?' said Benson sourly.

'Humanity committing collective suicide,' she muttered. 'I'm concerned. It's out of control out there.'

'What's the difference? In a few days we'll all be blown to bits anyway.'

She turned to him with a look of despair. 'Is there no chance Malone will convince Zweiger?'

'We're dealing with lunacy, Tamsin. Those guys have got one-track minds. Zweiger threw me out without so much as a second thought. The concept's too big for him.'

'You could try to reach the President direct. Appeal to his much-vaunted intellect.'

Benson snorted in derision. 'Anyway, I'd never get near him. He's probably in a shelter somewhere, flexing his button finger.'

From the street below came a loud crash. Tamsin ran to the window. A large grey Chevrolet had rammed into a tree, presumably avoiding the bodies lying in the street. She watched horrified as a mob converged on the car, dragged a woman from the driving seat, and instantly began tearing at her clothes.

'Do something! Oh, please do something!' she wailed.

Several more shots rang out as the troopers fired into the air, trying to scatter the mob, but they had no effect at all. Tamsin could see the commanding officer waving his arms, issuing orders. The barricades were shifted and a dozen men flowed through the gap brandishing guns, heading for the frenzied mob.

Suddenly a petrol bomb landed in the path of the troopers, then another in their midst. Two troopers fell to the ground and began rolling around frantically. Two more bombs landed behind the barricades. A crowd of men wielding stakes, knives and guns erupted from a side street and surged through the gap in the defences. The troopers began firing wildly, in panic. People fell and were trampled upon. The mob reached the steps of the hotel, and Tamsin could hear the sound of breaking glass mixed with gun shots.

'Andrew!' she screamed. Benson rushed to the window. The crowd outside had swollen to about two hundred chanting, screaming, hysterical individuals. Smoke billowed from the ground floor as more petrol bombs were hurled into the building.

151

'We're trapped!' yelled Tamsin, clinging to him.

Benson grabbed at the phone. It was dead.

Tamsin's mind reeled. If they took the fire escape they'd be torn to pieces by the mob. If they stayed behind they'd be burned alive.

'Let's get to the roof. Come on.' Benson tugged at her.

'Wait!' she yelled.

From the street below came the deep throb of heavy vehicles, then the staccato firing of automatic weapons. The mob broke up in confusion. People began running in all directions, some of them cut down by the gunfire. From both ends of the block armoured personnel carriers converged on the rioters, their occupants firing indiscriminately. As they watched, a half-track drove straight into a group of rioters, crushing them mercilessly. Soldiers leapt from the vehicles in full battle-dress, shooting wildly at the fleeing figures. A small detachment of soldiers rushed into the hotel entrance below.

Tamsin turned away, sickened. Benson strode over to the mini-bar in the corner of the bedroom, and poured two large brandies. They gulped them down eagerly, and waited.

There was a frantic rap on the door. Benson opened it cautiously. A soldier ordered them to the hotel foyer immediately, then ticked their names off a checklist. Benson grabbed their small suitcases and they ran for the stairs – the elevators were too dangerous.

In the foyer there was utter confusion. Hysterical women, foreign nationals ranting in a dozen languages, barking dogs, smoke. With a wave of relief Benson caught sight of Malone, aimlessly roaming the foyer in search of them.

'Thank God! I was about to give you up,' said Malone. 'Let's go!'

They followed the soldier out of the hotel and boarded an armoured vehicle, climbing in the rear with half a dozen soldiers. Malone squeezed in after them, slammed the doors shut, and the carrier lurched off.

'Where are we going?' asked Benson.

'Andrews Field,' replied Malone. 'There's an Air Force jet waiting to take us to Arizona.'

'Arizona?' said Tamsin. 'What's in Arizona?'

'Somewhere safe.'

16

To THE CASUAL passer-by the neat collection of buildings in the middle of the Arizona desert would have looked for all the world like a microchip factory. The passer-by would have been right; it was a microchip factory. What he would not have known was that four hundred feet beneath this innocuous establishment was located one of several top-secret command centres from which the Third World War could be conducted in peace and quiet.

Benson sat alone in a small, functional room officially designated a relaxation area, though how anyone could be expected to relax under the circumstances for which the command centre had been built defied imagination. Certainly Benson was in no mood for relaxation. It had been forty-eight hours since his disastrous meeting with Zweiger and still no word had come back about the release of the spy satellite. With only four days to go before impact, time was running out fast.

Tamsin had tired of his black moods and cynical remarks, and forsaken the relaxation area for the dubious comforts of their shared quarters – a tiny ten-by-ten concrete cell, with twin beds, a lavatory and shower, and a television monitor on closed circuit.

Crumpling up the empty plastic cup of his fifth coffee that morning, Benson flung it savagely at the door at the precise moment it opened. The spent cup struck Malone on the chest. He glanced down in brief surprise, then took a seat opposite Benson.

'Well?' said the scientist. 'Is there still a world out there?'

'Just about.' Malone looked Benson squarely in the eye. 'I've had word from Zweiger. The satellite's ours.'

Benson sat bolt upright. 'Well I'll be damned!'

'But there's a caveat.'

'Oh?'

'We can make a single pass only, and from as far out as is practicable to identify the Unknown. The President wants the satellite back on station in time for the main action.'

'Shit. They don't give much, do they?'

'We have to work fast, Benson. I've got most of the C7 team here, and they're computing the orbital correction now. We're patched in to the Goddard Space Flight Center – they've still got a skeleton staff, thank God – so we can control the satellite in real time from the command room here. We've also hooked in the White House so the President can see the pictures directly; make his own evaluation, if necessary.'

Benson jumped to his feet, grateful for something to do. Malone put a hand on his shoulder in restraint. 'Don't get too carried away. Remember, it only takes one minute speck of antimatter in the path of that satellite . . .'

'You mean Hendricks actually approved it?' said Tamsin in astonishment, gazing down at him.

Benson lay sprawled on his bed, his face grey with exhaustion, eyes red from lack of sleep. He stared at the featureless ceiling.

'Well, he didn't block it.'

'Amazing. So what happens now?'

'We've worked out an orbital correction that will boost the spy satellite out on an intersecting trajectory with the rock – these things are built to be manoeuverable. It means using up all the rather meagre fuel reserves, but there is enough, thank God. The main snag is, the President wants it back on station again after the encounter – if it's still intact, that is – so we need to keep some fuel back for the return trip.'

'He needs the satellite in case there's war, is that it?'

'I guess so.'

'Then they're obviously not convinced that the rock really *is* made of antimatter, are they? Otherwise they'd know that war is the least of our troubles. We'll all be annihilated anyway.'

Benson breathed deeply, rolled on his side and looked at her.

'I think I've convinced them that the fireballs are produced by antimatter, but even Malone won't concede that the rock is too. We're dealing with military minds here Tamsin, from the President down. They see the Russians behind the fireballs every step of the way. As far as they're concerned, the rock is a Russian space weapon.'

'Then why don't they confront the Russians with the evidence, or just blow it up, instead of letting us slide into a nuclear holocaust?'

'Until the probe gets some good pics of the object there *is* no hard evidence. The Russians could just deny everything; then what? And blowing it up would be no good. If it were a Russian spacecraft such an act would be interpreted as hostile and only serve to precipitate nuclear war. And if I'm right, and the thing up there is a rock of antimatter, exploding it would make matters worse.'

'What you're saying is that nobody's buying your theory, but so long as their strategy and yours don't conflict they're prepared to string along,' she concluded bluntly.

'That's about it, Tamsin. We'll just have to see how things pan out.'

She sat down on his bed and thought for a while.

'Christ, what a choice,' she mumbled. 'If it should turn out that they are right, and the probe shows this thing to be a Russian spacecraft, they'll probably go to war over it – given the wholesale devastation that the fireballs are causing. If you're right, and the rock can't be stopped, we'll be annihilated even more effectively.'

'Unless the President approves the use of the KEW.'

'The what?'

'Kinetic Energy Weapon. It's an orbiting pellet-shooter – part of the Star Wars project. Dead simple. It just shoots little pellets at Russian missiles with extreme accuracy. The momentum of impact at orbital speeds is enough to knock them out. The KEW is the only thing we can come up with that would stand even a remote chance of deflecting ten million tonnes of antimatter without breaking it into fragments.'

'You mean, a small pellet striking the rock will cause an explosion big enough to nudge it aside, but not so big as to fragment it?'

'Precisely. If we could get a succession of well-chosen hits, it might just work. Who knows? Got any better ideas?'

'I'll let you know,' she said. Then: 'What are the main uncertainties?'

Benson rubbed his eyes. 'Oh, one difficulty is that we can't really figure out the precise pattern of explosion when the pellets hit. The hope is that as the leading edge starts to annihilate, it will vaporize the rest of the pellet and smear it across the surface a bit – to spread the force of the explosion. It's a bit like trying to move an egg. If you prod it with a cotton wool pad it's okay, but jab it with a needle and it ruptures. The energy transfer can be the same, but if the energy is concentrated fragmentation occurs. The trouble is, nobody knows;

we've never had any experience with bulk antimatter. Theoretical modelling is all we have to go on.'

He sat upright on the bed, and reached for the bourbon.

'Then there's the problem of the spin. The rock's tumbling end over end like crazy. We have to get the timing exactly right, or the momentum transfer will be wrong. The KEW's designed for split-second operation, but without detailed information about the mass distribution we really have only the vaguest idea of what part to hit when.' He paused for a moment while he swallowed the bourbon. 'Apart from that, it should be a cinch.'

He offered her the bottle, but she shook her head.

'When's the encounter set up for?'

'Tomorrow night. That leaves about twelve hours for the President to evaluate the pictures and decide whether to release the KEW. After that it'll be too late. The rock will be too close for anyone to do anything about it.'

'But how likely is it that he'll divert such a vital component of his strategic defence?'

Benson shrugged. 'Pretty unlikely, I'd say. He'll demand watertight evidence before committing his favourite toy. The real problem is, it's a one-time system. It's not just a matter of diversion, as you put it. Once it's been used on the rock, it can't be used against the Russians.'

She weighed up the gloomy prognosis.

'I think I'll change my mind about that drink,' she said, and helped herself to a glass. 'Is there anything I can do? I feel pretty helpless.'

'So do I', he said, wearily. 'You could try praying.'

'For the release of the KEW?'

'If you like. Or pray that I'm wrong.'

'Andrew Benson wrong? That'd be something. You've been right about the whole business so far, haven't you, even though nobody believed you at first. Besides, if you are wrong, it wouldn't make a lot of difference, would it? From what you say, we'd still be annihilated in a nuclear holocaust.'

'Well, if there's going to be a nuclear holocaust, you're in the best place. Aren't you glad you came along?'

'Frankly no. I don't want to go on living if there's no world left out there.'

'There's not much left now from what I hear. Did you know Bombay suffered a direct hit from a fireball that makes the Patterson Creek pale into insignificance? They reckon it had an energy equivalent of the Hiroshima bomb. God knows how many were killed. If that had occurred in London or Washington, we'd probably be at war already.'

She shivered, and refilled her glass. Benson took the bottle from her and refilled his own.

156

'You were right, then – about the next cycle of fireballs being worse.'

'The Earth is nearer the centre of the ejected debris this time. There are some pretty sizeable grains coming down. We're getting explosions of nuclear proportions going on all over the world. It's horrendous.'

'Even in Russia?'

'You bet. But Zweiger and his crowd see it as a blind. Jesus, the mentality!'

They both sank back on their beds and lay thinking for a long while. Eventually she turned towards him.

'Andrew. If we ever get out of this mess . . .'

But he was fast asleep.

John Maltby drove his Porsche at 100 m.p.h. along the M62 motorway. This was well beyond the speed limit but he didn't care. There was almost no traffic and certainly no traffic police to enforce the law.

The sun shone from a clear blue sky, but this time no music issued from the radio. Nor was he singing; there was nothing to sing about. He checked the petrol gauge nervously. He'd tanked up just outside London, in the only remaining service station left open on the M1, and then only by giving the manager a hefty bribe.

It was 11.30; he'd left London at six in the morning, as inconspicuously as possible. It had taken an age to get through the two military checkpoints before he reached the open road, but once on the motorway he'd made good time.

Maltby smiled sardonically. Sir William probably thought he was well on his way to Glamorgan by now. 'Dispersal' was the term he'd used. 'All vital Defence personnel to be dispersed to regional centres until the emergency was over.' Just like that. Almost as though there'd been a gas leak in the office, or something, rather than impending nuclear war.

The man from the Ministry had prepared for this eventuality years ago. He had, after all, been privy to government's plans for civilians following a nuclear exchange, and frankly, it left a lot to be desired. An awful lot. Maltby's scheme hinged on the fact that his brother owned a holiday cottage on the Isle of Man, situated safely out in the Irish sea. When Sir William had delivered his instructions for Maltby to pack up, quit the capital and dig in at some do-it-yourself Welsh hideaway for civil servants, he knew the time had come to activate plan A.

Maltby's brother was an accountant who lived in a smart suburb of Liverpool. Like everybody else, he'd never taken the threat of nuclear war seriously, and had always been happy to trade a promise of sharing his cottage for the promise of an early tip-off. Now that the nightmare was really unfolding, he couldn't go back on it. Maltby tried to phone his brother from

London to set the ball rolling, but inevitably the telephone system had succumbed to the incessant fireball bombardment. The only possibility of direct contact had been through government radio channels, and for obvious reasons he was not going to attempt that.

A sign told him that Liverpool was only six miles ahead. So far, so good. If all went well, in another couple of hours he'd have collected brother, sister-in-law and nephew – plus cottage keys – and be on his way to the dockyard for one of the few remaining ferries.

Then he saw the barrier. It was a hastily erected affair; two Landrovers parked across the carriageway and a pole of some sort. A helmeted soldier waved him down. Maltby reached for his M.o.D. pass.

'Sorry mate, the road's sealed off,' said the soldier, without even checking the pass.

'What's the trouble, old chap?' asked Maltby. Then he saw the smoke.

'A big fireball explosion in Toxteth,' explained the soldier. 'Whole streets flattened. And now a major riot. The area's like a battlefield. Where yer goin'?'

'Norris Green.'

'Your best bet is to back up to the M57 and come in from the north. If you can get through, that is. There've been some pretty bad scenes in these parts.'

'Thank you, Sergeant,' said Maltby with a trace of anxiety. 'Mind if I bump across the central reservation?'

'Doesn't bother me.'

Maltby swung on to the eastbound lane and roared back to the M57 intersection. After a few miles he took the turn-off to Norris Green. Nobody stopped him. As he came into the residential area he could see the shops and some houses boarded up. A couple of army lorries and an ambulance passed him going the other way. There were no buses, nor any other cars, but that didn't surprise him, since private vehicles had been banned for all except those on official business. Like himself. To his left a pall of smoke hung over the city, blocking out the sun.

He was so intent on staring at the smoke that he almost ran into the next checkpoint. This time it didn't look so friendly. A gun-toting soldier bent forward as he wound down the window.

'That's as far as you go,' he announced.

Maltby reached for his pass. The soldier took it, held it up in front of his face.

'We got orders. Strictly no one goes through. There are gangs of marauders everywhere.'

'Now look here, my good man . . .' Maltby began.

'You'll 'ave to go back,' said the soldier.

'But I'm on official business for the Ministry of Defence, damn you. It's important that I pass. Now be a good chap . . .'

'Orders is orders, mate. Now do I 'ave to get you towed away?'

Maltby swore savagely under his breath. Then he reached in his pocket. The sight of five crisp tenners was all it needed to make the soldier see reason, even if paper currency would soon be worthless. The barrier was raised.

The suburb was like a ghost town. Street after street was either burned out or barricaded. There was no sign of life. He turned left into a residential road. A pack of dogs clustered around a dark object on the pavement. Maltby stared as he drove slowly past, and then felt the vomit rise in his throat as he saw what it was.

'Almighty God!' he muttered to himself. 'I hadn't realized it had come to this.'

He recognized his brother's road by the car dealer and service station on the corner. It was now a burnt-out shell, the cars gone. There was nobody in sight down the length of the street. A few old cars stood parked in driveways or in the road. He pulled up at number 28.

Climbing from the Porsche, Maltby made his way up the familiar path with rising anxiety. The freshly cut lawn and neatly trimmed flower-beds belied the sickening chaos that was enveloping them all. He reached the front door and rang the bell. There was no reply. He rang again.

Then he noticed blood stains on the porch. He pushed at the door; it was open.

Inside, the place had been completed ransacked. There were clothes, toys, discarded food scattered everywhere. The curtains had been ripped from the windows, the furniture overturned, glassware smashed. Maltby wandered round in a daze, stunned and nauseated. He checked all the rooms, then the attic. There was no sign of his brother or the family; they had vanished.

He stepped back out on to the front path and froze. Three youths, a tall white thug in a gaudy T-shirt and two black youngsters about 16 years old stood leaning against his car, swinging baseball bats. The tall one was grinning.

'I've always fancied one o' these cars,' he said simply.

Maltby said nothing, did nothing.

'Me 'n me mates feel like a bit of a spin, see. A rich bastard like you wouldn't miss it for a few hours, would you?' He waved the bat around his head a few times to make the point. 'Only thing is, we don't 'ave the keys.'

Maltby swallowed hard and reached in his jacket pocket. He stepped forward a few paces and held out his arm, dangling the keys. The white youth smiled and moved forward. As he reached out for the keys Maltby kicked him hard in the groin. The youth gasped in pain and doubled up. Maltby smashed his knee into the boy's face, sending him sprawling across the flower bed.

Quickly he seized the baseball bat and charged at the two black youngsters. They instantly broke and ran. Shaking like a leaf, Maltby jumped into the Porsche and shot away, the tyres screaming on the sun-baked road.

The dockside was crawling with military patrols. To reach it Maltby had to tour half the city, dodging stone-throwing gangs and army checkpoints, doubling back at least a dozen times. He used his special M.o.D. pass to gain access to the quayside, where he searched for the Isle of Man ferry. The normal operation of the sea terminus was halted, everything under police or army patrol. There were no signposts anywhere.

After half an hour's fruitless searching, Maltby pulled up at the customs house, its entrance guarded by two soldiers in battle dress. He used his pass again to gain entry. A duty Sergeant stood behind the counter.

'I have to cross to the Isle of Man,' said Maltby in breezy tones, as though he were a day-tripper on a village picnic.

'You'll be lucky, mate,' replied the Sergeant.

'What's the trouble, Lieutenant?'

The Sergeant suppressed a grin.

'A small matter of martial law, that's what's the trouble.'

'But I'm on M.o.D. business. It's urgent.' Maltby produced his pass.

The Sergeant scrutinized the pass carefully and made a face.

'There ain't no regular service runnin',' he said.

'But there must be something going across? Supplies?'

The Sergeant rubbed his chin. 'There's a special supply boat leaving at two, but I can't let you on without authorization.'

Maltby thought for a moment. 'Phone Whitehall,' he said. 'The number's on this card.'

'You must be joking, guv. The phones haven't been working for days. Anyhow, they'll all 'ave scarpered by now if they've got any sense, won't they?'

Maltby shifted guiltily. Then he reached for his wallet. The trick worked yet again, though this time the price was £150. He turned to go.

'How did you get 'ere anyway?' asked the Sergeant.

'By car.'

'You'll 'ave to leave that behind,' he said. 'Standing room only on this one.'

Maltby smiled wryly, shrugged, and went in search of the boat.

The afternoon sun blazed down from an azure sky on a calm sea. The scene might have been taken straight from a holiday brochure. The 'special' boat turned out to be a regular Sealink ferry commandeered by the Royal Navy, and packed full of essential supplies and medical equipment for the people of the

Isle of Man. Maltby stood by the rail, gazing at the receding coastline. With a start he realized that it might be the last time he would see it, at least in its present form.

'Fancy a drink?'

He turned to see a young sailor swigging a bottle of beer.

'The bar's well stocked. Nobody cares about the licensing laws no more,' he explained.

'No thanks,' said Maltby.

'Suit yourself. Wot you doin' on this ship then?'

'M.o.D. business.'

'Eh?'

'Ministry of Defence.'

'Oh. Reckon there's goin' to be nuclear war then, d'you?'

'It rather seems that way. Still, perhaps the powers-that-be will come to their senses in time.'

'Yeah. My mate, 'e reckons these fireballs ain't nothin' to do wiv the Russians anyway. Says it's some Yank Star Wars thing gone wrong. Is that possible, then? Wot d'you think?'

'Perhaps it isn't either East or West,' said Maltby.

The young sailor frowned. 'Well, it would 'ave to be one side or the uvver, wouldn't it? I'm going to get anuvver beer. Sure you won't 'ave one?'

'Quite sure, thank you.'

The sailor went below.

Maltby watched the creamy wake of the ship as it plied north-westwards, a dozen seagulls swooping in the slipstream. He checked his watch; 3.50. Should reach the cottage before dark – if he could find transport the other end. He turned to go below.

The searing white light caught his attention as he turned. Maltby's heart missed a beat. High in the western sky it seemed as though a second sun had appeared, only smaller. As he watched, paralysed with fear, the fierce white glow swelled, and arced slowly towards the zenith. He could see a blazing orange trail behind the thing, like the cartoon pictures of space capsules on re-entry.

Maltby gripped the hand rail and stared open-mouthed at the fearsome flaming entity as it kept coming on, plunging out of God's blue yonder, growing larger and brighter all the while till his eyes ached with the glare. But still he kept them riveted on the fireball.

There was no sound from the object; just the purposeful, menacing, inexorable progress downwards.

Maltby screamed. A pathetic, hollow, pointless shriek.

161

He flung himself down flat on the deck and covered his head with his arms. He could almost sense the intense light spilling over him, his bare hands registering the searing radiant heat. Still there was no sound.

The fireball struck the sea at high speed about half a mile away. The bulk of the antimatter, having been shielded by the intense radiation during its plunge through the atmosphere, annihilated more or less instantaneously with the force of a small nuclear explosion. The resulting shock wave burst the rivets on the ship's hull portside, and burst Maltby's ear-drums, leaving him stunned and bewildered.

Still lying prone, he raised his head and looked out through the port rail. Where there should have been blue sky, he saw instead an angry seething wall of water. In utter helplessness, Maltby watched the aqueous monstrosity rise up above the ship.

Sealink ferries are built to ride out the savage storms of the North sea and Irish sea, but they are not built to withstand tidal waves. The ferry rolled and capsized instantaneously as the huge mass of water smashed into its portside superstructure.

Maltby was pitched clear of the rolling ship, into the maelstrom. Tonnes of water poured down upon him. As his lungs filled with salty liquid his last thought was how strangely *warm* the water was.

17

THE COMMAND ROOM beneath the Arizona desert was circular, its walls lined with consoles, each attended by a swivel chair. Harsh white lights burned from the ceiling. The room was pervaded by the distinctive, oppressive smell of electronic instrumentatation.

The base commander paced about with proprietorial anxiety as the scientists supervised the final approach of the satellite. By good fortune, the rock lay at the farthest extremity of the antimatter stream, so that by a judicious choice of orbital correction it had proved possible to get the probe within a few hundred miles without disaster. The data was fed back initially to Goddard. The staff there had left the communications link intact, then headed for the shelters. From Goddard, the data came down the line to Arizona auto-matically, where it was processed on their computer, and then the re-constructed pictures were displayed on a large monitor.

Benson and Malone surveyed the flickering black-and-white image with intense concentration. The moment of truth was at hand. Both men knew that everything hinged on the outcome of the probe's encounter with the unknown object in space. Tension built up as the probe edged closer, its trajectory curving gently in the Earth's gravitational field to bring it on a precisely intersecting course with the target. The small repositioning jets had been activated for a few minutes thirty-six hours before, boosting the satellite way up into a high, eccentric orbit. Newton's laws of motion had done the rest.

The resolution was disappointing. Sunlight scattered from the antimatter cloud was interfering with the system. The rapid rotation of the object made analysis difficult, while slow-motion replay lacked the necessary detail. The command room was completely quiet, save for the soft hum of the instruments. Nobody spoke.

The image gradually swelled in the monitor, but still it remained puzzling, indistinct. Benson shifted nervously. Time was running out.

'Five minutes, Keeley,' announced Malone to the only other man in the room.

'Check,' replied the young, ruddy-faced engineer. Keeley was responsible for maintaining the link with Goddard and programming the orbital corrections for the satellite. He sat peering intently at a computer monitor decorated by a complex array of figures.

'We're getting near to our closest permitted approach, Benson. Then the President wants his satellite back, before it decommissions itself.'

'Turn up the magnification,' Benson snapped.

Keeley tapped in a few commands. Shortly afterwards, the image in the screen leapt closer.

'It's a rock, Malone!' shouted Benson. 'Those aren't vanes or membranes. Look!'

'I . . . I don't know. I couldn't say.'

'For God's sake, man! Does that look like a Russian spacecraft? It's huge, and its *solid*!'

'We can't be sure of that, Benson. I'm not prepared to make a positive recommendation to the President on the basis of that image.'

'Then let's get in closer!'

'We can't. We're overruled! Keeley, program the orbital corrections. Get that probe out of there in two more minutes.'

'Yes, sir!' Keeley began tapping in commands.

Malone seized a telephone. Benson stood rigidly as he talked directly to the White House. Malone's knuckles were white as he gripped the handset. Finally he laid it down gently on the cradle. 'The President says the game is over, Benson. The KEW stays firmly trained on the Soviet Union.'

Benson stood there in stunned silence. Above his head the reconstructed pictures of the rock flickered unnoticed.

So this was it. The end of the road. The last words of Leonid Burkov passed through his mind. *You'll have to save the world without me, Andy.* Well, he'd failed. *Sorry, old comrade.*

Malone turned to the base commander. 'Thank you, sir. Another minute or two, and it's your show.' Then he looked at Benson, who still stood rigid, staring at the consoles. 'Get back to your quarters, Benson. You're in the way here.'

Like a zombie, Benson shuffled out of the command room.

He couldn't accept that it was over, just like that. All the work, the battles with the authorities, the hopes and the anguish, the blood, sweat and tears – all in vain?

Benson turned, sick at heart, and watched the base commander emerge from the command room with Malone, in agitated conversation. *The rapport of military minds*. They strode off in the opposite direction, towards the commander's office.

On impulse, Benson doubled back and re-entered the command room. It was empty save for Keeley, engrossed in computing. Benson walked up behind the younger man, seized him by the collar and dragged him upright.

'What the fu . . .'

Benson flung Keeley savagely across the room. His head crashed against a console, and he rolled to the floor, motionless. In near panic, Benson studied the computer screen, analysing the data. Thirty seconds to go!

Furiously he began typing in new instructions, countermanding Keeley's orbital corrections. Twice he mistyped, and had to use the edit command. With only seconds to spare, Keeley's instructions were nullified. The probe was now heading on a direct collision course with the rock.

Suddenly the room was filled with the banshee screeching of alarms. Benson looked up to see military personnel bursting through the door.

'What the hell's going on?' he yelled at the leader.

'It's war!'

Then the man saw Keeley stretched out on the floor. He looked sharply at Benson.

'He fell,' said Benson. 'The alarm startled him; he struck his head. Get him to the sick bay.'

Then he turned and fled back to his quarters.

The image of a monstrous solid object slowly grew on the monitor screen, its features a medley of fluctuating black and white – the stark contrast of outer space. They could make out the detailed pattern of motion now, a chaotic tangle of changing shades as the sunlight reflected off the uneven moving surfaces. The probe was closing fast. They wouldn't get much of a look, just a glimpse before impact, and annihilation.

Benson leaned forward and adjusted the contrast on the monitor. Its quality was inferior to that in the command room.

'What are the chances?' asked Tamsin.

'Minimal. But we've nothing to lose, have we?'

'The President's lost his spy satellite.'

165

'The war's already starting, Tamsin. He doesn't need it.'

'If the probe makes it as far as the rock, what will happen then? Surely its mass is much too big for a controlled explosion?'

'The energy release will be equivalent to about one thousand hydrogen bombs. That's enough to vaporize most of the antimatter, and fragment the rest. It's bound to be one hell of a mess, but how much will fall to Earth is anybody's guess. There are so many unknown factors. I didn't want to do it this way.'

'How long till the probe hits the rock?'

'It's closing pretty slowly at this point of its orbit. I'd say it'll strike in about twenty minutes.'

'Won't they notice that the probe hasn't been pulled out? What happens when Keeley comes to?'

'It's the least of their worries. They're on full alert now. The missiles are being wheeled out. Anyway, I can always say the computer let us down. Keeley won't remember much.'

They sat for a few minutes, watching the screen, trying to make sense of the detail. The camera on board the probe and the data link continued to act flawlessly on automatic.

'What are the chances that the probe will make it all the way to the rock?' she asked.

'About fifty-fifty, I reckon. There's not much antimatter dust at this point of the stream.'

'And if it doesn't make it?'

'Then the rock will keep on coming. We've calculated it will enter the atmosphere tomorrow night, travelling around 21,000 m.p.h., at an angle of 45 degrees from the east – over New Guinea.'

This time it was Tamsin who reached for the bourbon. She filled two tumblers.

'Tell me, Andrew. Suppose the rock does keep on coming. What exactly will happen? If we're not already casualties of World War Three that is.'

'Let's not think about it.'

'I want to. I want to know what it will be like.'

Benson chewed his lip for a moment. 'If the rock were made of ordinary matter, like a very large meteor or small asteroid, it would plunge straight into the ground, vaporizing on its surface, but retaining enough mass to punch a big hole. Such things have happened; the craters still exist. It'd be a pretty awesome event for the guys underneath, but nothing compared to antimatter impact. With antimatter, annihilation will start the moment the rock touches the upper atmosphere. The energy release is so enormous it will disintegrate

166

the rock before it reaches the ground – even at that speed. The explosion will be the equivalent of a hundred million hydrogen bombs. That's enough to strip away the Earth's entire atmosphere and remodel its surface features. The oceans will simply disappear. And the gamma radiation across the eastern hemisphere will be unbelievable. No living thing could possibly survive.'

Tamsin stared at the television screen, expecting the image to die at any instant.

'Will it be over quickly . . . for us?' she asked in a husky voice.

'We're on the opposite hemisphere here, so the first we will know will be the shock wave. We'll be pulverized instantly.'

She shuddered involuntarily. Benson went to a small wall cabinet and removed another bottle of bourbon. He refilled the glasses and handed hers back. They thought in silence for a while. 'Andrew,' she said. 'Why us? Why in this big wide universe does it have to be our planet that incurs the wrath of the gods?'

'I'm a physicist, not a philosopher.'

'Doesn't it strike you as odd, though, that for billions of years the Earth has orbited the sun in peace, but as soon as man comes on the scene our poor old planet gets zapped?'

'Now you're getting mystical.' Benson refilled his glass. 'You're not suggesting it was meant to happen, are you?'

'No, of course not. But if this rock really is a piece of rogue antimatter from God-knows-where, it's pretty unlucky that we just happen to get in the way.'

'It was the moon that got in the way, remember.'

She shrugged. 'Same difference.'

'You're a scientist, Tamsin. You know that no statistical conclusions can be drawn from a single event.'

She still seemed unconvinced. 'So you're absolutely sure this thing is a natural event?'

'Of course it's a natural event! The only controlled production of antimatter on Earth has been in the form of beams of positrons or antiprotons. Even if somebody could figure out how to put them together in bulk there'd be the problem of confining the antimatter in a vacuum, not to mention the small difficulty of blasting it all into space.'

'Why couldn't the antimatter be produced in space to start with, to avoid the confinement problem?'

'But you'd need a huge laboratory up there . . .'

'A ten million tonne laboratory?'

'What are you talking about?'

She suddenly became very animated. 'Don't you see, Andrew? You've no

167

real proof that the so-called rock *is* made of antimatter. You yourself said that matter and antimatter look the same. Obviously the antimatter *grains* are associated with this object in some way . . .'

'Don't be absurd!' cut in Benson. 'Why should anyone *want* to build a space station to manufacture antimatter?'

'The ultimate weapon?'

'Christ, you're as bad as the rest of them!'

'All right then, for fuel, for propulsion, to power a spacecraft, heat a space station. I don't know! Maybe there's all sorts of reasons!'

'Like crashing into the moon?'

'A wreck? Perhaps something went wrong, released the antimatter. Maybe . . .'

'Tamsin, you're clutching at straws!' Benson's voice was shrill, slurred by the effects of the bourbon. 'There's no power on Earth that could build a ten million tonne space station!'

'I know that! No power on *Earth*.'

For a brief moment they stared at each other. Suddenly the door burst open. It was Malone.

'I've got the White House on the line! Something's happened. Come quickly!'

They raced after Malone to the command room. It was packed with military personnel manning consoles, supervising the deployment of missiles. The base commander looked strained, his face lined and grey. Malone flicked some switches and a crackle of static filled the room.

'The President's been on the hot line to the Kremlin, trying to avert all-out war,' explained Malone. 'A last-ditch attempt.' He wiped a perspiring brow with the sleeve of his uniform. 'Apparently the Soviets have finally admitted responsibility for the fireballs! Said it was some sort of accident!'

Benson listened in disbelief.

'They're getting some guy by the name of Rogachev to give a full explanation.'

'Rogachev, the scientist?'

'That's him. The one in charge of their space programme. The President patched us in so we can hear what he's got to say.'

At that moment an accented voice said in English over the loudspeaker: 'Mr President, this is Vladimir Rogachev of the Soviet Academy of Sciences.'

'I hear you, Dr Rogachev.' The familar voice of the President of the United States, edged with tension and suspicion, pervaded the command room. Nobody moved a muscle.

'Mr President, I am permitted by my Comrade President to engage in a frank dialogue concerning matters of mutual concern.'

'I am obliged to you, Dr Rogachev,' replied the President.

Rogachev cleared his throat noisily. 'As we are both aware, for several months all nations have been plagued by the periodic appearance of certain dangerous plasma balls – fireballs I believe you have come to call them. You have evidently discovered that these alarming phenomena are associated with a very large object in space, currently rushing towards the Earth at high speed. No doubt your specialists have been puzzling over the identity of this strange object . . .'

'You bet!' whispered Benson acidly.

'I have to tell you, Mr President, that we have known about this object for some considerable time. Last November, our radio telescope near Kiev began receiving some very strange signals from an unknown source. After careful investigation our astronomers discovered that the signals were emanating from an object in orbit about the moon. Soon the astronomers were able to see it through a large optical telescope. It became clear that we were observing an enormous artificial structure of extraterrestrial origin.'

Rogachev paused. Tamsin looked at Benson, then Malone. Both men seemed visibly jolted.

Then the President said: 'You mean an *alien spacecraft?*'

'Yes, Mr President. An alien spacecraft. Everything that we ascertained about this craft convinced us that it was the product of a technology hundreds of years in advance of our own – a fascinating yet frightening prospect. A small group of scientists was assembled in Moscow to determine our response. Some argued that we should immediately try to make contact with the intruders. Others felt that we should make an announcement of the discovery to the world and let the United Nations decide. We carefully weighed all the risks and advantages. In the end it became clear that there was only one responsible course of action. We had to destroy the craft.'

'What!'

The President's shrill expostulation echoed round the command room. Benson gasped in astonishment, and a murmer of shock rumbled among the assembled personnel. Only the base commander remained impassive.

'We had to destroy it before it destroyed us,' continued Rogachev. 'Surely you can see that, Mr President?'

'I can see nothing!' bellowed the President. 'What gave you the right . . .'

'Humanity was threatened! We bore a grave responsibility. The history of this planet shows all too clearly that when an advanced culture meets a more primitive culture, the primitive one soon disappears.'

'Dr Rogachev . . .' The President's voice shook with emotion. 'The nations

169

of the world will judge you most severely for this wanton and unilateral act of murder. You have taken it upon yourselves to destroy a unique opportunity for all mankind to participate in an event of . . . of cosmic significance. The arrival of this craft could have presaged the beginning of a new era for our planet, bringing undreamt-of benefit to all mankind. I am devastated by your callous disregard of these wider issues.'

'Mr President, you talk of murder, of great ideals. There is no murder; these intruders were not human. They represented not the salvation of mankind but its destruction! We believe that had you been in the same position you would have acted similarly.'

'Do you, by God!'

'Naturally we regret the need to have taken this pre-emptive action.'

'And the fireballs, do you regret those?'

'This we did not forsee, Mr President. We planned to destroy the alien craft cleanly, with a single knockout blow. Last February we launched a spacecraft towards the moon containing a large nuclear device, which we detonated on approach to the orbiting object. What we did not – could not – know was that in the bowels of this colossal craft was a sizeable quantity of antimatter, evidently a power source. The shock waves from our nuclear device must have caused the antimatter to come into contact with the ordinary material of the craft's hull. The resulting explosion was of substantially greater proportions than we had envisaged. It propelled the wreckage of the alien craft away from lunar orbit and into an eccentric orbit around the Earth. In the ensuing turmoil some of the antimatter must have escaped and been spewed around. As far as we can tell, most of it fell harmlessly on to the moon, producing a great eruption and a large burst of gamma radiation. Only minute fragments remained in space, some of which have regrettably found their way to Earth and caused these fireballs.'

'Are you saying, Dr Rogachev, that there is no danger from the wreckage itself when it hits the Earth tomorrow?'

'The wreckage has a very great mass, Mr President, and it is travelling very fast. It will hit the ground somewhere in New Guinea. The impact will be extremely violent, causing a large crater and a shock wave that may bring about great destruction in that country. We have already alerted the New Guinea authorities to the dangers that they face. The damage will, however, be confined.'

'And the fireballs?'

'These may continue for a while, but the wreckage lies near the extremity of the antimatter stream. The present cycle of fireballs is nearing the end, and

170

our calculations suggest that gravitational perturbations will shift the remaining material away from Earth.'

There was a long pause in the conversation. Finally the President said: 'Dr Rogachev, I thank you for your frankness, but for which the world may well have embarked upon a nuclear holocaust. Your excuses I cannot accept. No doubt you will answer to the councils of the world for what you have done.'

'So be it, Mr. President.'

The line went dead. Nobody in the command room spoke for at least a minute. Then Benson said softly: 'Such a waste. An immeasurable loss. Will humanity never rid itself of the military mentality?'

'Were the Russians so wrong?' responded the commander.

Tamsin put her hand gently on Benson's shoulder. 'What did they want Andrew, these aliens?'

Benson shrugged. 'Who knows? Maybe they were just cruising the galaxy looking for friends.'

'Or a home . . .'

Malone stared, his eyes catching sight of the monitor. In all the excitement he hadn't noticed that the spy satellite was still plunging towards its rendezvous with what had been the Unknown. He didn't ask why the orbit hadn't been changed. His attention was riveted to the picture on the screen. The others looked up.

A monstrous object filled the screen with a dancing pattern of light. The probe was closing very fast, and the image swelled rapidly as they watched. For the briefest instant they glimpsed a whirling, mangled wreck.

Abruptly the screen was filled with snow.

EPILOGUE

THE MEDICINE MAN sat immobile, ringed by the bones, rotting entrails and pebbles that were the tools of his trade. For three whole days and nights he had sat thus, oblivious to the sounds of the jungle, moving only to take a little water or to rearrange his sacred pig's teeth.

All his life he had prepared for this, the final coming. For five generations his forebears had passed down the secret, in the cryptic ways known only to those educated in the mysterious arts of the tribe. Now the moment was at hand. The medicine man had to be properly prepared.

He had carefully covered his skin with the kuwala oil and shaved his head and armpits. The long litany of sacred chants had all been methodically executed. It only remained to wait . . .

Night fell.

The medicine man pondered on the wickedness of his people. On how the young men had turned away from the traditional laws of the tribe, following the evil white people from the city at the mouth of the Najimba river, imitating their corrupt ways, wearing their devil's clothes. On how the women no longer followed their ancestors' codes, accepting strange tablets and lotions from the evil one who dared to call himself doctor.

For two hundred years the downfall of his people had been foretold, in the enigmatic stories of his predecessors, full of dark, hidden meanings and subtle warnings. How he had fought to preserve the true path for the tribe! Had he not sought out the wickedness wherever it erupted to destroy them?

Now, with the ancient prophecies about to be fulfilled, with the final justice at hand, they had deserted him, thought him mad.

The old man surveyed the night sky with tear-filled eyes, the burden of his people's wickedness somehow concentrated in this one body and soul.

He knew the spirits would bring forth a sign before the final transformation, so it was with a thin smile of expectation that the medicine man noticed the bright new star in the east, from the direction of the ancient spirit kingdom.

How strangely it flickered!

As he followed its progress, higher and higher in the sky, its flickering brilliance grew in intensity. The spirit-star seemed to approach directly, sensing his presence, seeking him out.

It was as the sacred chants had predicted!

Presently the medicine man could observe the movement of the fiery object clearly against the background of the star-studded sky. His neck craned backwards as he looked above to watch its final descent and the realization of his ultimate destiny.

The spirit-star visibly swelled and flamed in brilliance, searing the old man's eyes. Yet his gaze remained riveted to the heavens, his heart pounding in anticipation.

Then it was as if the star spread out across the whole sky, turning night into day, fingers of white heat radiating to the four corners of the Earth.

The old medicine man shook in the terror of absolute knowledge, watching his universe convulse before him.

The flame and light seemed to engulf him. The agony in his chest became unbearable . . .

When the leading edge of the shockwave struck him moments later the medicine man was already dead.

Author's Note

The events in *Fireball* are, of course, largely fictional. However, they do have a basis in scientific fact. In particular, the alarming phenomenon of ball lightning remains a scientific enigma, even after many years of careful investigation. Interested readers may consult two books that deal with the subject in depth: *Ball Lightning and Bead Lightning* by James Dale Barry (Plenum, 1980) and *The Nature of Ball Lightning* by Stanley Singer (Plenum, 1971).

Ball lightning behaves more or less as described in this book. Luminous spheres, ranging in size from a centimetre to a few metres, and usually orange or yellow in colour, appear from nowhere and float about for seconds or even minutes before vanishing, often explosively. Although these balls are frequently associated with stormy conditions, and are occasionally called thunderbolts, this is not necessarily so; hence the expression, 'bolt from the blue'. In this respect the appellation, 'lightning', is something of a misnomer.

Perhaps the most terrifying aspect of ball lightning is its curious attraction for interior spaces. The phenomenon is often observed inside buildings and even aircraft. Needless to say, there are many recorded instances of injury from such encounters. The experiences of George Todd in Chapter 6 are an embellishment of a real-life incident reported by R.C. Jennison in *Nature*, volume 224, page 895, 1969. (The fictional character of Todd bears no relation, of course, to that of Professor Jennison.)

Attempts to produce ball lightning in the laboratory have been largely unsuccessful. Intense electric fields will occasionally produce corona discharges, St Elmo's fire and other luminous effects, but coherent detached balls seem peculiarly difficult to create. Those balls that have appeared have tended to fade away almost immediately.

Some of the earliest experimental research on ball lightning was carried out at the turn of the century by Nicola Tesla, a rather enigmatic Yugoslav who worked mainly in the United States. Tesla's 1899 diary was only recently published, and contains fragmented accounts of the production of laboratory fireballs. Tesla has become something of a mystical cult figure in certain quarters, though his scientific standing remains high. As reported by Maltby, Tesla did indeed believe he had found a way to transmit electromagnetic power without wires; Benson was entirely correct in expressing scepticism.

Theoretical studies of ball lightning face the challenge of explaining the source of such a large quantity of energy, and how that amount of energy can be encapsulated in a stable manner over the rather long lifetime of a typical ball. Theories divide into two categories, according to whether the energy source is internal or external. Thunderstorms can deploy enormous quantities of electrical energy, and some theorists have tried to construct scenarios in which this energy is somehow channelled or concentrated.

Perhaps the most famous attempt is that due to the Russian physicist and Nobel laureate, Pjatr Kapitza. In Kapitza's theory the ground and the clouds act as partially-reflecting surfaces for long wavelength radio waves that are produced by ordinary lightning discharges. With this configuration, it is conceivable that standing wave patterns can be created, where an electromagnetic field is trapped between the clouds and the ground in much the same way as the standing wave on a plucked guitar string. Under these circumstances, the field strength at the positions of maximum amplitude (the anti-nodes of the wave) could be great enough to ionise the air, and produce a glowing ball. Energy would be fed into the ball continuously from the wave, and the ball would tend to shift about as the clouds move. It was this sort of model that occupied Professor Benson's attention at the outset of his investigations.

Among attempts to explain ball lightning by an internal energy source are those that appeal to chemical reactions, unusual physical conditions, and even radioactive processes, following a conventional lightning strike. In the case of the last of these theories, published in *Nature*, volume 228, page 545, 1970, a serious radiation health hazard would ensue.

Finally there is the theory of D.E.T.F. Ashby and C. Whitehead, who proposed that ball lightning is produced by micrometeorites of antimatter. This idea was published in *Nature* in 1971 (volume 230, page 180), and attracted a certain amount of comment. The authors advanced some experimental evidence in favour of their theory, in the form of several unusual cases of gamma ray bursts from electron-positron annihilation events in the atmosphere close to their detecting equipment. Though no balls were seen (the apparatus was monitored automatically), Ashby and Whitehead considered the origin of the gamma rays to have no conventional explanation. I first became interested in this theory following a visit about that time to the Culham Laboratory in Berkshire, where Dr Ashby was working. As luck would have it, the day was a stormy one, and I well remember him rushing around tending his equipment. The idea of using the ball lightning phenomenon as the basis for a novel was later proposed to me by Dr David Robinson of King's College, University of London.

The concept of antimatter that is so crucial to Professor Benson's theory is a well established scientific fact. Antielectrons, or positrons as they are better known, were first predicted by the British physicist Paul Dirac on the basis of his mathematical work, carried out in the late 1920s, aimed at amalgamating the quantum theory with the special theory of relativity. Dirac noticed that the theory had a place for electrons, but also for mysterious unknown particles that are in some sense the mirror image of electrons. These antielectrons have the same mass as electrons, but opposite electric charge.

In 1932 the American physicist, Carl Anderson, announced the discovery of Dirac's antielectrons from his observations of cosmic rays. In later years, physicists were to discover that all elementary particles of matter possess corresponding antiparticles: thus there are antiprotons, antineutrons and so on. In bulk, collections of antiparticles constitute 'antimatter'. Today, the production of antiparticles in the laboratory is fairly routine. At the CERN laboratory near Geneva, for example, large quantities of antiprotons are made and stored by magnetic confinement for the purpose of high energy collision experiments in particle accelerators.

Was Benson right in dismissing Maltby's conclusion that the Russians were manufacturing and deploying antimatter weapons? Perhaps not. In 1986 a study by the American Rand Corporation concluded that it is entirely feasible that antimatter be used for rocket motors, beam weapons and in X ray lasers (*Nature* , volume 322, page 678, 1986). They set a time scale of only five years for the development of such systems. Noting that CERN collects and stores some hundred billion antiprotons per day for experimental purposes, Rand addressed the problem of the bulk manufacture and storage of antimatter in 'militarily interesting' amounts, which they put at ten milligrams per year. They estimate that the manufacturing process would consume 4 gigawatts of power – expensive, but not absurd. On the basis of the Rand report, the US Air Force has now embarked upon an antimatter research programme.

What about the astronomical implications of antimatter? In his Nobel Prize speech delivered in 1933, Dirac stated that it is merely 'an accident' that the solar system is made with a preponderance of matter over antimatter. 'It is quite possible,' opined Dirac, 'that for some of the stars it is the other way about.' Physicists and cosmologists subsequently began to deliberate on the question of whether the universe contains equal quantities of matter and antimatter. On the face of it, the laws of physics are entirely symmetric between matter and antimatter, so whatever processes have produced matter, there should be some corresponding processes that have produced equal amounts of antimatter. Certainly they are produced symmetrically in the laboratory.

The problem is, astronomers can tell that almost all our galaxy is made of matter. When matter and antimatter meet, they mutually annihilate amid an intense burst of gamma radiation of a characteristic energy. Because encounters between stars, gas and dust frequently occur throughout the galaxy, if it did contain substantial quantities of antimatter, a significant background of distinctive gamma radiation would ensue. Gamma ray satellites fail to detect such radiation in abundance, from which one may conclude that antimatter is very rare indeed within the Milky Way.

The possibility that other entire galaxies might be composed of antimatter has been taken quite seriously. Galaxies are self-contained entities separated by millions of light years of empty space, and galactic collisions are rare, so the absence of gamma radiation from annihilation events might not be a problem in this case. A great deal of attention was given to modelling such a theory in the 1970s.

This idea fell out of favour for two reasons. The first was the absence of any convincing mechanism that would cause matter and antimatter to separate on a large scale; presumably they were thoroughly intermingled when first produced by the big bang that marked the origin of the universe. Secondly, in the mid-1970s a number of theories aimed at unifying the force of electromagnetism with the nuclear forces gained credibility. These so-called Grand Unified Theories, or GUTs, feature a built-in lopsidedness between matter and antimatter, thus breaking the essential symmetry on which the matter–antimatter symmetric cosmological models had been based. For the first time it became possible to conceive of a universe composed almost exclusively of matter.

In spite of their appeal, GUTs have not yet been confirmed by experiment, and some physicists remain open-minded about the existence of large quantities of antimatter in the universe. Balloon experiments have detected unusual quantities of low-energy antiprotons from space that are hard to account for. Plans are afoot to launch an antimatter detector in the mid-1990s. Called Astromag, it will search for composite antinuclei such as antihelium which could only be produced in antistars.

If antistars and antigalaxies exist, it is certain that from time to time they will eject material which would eventually enter a galaxy made of ordinary matter. Any direct encounter between the ejected antimatter and material in the receiving galaxy would lead to dramatic effects, as related in *Fireball*.

In 1965, the nuclear chemist W. F. Libby (also a Nobel prizewinner) published with some colleagues a curious paper in which the effects of an antirock entering the Earth's atmosphere was studied. The authors had a theory that such an event actually occurred – on 13 June 1908. On that date there was a huge explosion, equivalent to the detonation of a large hydrogen bomb, in the remote Tunguska River region of Siberia. An expedition to the area in 1927 revealed extensive heat and blast damage, but no trace of a crater. The Tunguska event has become a famous mystery. If an ordinary large meteor was involved, why was no impact crater or meteoritic material found? Libby and his colleagues argued that an antimatter meteorite was responsible. The paper was also published in *Nature*, volume 206, page 861.

Of course, the chances of such an encounter with an antirock randomly ejected from a far-flung astronomical system are extremely remote, and Tamsin was quite justified in questioning Benson's theory on this count: bulk antimatter is more likely, perhaps, to originate from an alien spacecraft. Indeed, as a source of power in space travel, antimatter is unequalled. In space, it can be accommodated in isolation without difficulty, and would represent a huge energy resource with negligible bulk – ideal, in fact, for powering a 'space ark' that could ply the galaxy as a self-contained ecosystem. Who knows, there may be such an ark lurking out there in the solar system . . .

Milchester University and its staff are entirely fictional. Any resemblance between the characters in *Fireball* and real individuals is purely coincidental.